FIRE

MOUNTAIN

FIRE
MOUNTAIN

RICHARD BLANCHARD

Also by Richard Blanchard…
Mounted in the City by the Bay
a graphic story of police work

Cover design by Pete Masterson
Interior design by Val Sherer

Copyright © 2004 by Richard Blanchard
ISBN 0-9663942-3-2
Published by
     Forever Fine Art
     2 Del Paso Drive
     South San Francisco CA 94080

Printed in the United States of America

Inspiration
"Claire Driscoll"

Thanks to
Professor Neal Loughlin
for encouragement and advice.

&

Sincere thanks to
Chip Roberts
Hugh and Kathy Barker
Joan Lannertone

CHAPTER 1

LONG AGO

The golden October moon shone on the face of the large quartz outcropping. It radiated tongues of fire in the clear night air and, in some areas, could be seen for miles. The Indians camped on a nearby slope looked with reverence as the mountain appeared on fire in the bright night. They knew the large bear would be extending his range tonight. One of the braves would have to stand watch and keep the fires going.

Fish Finder's Wappo clan had traveled up a side stream from the Maccama River to the steelhead breeding grounds. They had found a small canyon five miles up the stream from the Maccama. Deer and quail were plentiful. Oak trees and berry bushes grew in abundance on the hillsides. Several months after having established a camp above the stream, Fish Finder first saw the glow of what looked like fire on the mountain. He told several others to look. They were wondering if the fire would come toward their camp. They watched for several hours, but the fire seemed to stay in place. "I will scout in that area tomorrow," Fish Finder said. Two of the braves offered to go with him.

The next mid-morning, Fish Finder, Flowing River, and Coyote Man left camp. They moved quietly as they traveled down the canyon. Soon they were passing through larger tree growths. In a grove of redwood trees, they saw large droppings. "A bear," they thought. They could see tracks of the large animal where it had moved to rocky ground just outside of the grove. They drew arrows from their quivers and continued slowly and silently up the side of the canyon wall toward where they thought they had seen the fire the night before. Near the top of the mountain they saw a large cave. So large they were in awe. To the right of the cave was an enormous outcropping of stone with much of it in clear quartz. They could see it contained a surface that looked like water.

Fish Finder broke the silence. "The moon shines on that surface and looks like the fire we see from our camp."

Coyote Man said, "A great bear guards this mountain." The others agreed. They moved back down the canyon side and crossed the stream, and along the way they saw several deer and a great orange and brown-colored cat sunning himself on a ledge above the far side of the stream. He rose and watched the men as they passed.

When they returned to camp, the women were already starting the evening meal—a mush of acorn meal and deer stew. The men told of the great cave and the large stone that had a surface like still water. When the moon rested on this great stone, it reflected the glow of fire. The men also told of the large sign left by a great bear who lives in a cave near the great stone. Everyone must avoid the area and no one is to hunt or fish alone. Women looking for wood or food must be accompanied by an armed brave. The first real fear had come into their lives near their camp of plenty.

The Wappo had only recently returned from their annual gathering of the clans at the lower end of the great lake above the Mount St. Helena area, as it was to be known in later days. The clans would gather and net the small fish who, after breeding, schooled between the lake and the mountain stream. These fish were highly favored for their oiliness. The Wappo would also trade with the Miwok and Patwin tribes in the area. There would be much dancing and several young people would make their commitments to each other and a marriage feast would take place. A woman would go with her man to his camp and learn family ways from her mother-in-law. Then the couples would return to the wife's clan. At night they would sometimes hear the great bear growling. The braves would build the fires up and have their arrows ready. They would listen and watch, but the bear never entered the campsite. In the morning, signs would sometimes be found nearby.

Fish Finder lived out his days in the high canyon and his son, Red Tree, succeeded him as leader of the clan. Later in life he would hear from other Wappo camped in the Napa and Sonoma Valley area tales of strange men who had much hair on their faces and were enslaving the Indians, making them work, and beating or even killing them.

Red Tree asked, "Can't we gather together and kill them or drive them away?" He was told they had spears that made loud noises and killed a man. They also had a large, round spear the size of a young tree that caused thunder in the day and could kill many.

Red Tree was also told, "These strange people are taller than us and very pale-skinned."

Red Tree replied, "I must see them."

"If so, then be careful."

Several moons later Red Tree and two braves traveled upstream and crossed the mountains where the great rock trees lay from ancient times. Traveling down the spine of the mountain to the Sonoma area and staying hidden as they moved near the strangers' area, concealed in bushes, they watched as these men in their covered bodies gathered the Indian men and led them to a long table. They saw the men drinking from some kind of hand held bowls and eating bread. After a few minutes, the captives were led to an area near a small stream. Red Tree and his two braves could see the men mixing mud and dried grass and forming them into what looked like small rocks.

Sonoma Mission was being created. Occasionally a man with a long cord would hit one of the Indians. Red Tree and two braves looked at one another. They could see no women. They watched for hours. Then they saw two Indian women with no clothing on them, moving to the nearby stream and washing themselves.

Red Tree said, "Stay, I must talk with them."

"Careful, you'll be like the other men if they catch you."

Red Tree moved from bush to bush and reached the stream where the women were bathing. He sounded the quail call several times. The women looked up and he beckoned to them. They looked around and saw no one watching them. They moved up stream to him. He said, "Follow me. I'll lead you away." The women followed Red Tree, looking behind, scared, but wanting to be free. Every night for weeks, the hairfaced men had come upon them and used them until late in the night.

Going with Red Tree and the other braves, the women traveled 'til dark. Red Tree and the braves shared their food and blankets with the women and took turns standing night watch. At the first faint rays of light, Red Tree woke the others and they moved through streams and other rock formations in order to leave no trails for any followers. They captured or killed small game as they circled back to their camp, taking two days longer to return home.

"After you have rested, we will return you to your people," said Red Tree. They said their home was on the lake above Mount St. Helena at Cimi To Co No Ma Campsite (home of the humming birds). "We will take you there when the clans gather," said Red Tree. The women replied, "You must be very careful, so the hairfaced men do not find you, and work and beat you. They feed you little, and a man in a black robe with crossed sticks hollers words at you. We think he was trying to put a spell on us."

Several months later one of the women became quite sick and died. Even the woman of healing herbs could not help her. She festered from her childbearing part. The other women had moved in with a widowed brave. In time they both became sore in their genitals and a child eventually born of the two was quite sickly. The medicine woman talked to Red Tree. "These hairfaced people cause sickness where they touch a woman and it spreads to her mate. If you bring back any more of these captured women, they must live alone."

"Yes, the hairfaces are bad; I would like to kill them all," spoke Red Tree.

"Our clans are too few," said Owl Lady, the medicine woman. "We are fewer at the lake gatherings each year, and some of the young are marrying into other tribes. The Wappo Nation is ending. The great dream of finding a new country that our elders had after leaving the northern forest is ending. I do not know why, but each year fewer children are born. It is as if the Great Spirit is making our women barren. Maybe we are being punished for old ones leaving their sacred ground."

Red Tree replied, "We must be careful. At the first sign of the hairfaced men, we will move to the great mountain and live along its streams and go down to the lake at the humming bird place. It will be colder in the winter and hotter in the summer, so we will have to learn to live with what the Great Spirit gives us."

In time Red Tree's remaining clan moved to the eastern slopes of Mount St. Helena where they spent the warmer seasons. They started to paint their faces with the red dust of the mountain. In later years the whites would mine mercury in this area. Eventually, the last pure Wappo, a grandmother, passed away in the 1940's. Several scholars tried to learn the Wappo language, which had become very mixed with other tribes' languages, and even some Spanish. Finally, except for game and fish, the Wappo's former home high in the hills above Calistoga on the stream that fed into the Maccama River became deserted.

CHAPTER 2

HANS

In the late 1890's, the first whiteman, a backpacker, had found the Wappo's caved-in huts above the stream flowing below. He wondered how long the Indians had been gone. He had heard there were Indians still living up in Lake County, and a few at Glen Ellen. He gathered wood for a small fire, rolled out his bedroll and canvas-covered blankets, and unpacked his knapsack, small coffee pot, fork, knife, spoon, and tin plate. In a small towel he unfolded was dried fruit, sausage, coffee, and rye rolls. He emptied some of his canteen into the coffee pot and added a little coffee. He started a fire with a handful of shavings from a leather pocket on his vest. The wood caught fire. Then he picked up several stones lying nearby, placing them so he could rest the coffee pot on them. He walked forward a few yards and could see deer moving down to the stream to drink. A doe looked up at him. He remained motionless. As she continued down to the water, he turned and went back and ate his dinner. After eating and tying his knapsack up, he tossed a rope over a limb and tied it off, so that the smell of food did not attract some animal into camp. He unrolled his bedroll, crawled in, and drifted off to sleep while looking at the stars. An owl hooting awoke him in the middle of the night. He sat up looking around and looked again to the northwest.

There was a fire on the mountain. He watched for the longest time. It seemed to be contained in one location. He watched a little longer. The owl had quieted. He lay back wondering, looking at the stars until he fell back to sleep. When he awoke the next morning, the air was crisp and the day was bright with a few high clouds. Birds were singing and calling in the nearby brush and trees. Squirrels were chattering and scolding.

"Good morning, little ones." He crawled out of his bedroll, slipped into his hiking boots, and walked over to a nearby bush and did his duty. Then he walked back, lowered his knapsack, and took out several pieces of dried fruit and some coffee for his morning breakfast.

Soon he rehung his knapsack and started down to the stream below. He could see, as he meandered along, that the grass was starting to dry and wild flowers were coming into bloom. He spied a large-eared rabbit nibbling the wild rye grass who rose up to watch him. Continuing towards the stream, he saw a family of raccoons washing; as he reached the stream, they watched him and then continued their cleaning. He looked at the stream. It widened out in this spot making a large pool. Some water was still flowing out of it and continuing on down the canyon. His eyes had become more focused and he had seen several large fish lazily swimming in the shallows. He looked in wonderment at their size. What large trout! (He would in time learn they were California steelhead.) His next trip he would have to bring his fishing pole. Hopefully it was strong enough for a fish this size. He filled his canteen, went back to his camp, thought about the fire he had seen, and looked in that direction. There was no smoke that he could see.

He spent the rest of the day exploring the mountainside. He could see where Indian maidens had pounded acorns on the lava rock. The lava had been indented and he found a pounding pestle that had been used to make flour from the acorns. He then came across a large clump of wild berries, quite a few were ripe enough to eat and he ate his fill. He would remember this spot in future trips.

When Hans arrived back in camp, he started making coffee, took the two rye rolls out, finished eating, and then looked around. He really liked this place. It was special. This would be his camp from now on. He took out a small ax and hand-held pruning saw and started to prune and remove some of the shrubbery, widening his campsite area to room size. As the sun set, he stopped, drank from his canteen, and answered nature's call. Returning to his camp, he lowered his bedroll from the crook of a tree he had placed it in and rolled it out. His eyes drifted to the northwest.

The fire looked as if it were starting again. Hans watched for the longest time. It grew brighter as the night darkened and the moon climbed higher. He went to his bedroll, got in, and continued to look until he fell asleep. The next morning after eating his breakfast, he continued to develop his campsite, 'til the sun was overhead. He stopped, sat down for a while, and decided he would leave his saw, hatchet, coffee pot, and utensils here. He put everything into his knapsack and hung it in the oak tree again. He would make a new and larger knapsack in the evenings after finishing work.

Hans had come to the Napa Valley as a cooper from Austria. He had completed his apprenticeship in Germany as a cooper and at age 28 he had read of the large vineyards being planted in California. His mother's second marriage in her late 40's had been to a wealthy diamond merchant in Vienna. The merchant had offered Hans the chance to apprentice in the diamond business, but he enjoyed his cooperage work and the travel it offered. He had worked in France and Spain and the thought of a trip to America fascinated him. Hans was a little short on the boat fare to America, so he asked his stepfather if he would lend him $200.00 for his trip. Franz talked to his new wife, Marta, who didn't like to see Hans go so far away, but knew she could not stop him because he loved to travel.

A month later Hans sailed for America. He arrived in New York, cleared customs and immigration, and spent the night sightseeing with a young Italian man named Rico. Hans had met Rico on the boat and talked of going to the Napa Valley in California to work in his uncle's new vineyard. Together, Hans and Rico took the train across America. Looking out the windows while crossing rivers and the mighty Mississippi, passing through never-ending forests and fields, they saw small bands of buffalo, many deer, elk, and a few bear. They traveled up and over the mighty Rockies and then down to Oakland, California, a city by San Francisco Bay.

Ships lined the shore, many abandoned from the gold rush days, in poor condition, or torn apart for salvage or scrap. The two men checked into a small hotel for the night. The clerk informed them that trains to Napa and on to St. Helena and Calistoga left the depot at 8:00 a.m. and 2:00 p.m. They stored their meager belongings, went for a walk in the surrounding area, and were approached by pimps and solicited by prostitutes. The language was universal, but this night Hans and Rico returned to the hotel and ate in the dining room. Dinner was pot roast, potatoes, vegetables, and apple pie for dessert. Dinner finished, they went to their room and talked of their coming trip to the wine country. They awoke the next morning to a breakfast of bread and coffee, then collected their belongings, and checked out of the hotel. After walking two blocks to the train depot, they waited two hours for their train, then boarded, and were on their way to Vallejo, and then on to Napa and St. Helena. Rico met his uncle, Luigi, at the depot and introduced Hans to him. He explained Hans' trade to his uncle. "Yes, Rico, he has come at the right time. There is need for coopers all through the valley as more and more wineries are being built. Tomorrow I will introduce Hans to a master cooper in Rutherford, a small town near St. Helena."

They climbed into Luigi's old truck and twenty minutes later were at his vineyard. They were greeted by Rico's aunt, Rosa, and half a dozen excited children, ranging in age from three to twelve. Luigi showed the two men to a small shed alongside the main house and told them where the outhouse was. They stored their belongings, looked at the old single beds they would sleep in, and wandered back outside. Chickens had the run of the grounds and a large dog was tied to a nearby tree.

Uncle Luigi returned and led them on a tour of barns and sheds, then into a deep cave with wine vats, and then out into the vineyard. Luigi had just acquired forty more acres, on which he would plant white grapes, in addition to his existing one hundred twenty acres of red grapes. He would start clearing the new land in a couple of days. Later the three men returned to the main house and feasted on deer meat, quail, pasta, a large salad, and homemade bread. Even the children drank wine. They talked late into the evening, mostly in Italian and some broken English. In the morning, Rico and Hans helped with chores and then joined Luigi overhauling a disk in one of the sheds. After lunch, Luigi drove Hans into Rutherford and introduced Hans to Otto Schalk, the cooper. Luigi said, "You men talk. I come back after going to the market." Hans and Otto slipped into their native German and Austrian languages, in which the dialects were quite similar. Otto continued, "Hans, you'll have to learn the English. It's the language most people use here in America."

Until Hans' arrival, Otto had been working alone and the demand for barrels was great. Otto told Hans he could stay in the back of the cooperage, where there was a wood stove and well water out in back. Hans nodded that this arrangement would be fine. Otto said he would lay in some supplies for Hans and come early in the morning to pick him up. Luigi returned from the market, goodbyes were given, and Hans returned to Luigi's vineyard. They worked on farm equipment until dinnertime and talked about Hans' luck at finding work and a place to live. They ate a large dinner again, and in the morning after breakfast, Otto arrived. Uncle Luigi said, "Hans, you come and see Rico and me and have dinner. Always plenty."

In his limited Italian, Hans thanked Luigi. "Thank you and your family for your kindness. I appreciate it and if I can ever help, I am at your call." Goodbyes were given and they returned to Otto's cooperage and began building barrels. Some of the work was building great holding tanks twenty feet high. The wood had to be perfect. They worked without lunch until near dark.

"Hans, tonight you come home with me. I live near. You can eat, stay the night, and we'll get you better arranged at the shop tomorrow."

"Fine, Otto."

Otto introduced Hans to his wife, Freda. "We have a dinner guest and I have a good man to help me at the cooperage." She shook Hans' hand, an American custom, but they spoke in German. "Otto, you and Hans wash up. I'll finish up in the kitchen." Freda loaded the table with rolls, sausages, cheese, and a large duck she had prepared. A pie was also on the table. They ate, talked, and enjoyed one another's company. After dinner and when the conversation was through, Freda showed Hans to a sewing room with a cot. He thanked Freda and went to sleep thinking of his first day's work in America.

Otto called to Hans in the morning when it was still dark. Otto had placed a lighted candle in the room. "Bring the candle to the kitchen, Hans."

"Yes, Otto."

Hans quickly dressed, picked up the candle, and went to the kitchen. Freda had rolls and sausages and coffee ready. He sat and ate with Otto. Then they thanked Freda, and said goodbye to her, Otto kissing her cheek as they left. They returned to the cooperage and started work. Midday, Otto took Hans into St. Helena for a new blanket and other supplies. Hans had to use the last of his funds. Otto told him that he would advance any funds that he might need and pay him on the 15th of each month.

Although they worked long hours, Hans enjoyed working with his hands. It pleasured him to create even these simple barrels. Sunday was the day of rest, but Hans would wander the Napa Valley floor and look up at the surrounding hills and Mt. St. Helena to the northeast above Calistoga. Someday when he had more time, he would hike these hills and climb the mountain.

There finally came a time when their worked slowed and Otto said he and Freda would go home to Germany for a visit. They would be gone for three months. Train and boat travel took time. They left the first of September.

That was when Hans started his hikes to the surrounding hills. A month and a half later he stumbled upon his campsite. When Otto and Freda returned, Hans asked Otto how he might obtain the land where he had made a campsite. Otto said, "We will have to go to the county seat and see who owns it or if it might be possible to homestead it." Hans asked Otto about homesteading and Otto explained the process to the best of his ability. After a visit one morning to the county seat at Napa, they learned which of the hillsides above the valley were opened to homesteading and obtained the necessary papers.

In time, Hans was able to homestead forty acres in the area of his campsite and Otto also homesteaded the adjoining forty acres. Hans and Otto decided to build a large cabin across the dividing line of their properties. It had a large room and kitchen in the middle with an oversized fireplace made from petrified wood, with a large bedroom on each side of the cabin. Whenever Hans could get away, he would hike to the cabin. Occasionally, Otto, Freda, and he would ride up to it in Otto's truck. They would also come up for a ten-day stay at Easter, when the steelhead were running.

The second spring, Otto and Freda had visitors from Europe. They took the visitors to the cabin. They hiked and fished, saw deer and other animals, and proclaimed it the highlight of their trip to America. In time the cooperage business slowed and Hans started working as a carpenter. He was now living at the cabin and walking five to ten miles to work. Eventually, he saved enough for a trip home.

His mother was elated to see him again. She had again been widowed and had been left very well off. She was now in love with a baron from Germany who was also in the diamond business. After two weeks, Hans was homesick for America. His mother begged him to stay the remaining two weeks of the month he had planned to be with her. Hans did stay on one more week. The baron was a very friendly fellow and quite jolly when in his cups. As he smoked his big cigar, he asked Hans to stay. "Son, I'll make you a wealthy man."

"Thank you for the offer, Fritz, but I have my beautiful place in America that I am developing. Someday you and mother must come and visit me." When leaving his mother, Marta had slipped a leather throng over his neck with a small, but heavy bag of diamonds and gold coins. "Fritz and I want you to have this."

"Mother, there's no need."

"I know, but I love you so. Fritz is a very happy man and we can afford it."

"Thank you, mother, and please thank Fritz." Fritz had returned to Amsterdam on business two days before.

Chapter 3

Eva

Hans sailed for America. Aboard ship he met a young, eighteen-year-old German girl going to America to be a maid. She was brown-haired, pretty, and athletic. The sixth of nine children born to a baker and his wife, she had lived near mountains and loved hiking. With her limited education, the most she could look forward to at home was marriage, and the men were few. Working as a maid for twenty years and saving money, maybe she could open a little store or find a widower with children who needed to be cared for.

Hans and Eva met daily and walked the deck, talking for hours. By the end of the voyage they had fallen in love. Hans asked Eva to come to California with him. He owned property, had good working prospects, and a little money saved. Eva hesitated because she had a contract to work for a couple who had paid for her passage. Hans told her he would send her employer the passage money and an extra $100. The couple could find someone else. Hans and Eva could get married during their layover in New York City and be husband and wife on their train trip to California.

It sounded so exciting to Eva! She listened to her heart. They found a small hotel operated by an old, German couple who said they could get a Lutheran minister to marry them tomorrow. Hans found a jeweler to put one of the diamonds and gold from two of the gold coins which Fritz and his mother had given him into a ring. They were married the following afternoon with the hotel owners standing up for them. After a nice dinner with the owners, they drank lots of beer and talked until late in the evening. That night they slept in each other's arms. Hans did not want to rush Eva. They were both virgins. When the hotel owners came to the train station to wish them goodbye, Hans invited them to come to his cabin in California when they took a vacation.

The views from the train enchanted Eva and as it traversed the country, they gently came to know each other.

Chapter 4

Calistoga

When Hans and Eva finally arrived in Calistoga, they purchased supplies, blankets, sheets, pillows, a mirror, a vase, and other assorted necessities. When they reached Hans' cabin, Otto and Freda were vacationing there. Otto exclaimed, "Freda! One leaves and two come back!"

"Eva, this is Freda and this, Otto—my dear friends. Freda and Otto, this is my dear and beautiful wife, Eva, who I love so very much. We met on the trip to America and were married in New York."

"Wonderful, wonderful!" Freda exclaimed.

Otto followed, "Congratulations to you both. We will have a wedding dinner for you. I have some of Luigi's good cabernet and I caught a large steelhead this morning."

More conversation ensued and then Hans led Eva into his room. Following Hans, Eva closed the door and jumped into his arms. They kissed and then he gently put her down on the bed. "Hans, you've brought me to heaven."

"Wait 'til I show you the wonders of these hills."

Then they returned to the others and found Freda fast at work, preparing food. Eva asked to help and Freda put her to helping. Otto opened two bottles of wine, poured four large glasses, and gave one to each of them. Then he proposed a toast to the newly married. "Happiness, a long life, and many children."

"Ja, Ja!"

Otto and Hans talked of work while the women busied about in the kitchen area. After a lengthy dinner and much wine, they moved onto the porch that Hans had built. Overlooking the canyon, the porch provided a magnificent view of a golden moon shining brightly. Eva exclaimed, "Look! The mountain's on fire!"

Freda responded, "No, dear. That's what we thought the first time we saw it." Hans then explained, "There is a large rock outcropping of clear quartz. When the moon is full, it looks like the mountain is on fire. I am sure the Indians living here many years ago thought as you first did, Eva. They might even have worshipped it."

"How very amazing. It's like a natural wonder."

"Yes, Eva, but only when it's reflecting. Still it's very special to all of us who live here." Otto and Freda said good night and retired to their bedroom. In love and enchanted with Fire Mountain, Hans and Eva held each other as they sat on the porch. When they retired, sedated by the wine, they fell asleep quickly.

The next morning Eva caressed her husband for the first time. She whispered, "My husband and my home." They quickly became one.

After Otto and Freda left following breakfast, Hans led Eva down to the stream where she gazed in amazement at the incredibly large fish. "It's so beautiful here, Hans. I am so lucky to have met and fallen in love with you." She removed her shoes and waded into the water. It was cold, but not as cold as the mountain water in the Alps.

Hans asked, "Is it too cold?"

"No, but I don't swim with my clothes on." She then removed them.

Gazing with amazement and desire, Hans said, "Eva, you are so beautiful."

"Hans, come join me."

He removed his clothing and swam to her. They swam in small circles and then back to the shallow water where they caressed and kissed before returning to the bank. There Eva placed their clothes in the shape of a bed and lay down upon it. "Come to me, husband mine." Hans knelt between her legs and kissed her lovely body until she asked for his entrance. Eventually they rinsed off in the water, put on their clothes, and returned to their bedroom for more lovemaking. After sleeping a few hours, they awakened hungry, ate some leftover rolls with jam and drank coffee.

Hans told Eva it might be lonely for her when he went away to work for a few days. Thus he would buy a large dog; and a car, which he would learn to drive.

Later that day they hiked to the berry patch, finding a family of raccoons feasting there. After the raccoons vacated the berry patch, albeit slowly, Hans removed his shirt and they picked a lot of berries, some of which they ate. Eva said she would bake a pie with those remaining. They returned to the cabin and Hans brought in firewood while Eva made the pie and baked a couple of potatoes which Otto and Freda had left behind. After they consumed a bottle of wine, Eva cleared the table while Hans gathered more firewood. As the fire grew in intensity and the cabin got warmer, Eva joined Hans in front of the fireplace. Kissing him, she said, "Hans, I am in heaven."

"Almost, dear."

The fire coals reminded Eva of Fire Mountain and she mentioned this to Hans. "Yes, my dear one. But the mountain is not this warm, nor does it have the love I have here in my arms." She kissed Hans deeply and soon they lay naked on the sheepskin rug in front of the fireplace. Hours later the fire had burned out and they awakened because of the cold. They retired to their bed, caressing, and ultimately fell asleep.

Over the next few days, Hans showed Eva much of the surrounding area, including the young fruit trees he had planted. There were apple, apricot, pear, and fig trees. As he walked with Eva, he said, "In the lower areas toward Calistoga, there are also many wild St. George grapes. We will have a lot of fruit to can or dry and I will start a garden of vegetables."

"I will help you, Hans."

The following week Otto and Freda arrived with more food and supplies. Otto said he had work for Hans. He would pick him up in the morning and return him in the evening. The work was near St. Helena, building tanks for the Christian Brothers. Hans said, "Otto, you must teach me to drive."

"Sure, Hans. At lunchtime each day." A good student, after a few weeks Hans was driving like a veteran.

That night at dinner, Hans told Eva he would sell some of his diamonds in Santa Rosa, buy a car, and teach her to drive. Eva hated to see the beautiful stones leave their possession, but she realized the car meant Hans could find more work and not be away from her for long periods of time.

In the days which followed, Hans taught Eva how to fish, and trap cottontails near rocks. He also warned her of rattlesnakes. If she heard or saw one, she was not to move until it was out of striking range. If bitten, she was to lie as still as she could for at least six hours. Eva was nervous about the snakes, but Hans calmed her by saying he had heard of no one dying from their bites, although some people got very sick.

The first day Hans left with Otto to work, Eva busied herself rearranging things in the cabin and airing the bedding on a line she found tied between two trees. She also explored her surroundings, enjoying the freedom and beauty of the area. When Hans returned at night, dinner, conversation, and lovemaking was all part of their "diet."

A few months later, Otto and Freda came to the cabin to spend a weekend with them. A little before leaving, Otto told them, "We are going to be moving to Southern California. We have purchased a small hotel in Santa Barbara. We just received confirmation Friday. We will semi-retire."

Hans asked, "What about the cooperage business?"

"I am giving it up. If it were worth anything, I would give it to you. But I think we built all the barrels and tanks needed for a long time. Keep working as a carpenter and you'll make a good living. And develop your acreage. You can sell produce in town."

"That's a good idea, Otto."

"Hans and Eva, we may never return here and we felt we should offer you our half of the cabin and our forty acres."

"What price are you thinking of, Otto?"

"I think twelve hundred dollars would be more than fair."

"Do you need cash? We could work something out. I have something to show you." Hans left the room and returned with four diamonds and six fifty-dollar gold pieces. Otto's and Freda's eyes opened wide.

"Where did you get these?"

"My mother and her husband. He's a diamond merchant. These are very expensive diamonds from Amsterdam." Otto and Freda looked at each other. Freda said, "Maybe two more gold coins and we could make a deal, if Otto agrees."

Otto said, "Yes, that would be fine. We can go to the courthouse and I and Freda will sign a deed to you and Eva. I have another day of work. We can go to the courthouse on Thursday."

"Yes, that's agreeable. Eva and I will meet you there. Is 10 a.m. good for you folks?"

"Yes."

After Otto and Freda left, Eva said, "Hans, we didn't even talk about it."

"Eva, I'm sorry. But I realized that the last thing we wanted was for strangers to be moving in with us. And with more land, we can increase the orchard and gardens."

Four days later the two couples met, signed the deed, and recorded the transaction. Otto said, "You must come to Santa Barbara for a visit."

Both Hans and Eva replied, "We will, for sure."

"Good luck to you in Santa Barbara," Eva said. "Yes," Hans echoed.

On the way home, Hans and Eva stopped at Luigi and Rico's home and were invited to stay for dinner. They had a fun-filled evening during which Rico told them his girlfriend from Italy was to arrive in a month. There would be a large wedding and they were invited. They enthusiastically said they would attend.

CHAPTER 5

GEORGE

On one of his carpenter jobs, a fellow worker named Sam mentioned that his wife's brother-in-law needed a place to live. He was a bit sickly because he had a lung problem, but was not contagious. He had once been studying to be a priest, but gave up his calling because of his poor health.

Sam said, "I know you worry about your wife being alone at the cabin. George could learn to shoot a rifle and be protection and company for Eva when you're working, especially when you're on a job which takes several days." Hans replied that he would think about it and talk to Eva, which he did that night. Eva replied, "I would enjoy having someone around, but can I trust him?"

"The man wanted to be a priest. I don't think you would have to worry. Just wear something when you swim and keep your clothes on around the cabin. Your beauty is only for me to see, dear one."

"Yes, my husband. Let's meet the man of God."

The following Sunday, Sam, his wife and four children, and George arrived with a picnic basket. George, who was a little frail looking, but with good color, also had a small suitcase with him. He was a nice man. Eva could tell that immediately.

"I would really appreciate the chance to live here in the mountains and in time I think I will grow stronger," he said. Hans and Eva quickly welcomed George into their home.

Sam and his family had set up the picnic basket on a table on the porch. All enjoyed the picnic. After eating, Hans led everyone down to the stream where they looked at the big fish and the children waded. Later, goodbyes were expressed and that night George moved into Otto's and Freda's room.

The next morning Hans left for work before George arose. Having made Hans coffee and rolls with homemade berry jelly, Eva did the same for George when he entered the kitchen dressed in work clothes. After he had eaten, she showed him the orchard and vegetable garden. Then they hiked down to the stream since George had stayed at the cabin the day before. George also was amazed at the size of the steelhead. Eva explained, "A lot of them come up the stream in the spring. In a dry year, many of them become landlocked. Hans has told me they then spend the winter here with us."

"Why is that, Eva?"

"When it doesn't rain enough, about a third of a mile downstream, it widens over a lava bed and becomes very shallow. When that happens, some of the wild animals wait for them to struggle across to deeper water. In early September, you can see them fishing for the steelhead, each in their own style."

"That's sad, Eva."

"No, that's nature, George. George, turn your back for a few minutes and I'll quickly bathe. And no peeking."

"Oh no, Eva. I wouldn't do that." Eva quickly undressed and George heard her exclaim, "Oh my! It's a little cold today." George also heard her splashing and then she was quiet. He was tempted to look, but only to make sure she was okay. Eva swam back and forth a couple of times and then returned and dressed. "Give it a try, George."

"Maybe another time, Eva." They returned to the cabin. "What can I do, Eva?"

"Bring in some kindling and a couple of pieces of firewood."

"Yes, Eva." Eva thought about dinner. Some deer stew, biscuits, and late greens from the garden. She also decided to bake an apple pie. George returned with the wood and she asked him to pick a dozen and a half granny smiths.

"Which ones are they? I know there's several trees with apples on them."

"George they're the greenest, shiniest ones to the right of the orchard."

Twenty minutes later he was back with the apples.

"Can I peel them for you, Eva?"

"It's too soon, George. Sit down and rest. I don't want you to overtax yourself. You're here to get healthy again."

"I think I will. It's so peaceful and beautiful here."

"Yes, it is. I also feel I've come to a very special place."

That night Hans returned home about 8 p.m. The long day of work and the ride home added to the day's length. The men enjoyed the hearty meal. George talked of the large steelhead he had seen and the overall beauty of the area.

"George, in time you will see our great secret. Yes, in a few days the new moon will shine and you will see what has come to mean so much to us."

"I'm anxious to see what you're talking about."

Each day Eva would lead George along some new trail to help familiarize him with his surroundings, just as Hans had done for her. They always carried the 22 and occasionally they would gather in a deer. They would field dress it, sling it on a fresh cut pole, and carry it home. Hans had shown Eva how to hang the carcass covered in gunnysacks in the nearby bay trees high among their thick leaves. As long as the weather was dry, the meat would season and dry with a thick crust until they needed it. They always jerkied some in the summer for use during the winter or to take along on long hikes.

One day they received a letter from Hans' mother, Marta. She and Fritz would like to come for a visit next July with another couple. Hans and Eva were very excited. Hans told Eva, "George and I will add two more rooms overlooking the canyon when my work slows in the winter."

"Hans, that will be wonderful. The garden will be peaking and there will be a lot of fruit in the orchard. I'll also smoke several steelhead in the spring. I hope they like deer meat."

"Eva, I am sure Fritz does, especially the way you bake it." All through that winter, weather permitting, the men worked at building two improved cabins, along with two new outhouses. They increased the size of the garden. Their dog, Rags, helped to keep the raccoons and deer away.

That July Marta, Fritz, and their friends, Karl and Sofie, arrived in Calistoga and took a sedan service to the ranch. The greetings went on for half an hour. They were shown to their cabins and where the outhouses were. There was cold running water in the cabin. George had fashioned an outdoor shower with a pipe running to a perforated bucket and there were pipes leading out of a 200-gallon metal vat which was set on bricks. For hot water, George would build a fire under the tank and when a plug was pulled, gravity fed the shower. Eva and Hans had kidded him about his Rube Goldberg contraption, but it did work.

Poor Eva was constantly cooking for what turned out to be a three-week stay. Hans missed some work for a few days to socialize and lead the guests on hikes or a day of fishing. The men really enjoyed the fishing and could not believe the size of the fish they caught. A picnic to the berry patch was also a delight. The wild game excited everyone. The first night, Sofie came running to the main cabin after a visit to the outhouse. "The mountain's on fire."

"Is it?" Hans asked.

"Yes, yes! It really is."

"Let's all go out on the porch," Hans said. They did so.

All the guests exclaimed they could see it. Smiling softly, Hans explained about the large rock outcropping on the side of the mountain and the large quartz face upon it. It was picking up the moon's reflection. Fritz said, "Maybe you should call it Diamond Mountain."

"That would be good, Fritz, but a neighbor has a small mountain by his place that already carries that title due to the large quantity of broken quartz on it."

Several days later after the guests had left, when Eva was changing the linen in Fritz and Marta's cabin, inside a pillowcase she found forty $20.00 gold pieces and a letter from Marta saying how happy she was to have Eva for a daughter-in-law. Eva also found $100.00 in paper money in the other cabin's pillowcase and a "Thank you" note.

This was the first time she ever held money in her hands.

When Hans came home that night and started to undress, Eva said, "I have something to show you."

"I am tired, dear Eva."

"It will only take a minute." He sat on the edge of the bed and she came to him with a cigar box left by Fritz. She opened it and Hans' mouth fell open. "Where did this come from?"

"The gold coins, Marta and Fritz. The $100 from Karl and Sofie."

"Keep the box hidden. We will have to spend it wisely."

"How generous they were, Hans. We must write and thank them."

The next morning Hans did mention what had happened to George and gave him $10.00. George said Hans didn't have to do so, but Hans insisted. "You worked so hard on the cabins with me last winter and your warm shower contraption is very helpful."

"Thank you, Hans. I could use a new pair of pants and a few other things." George continued, suggesting, "Hans, you could do this and make some extra money with a little advertising in the

San Francisco papers. Rent the cabins between mid-May and the first of October each year. The weather's good, and city people enjoy the country. You wouldn't have to work out so much, or maybe never if we built a few more cabins."

"George, do you really think so? How much does advertising cost?"

"It's not too expensive, Hans. You write a few words telling about the place and what you are offering and what your rates are. I'll help you with the advertising."

"Good. We can plan for next May. We'll build several more cabins."

By late April, they had completed three cabins and three tent cabins. They would finish more next year. George drew up the ad which had a drawing of a moon over a mountain and trees. It read: "Room and board. Escape to beautiful mountains. Home grown food. Quiet cabins – $6.00 per day. Tent cabins – $4.50 per day. Minimum stay 5 days. 50% deposit to hold a reservation. Please write early for dates you plan to vacation and we will try to meet your desires. Buses and trains run to Calistoga. We will pick you up at depot. Mail requests to 4822 Petrified Road, Calistoga, California."

By mid-July, Eva realized she was pregnant; she had almost no morning sickness. It was the fourth month she had missed her period and she was starting to fill out a little. Hans had taken several days work at one of the wineries and was sleeping in his bedroll at the worksite. Eva decided to tell him the day he came home. She and George were busy with their fourteen guests—ten adults, and four children. George led several hikes. Last spring he had found a spot in the stream safe for swimming with a little caution. Each week there was also a large picnic to some place of interest or beauty. The picnics became a favorite with the guests.

When everyone had been fed one evening and George and Eva were cleaning up the kitchen, Eva said, "George, I am missing my Hans."

"He's a good man, Eva. A few more guests during the season and he won't have to work away during the summer."

"George, I think you and Hans will have to build a few more cabins."

"Yes, Eva. If the winter is not too severe, we could have them ready by June 1st next year."

"By the way, George, you're putting on weight and I see you hiking like a young deer."

"Eva, my health has steadily been improving due to the air and your good cooking."

"Thank you, George. I think it's the hiking and gardening."

Hans returned home three days later than expected. He had the good sense to bring added provisions from town—staples, wine, and soft drinks. He picked up mail at the post office and a local paper that was starting to carry all the news of the valley and surrounding countryside. That night Hans was the man home from the sea for Eva. They were both starved for each other. Eva decided to wait a couple of more days to tell Hans of the baby that was coming.

One of the letters Hans had picked up from one of the recent guests mentioned that their child had a very itchy rash. The doctor thought it might be poison oak, a low growing bush that was spreading in California. Hans told Eva and George, "We will have to find out about this bush."

The next spring there was an article in the local paper about poison oak. It was described as a three-leaf, green-to-red bush. Contact with it made one extremely itchy, but the condition was rarely fatal. It was not to be burned because smoke could cause a rash. Calamine lotion was the prescribed remedy. George said he would try to attack it with a hoe wherever he could see it.

Four days after Hans was home, Eva told Hans she was going to have their baby. He was surprised. Then gently putting his arms around her, he said, "Darling, you should have told me. We could have refrained from lovemaking."

"No, Hans. I wanted you so very much and it is still early. I love you so very much."

"Eva, our own child! We must tell George and send letters to our parents."

"Yes, that would be nice."

That night when they told George, he was all smiles. "Eva, I'll help you more in the kitchen, just tell me what to do."

"I'll be fine. I can do my work. The season will be over when I really start to get big." Eva noticed George was always readily available that summer.

One morning after Hans had left for a three-day cooperage work contract in the Russian River area, Eva started to experience labor pains. George was working in the garden doing some cleanup work before winter set in. She went out to the porch and called to him. George answered, "I am on my way, Eva."

"Go, and bring Mrs. O'Malley. I think the baby is coming."

"Yes, Eva." The O'Malley residence was a good two miles away, out on Petrified Road. George left at a trot—something he could not have done two years before. He got to the O'Malley residence and saw their car was gone, but he hollered and knocked at the door. A young man eventually answered.

"Where is your mother?" George asked.

"She and dad went to Santa Rosa to look at some sheep at the auction."

"Hans' wife is going to have a baby and she needs your mother. Tell her to come as soon as she gets home. Please."

"Yes, I will."

George headed back to Eva. He called out her name when he entered the home.

"I am in here, George." Her voice was strained. George entered the room. Eva lay there, her hair moist with perspiration. "My water broke, George."

"What can I do, Eva?"

"I know they always say to have hot water ready. Use the large soup pot." He went to the kitchen, filled the pot, and put it on the stove. Then he went outside for kindling and wood. He was putting wood into the stove when he heard a loud scream. Running into the room, Eva groaned, "There was a bad pain, but not yet, I think." George went to the kitchen and returned with a damp cloth and rinsed her face. "Thank you, George." Then she screamed again.

Mrs. O'Malley arrived almost six hours later. As she entered the house, she called, "Am I on time?"

George replied, "In here." Eva's face was contorted with pain.

Mrs. O'Malley started cooing to Eva like a little child. "Now, now, darling. It's going to be fine. Just a little more." Kate lifted her dress after chasing George out of the room. Eva's vagina was spreading for the delivery that would be soon. "You have to push now, darling. A deep breath, then push."

It was almost another two hours before the baby was in Kate O'Malley's hands. "It's a lovely little girl, Eva. She's lovely!" She called to George to bring in a basin of water. The child had arrived noisily. "The lungs are good too, Eva."

"Give her to me. Please."

"Just a couple of minutes, dear." She cleaned the child and wrapped her in a heavy towel. Then she returned the baby to Eva as the afterbirth was passing. Kate cleaned Eva and removed the soiled towels from under her while the little one was still crying. "Is she okay, Kate?"

"She's fine." Kate placed a couple of clean towels under Eva and then wiped her brow, face, and hands ever so gently.

"Thank you, my angel," Eva said to Kate. "I wish Hans was here."

"It's better he's not. You need a little time with your new baby."

Kate went out to the kitchen and George poured her some fresh coffee.

"George, would you have a little drop to put in my coffee?"

"I'm sorry, Mrs. O'Malley. The only thing in the house is some red wine."

"Well, give me a glass."

"Yes," he replied and brought her a glass from the cupboard.

When Kate returned to the room, Eva was still beaming and the little one was opening and closing her mouth.

"Eva, she wants the breast. Give her a nipple."

"Kate, I started flowing a little the other day."

"That's good, Eva. Sometimes it's hard to start."

Eva bared a breast and the little one quickly found the rich, life-giving liquid.

"Kate, this feels so nice."

"Yes, one of the little gifts of motherhood." Kate knew, having had five of her own. Then she went to the outhouse. She was tired. It had been a long day and night for her. Gazing to her left, she saw a doe grazing near the garden fence and, as she sat, she watched a fly entangling itself in a silken web. "Life begins and does end," she thought. Then she crossed herself and hoped there would be no webs in this child's life for a long time to come.

CHAPTER 6

ANNA

Hans and Eva named their daughter Anna, and by the time she was six month's old, they took her on hikes and picnics. They taught her to swim at three and by four she was a little fish. Anna would accompany her mother or George during trail-clearing time and by age six she was going on hikes with guests.

She was a happy child. She loved the animals and birds. As time passed, Anna wanted to catch a fish by swimming after it, but they were too quick. One year when Max was camping down by the river, he told her, "If you are very patient, child, I will show you how I catch fish in the high Sierra's."

"Okay, Max. I'll be patient."

Max took off his shirt and walked down to a rock which jutted out into the stream. He lay down on his belly and put his entire arm into the water.

"You can't *grab* one, Max."

"Sh, sh."

Eventually Anna saw a few fish coming to investigate the intruder in their territory. One fish came to rub his back against Max's hand. Max waited until the fish was no longer suspicious and then grabbed its back and slowly lifted it out of the water. Anna was amazed.

"Max, you did it!"

"Usually not quite that fast, Anna. I guess there isn't a thing God made that doesn't like fingers on its back."

That night at dinner, Anna told everyone what Max had done. George commented that he had heard of it, but there was a law being made which would outlaw trout being taken that way. Hans said, "To protect the fish that should be the only way." They all laughed.

Eva asked, "What did he do with the fish, Anna?"

"He said he would have it for breakfast."

"Clever man," Hans observed.

As time passed, Anna began helping George in the garden and came to love planting and helping until the plants grew to full size. She was especially proud raising carrots, beats, and potatoes. She also loved climbing the trees to get fruit that was too high to reach from the ground. George would tell her to forget a piece that was too high, but she would still struggle to get it. A few times, he thought he would have to catch her because she looked like she was going to fall. But she always slid down safely.

Anna liked school and was a bright student. In high school she began to "discover" boys. "Mother, they want to touch you."

"They're just experimenting, Anna. But don't let them touch you. A girl can get a bad reputation and people talk. If a boy takes you out at least three times, then he can kiss your cheek once goodnight. It's good to want a man someday, but marriage is the time for more romantic happenings."

"Yes, mother."

By age sixteen, Anna had explored every canyon and mountain around her family's home. Halfway to Fire Mountain, she had found a blow hole above the stream. In August you could put a hat or light object over it and it would be blown away several yards. If she straddled it, her dress would blow up over her face. One day she followed the stream farther down the canyon to where it went under a large boulder. When she went around the boulder, the stream seemed to have disappeared. Bunch grass grew in a thick cover straight to some Manzanita which, in turn, led to the hillside. Crawling on hands and knees, she worked her way through the Manzanita and came to an opening in the hillside where the stream reappeared as it entered a cave. Inside the cave, Anna saw what looked like tracks and sign.

It was a large, dry animal scat. Lion, or bear? Anna wondered. She thought the bears had left this canyon. Maybe this was one down from Lake County. She didn't think she should chance entering the cave to follow the stream any farther. She would bring George back another day with his new 30-30. Anna returned home and told her family and George where the stream led.

Hans said, "Maybe that's another hike for our guests next summer, if it is varmint free."

Being the slow season, one evening Anna asked George if he wanted to see the cave where the stream entered. "Sure Anna, there's nothing that I was going to do tomorrow that won't keep." Anna then told her mother.

"What about school?" she asked.

"One day won't matter, Mom. And it may be good for business."

"Anna, I'll pack a lunch for you. Your father is due in from San Francisco later this evening. We can have a day together while you two are off exploring."

"Thank you, Mom."

"I am turning in early. Good night, all."

The next day Anna and George thanked Eva for the picnic basket and went down to the stream and followed it to the boulder. "It's just a little ways behind this boulder and through a clump of Manzanita, George. That's why I brought these pruning shears. We can get through without crawling like I did."

"Good idea, Anna."

George could see the opening to the cave; it was about six feet wide and the same in height. The stream entering the cave was about four feet wide and looked deep. A little ways in George lit his kerosine lamp. They continued on and soon could see light ahead. When they reached an open area, the stream widened inside the rock formation to almost 30 feet across. There was grass, brush, and one large, old oak tree growing there. They could see several steelheads in the depths of the stream. The stream continued its flow back into the cave again narrowing as it left the open area. They followed it to where they would have had to crawl to follow it any farther.

Then they returned to the open area, sat down, and unpacked the lunch Eva had made for them. After eating and talking about what they had discovered, Anna removed her clothes, dove into the water, and swam across to the other side. George watched her as she swam. He was used to her nudity ever since she was a child, but she was becoming a voluptuous creature as she matured.

"Cold?" he asked as she climbed up the other bank.

"Not too bad."

She walked on the tender grass to the oak tree. She looked at its branches and saw an owl flapping away. They both noticed "Old Smarty" hiding up there.

Anna observed, "It's a good safe place for him to winter. He must fly out to feed because there's nothing here for him to eat."

She dove back into the water, swam a few yards, and then surfaced.

"George, there's one really big old fish down there. He must be a grandpa."

George did not reply. As he looked around, he saw another scat in the cave, but it was quite old. No lion has been here for a long time, he thought.

"That is a very old scat, Anna." As she dressed, she replied, "I thought so. But I didn't want to chance it."

"You were smart, Anna. Always play it safe. Accidents can happen here in the wilderness."

They returned home just as it was getting dark. Hans was on the porch looking down toward the stream for their appearance. When he saw them, he called to Eva, "They're coming up from the stream now, darling."

They had had a very endearing day together. The privacy was nice at times. "Eva, dear, George *does* know when it's dinner time. He's really gotten quite healthy here, hasn't he?"

"Yes, I think he's adopted us permanently. He rarely goes to his brother's place any more."

Anna and George came through the Dutch doors. She moved quickly to Hans and kissed him warmly.

"Hi, Mother."

"No kiss for me."

"I am on my way."

They kissed and Eva said, "Set the table."

"Yes, Mother."

"Hans, how's work?" asked George.

"Busy, but I like it."

"Anna's found a very exciting location on the stream inside a cave which has an open area in the middle of it." George told all the details of the cave and stream to Hans, and Eva listened as she was setting dinner on the table.

"Your father brought some hamburger home with him, so we're having meatloaf, vegetables, and baked potatoes. There is also homemade bread and fresh green onions from the garden." Eva had also made a cobbler out of mixed dried fruit.

During the vacation season, it was almost always families or couples that came to the resort. While walking around, Anna would sometimes see a couple making love and if she wasn't noticed, watch in wonderment. She would leave curious about the moanings and murmurings. People really seemed to like what they were doing. She talked to Eva about it.

Eva said, "Lipschun, you shouldn't watch. That's very private. It is how people have babies."

"The only way?"

"Yes, dear."

"Does it always make a baby?"

"Quite often. We'll talk again next year, dear."

A year later, Anna went with one of the football players to a party after the senior prom. She had a glass of wine and the boy had several beers. On the way home he parked about two miles from her house. They were kissing when he placed his hand between her legs.

"Justin, no."

"Oh, come on, Anna. I just want to touch it."

"No, Justin. Married people do that."

"Don't be so old-fashioned." He started to pull up her dress.

"No, Justin." He touched her panties and the heel of her hand struck his nose.

Although she had aimed for his chin, tears were in his eyes and blood was pouring out of his nose as she jumped out of the car. Anna started to walk toward home. A few minutes later, Justin's car came speeding down the road. Anna jumped into the brush. Justin stopped a little past her and started calling, "Anna, Anna, come back. I won't do anything."

Anna thought, "You just tried to run me down."

She was tearing her prom dress in the brush, but she knew where she was and was sure she could make it home. When she finally arrived at the resort, a light was on in the dining room. When Eva saw Anna come through the door, she exclaimed, "My god, Anna! What happened?"

Anna told her what had taken place. The prom and the party had been wonderful, but Justin wanted to touch her.

"I tried to shove him away and I made his nose bleed. Then I jumped out of the car. He tried to hit me with the car, but I ran into the brush and made it home."

"Honey, I am sorry a nice evening had to end this way."

Hans came into the room. Seeing Anna, his mouth opened and the story was told again.

"I'll talk to that young man."

"Dad, don't say anything. I don't want anyone to know."

A few months later at a gas station where Justin was helping out, Hans confronted him.

"My daughter said you fell and hurt your nose. How is it?"

"Oh it's fine."

Hans thought, "I guess it's best not to say anything more."

CHAPTER 7

DON

Over the years Anna would take guests to the blow hole, the cave where the stream flowed, or sometimes for an overnight campout to the big cave near the quartz-faced rock that reflected the light of Fire Mountain. This was for the more adventurous city folk. She always went for a swim in the buff in the stream in the cave and occasionally one or two vacationers would join her, especially the foreign guests that would make the long trip from Europe. During summers when she was home from junior college, she was still leading some of these hikes, especially when the resort had a lot of guests. She and George would split them up and each take a different hike. Once quite late in the season George had left with a group when a young man who had arrived that day on a motorcycle for a week's vacation approached her and said, "Hi, I am Don White. I'm a student at U.C. Berkeley. I missed the hiking group. Could you direct me as to how I might catch up to them?"

He was a large man, but quite pale and a little frail. He had the waviest red hair Anna had ever seen and a wonderful smile.

"Do you really think you're up to a hike today? Maybe you should rest for a day. Suppose I knock on your door in the morning and I'll take you for a very special hike if you think you are up to it. If you are, I am too."

"I am, Anna."

Don woke to a light rapping on the tent cabin door. He was a couple of months over a serious bout of pneumonia that had sapped him and reduced his weight by almost thirty-five pounds. He heard a female voice calling, "Mr. White, Mr. White?"

He replied, "Yes, yes."

"Do you still want to hike?"

"Yes, I do."

"Are you okay? George looked in on you yesterday and you were snoring quite deeply."

"Yesterday! Do you mean I've slept around the clock?"

"You must be starved."

"I am."

When he had arrived Sunday, Hans had led him to his tent cabin, told him where the outhouses were, and what time dinner would be. Although he had left the cabin, talked to Anna, and eaten with the other guests, he was still quite hungry. Anna's mother was in the kitchen when he entered the dining area.

"Good morning, Mr. White."

"Good morning, Mrs. Dobling."

"Please call me Eva. Everyone does."

"Yes, Eva."

"Most of the guests are already out hiking with George this morning. Sit down and eat; you must be very hungry."

"Yes I am, Eva. Did you call me a few moments ago?"

"No, that was my daughter, Anna. I told her to check on you. Then she was going to town to pick up supplies. You'll meet her later."

"I think I did Sunday afternoon for a moment."

"Good. You'll see a lot of her, helping in the kitchen and waiting tables or maybe on one of the hikes."

A few minutes later Eva was placing a large omelet, ham, potatoes, a fresh roll, a bowl of prunes, and a glass of orange juice in front of Don.

"Would you like coffee or tea?"

"A cup of coffee would be fine, Eva."

Twenty minutes later Don was telling Eva how much he enjoyed the breakfast.

"I think you need a couple of good meals, Mr. White."

"Please call me Don."

"Okay, Don. You should take a little walk. Just down in the canyon you can see the beautiful stream."

Don did as Eva suggested. The weather was mild and he took his time. He noticed birds eating seeds at a nearby bush and a large gray squirrel was chattering in an oak tree. Coming upon the stream, he saw that it was incredibly clear. As he looked at it, he noticed fish swimming and, as his gaze lowered, he noticed a couple of large steelhead that hung suspended at the current's edge. He gazed at the water and fish for quite a while and then a doe came down to the other side of the stream to drink. She must have been there looking at him as he squatted by the water's edge quietly and motionless. She did not seem alarmed, and moved to the stream to drink her fill, checking on him between sips. He realized he couldn't move even though he was getting tired of squatting so he steeled himself to stay still so she wouldn't flee. A hawk's call broke the silence and Don and doe both looked up. A second hawk flew near to the first one. Don eased himself up slowly. The doe watched him rise to his full height, turned, and climbed back up the slope and disappeared in the brush. Don smiled. He liked this place. Needing a rest, he hiked back to his cabin, used the outhouse, and then lay down to rest.

The dinner bell's clanking woke him. He moved to the bureau. Looking in the mirror, he could see a day's growth of beard. Well, he would shave tomorrow. When Don entered the dining room, everyone was talking to one another while waiting to be served. Anna came over and said, "Wait a little and we'll eat together after I serve the others." She guided him to a table near the kitchen. He thanked her and she was back quickly with a glass of wine. "This will hold you 'til we eat."

Don watched Anna and a middle-aged man take bowls and plates of food to the tables of the other guests. As she was setting a tray of food on the table, Don observed her. About seventeen, he thought. Her hair was brown, her eyes, dark. She was just over five feet, well endowed, and had nice legs. He could tell even though she wore Levis, a white blouse, and hiking boots. Her hair reached almost to her waist. Her face was tan and her lips full. A very pretty girl!

When she finished serving the other guests, she sat down across from him, filled his glass with wine, and poured herself a glass.

"Thank you, Anna."

He offered her a bowl of salad, but she said, "Oh no, Don. Guests first or my mother would have a fit…"

"If you insist."

"I do."

Her voice had a melody to it. It was a happy voice. She seemed so vibrant. Anna seemed to have found so much beauty in her surroundings and so much happiness with her parents and faithful George. The birds and animals were her personal friends. He guessed the hardest part for her was the taking of deer for the table. But often that was the only food available.

"What do you do, Don? Besides college?"

"I plan on being an architect and I work nights as a waiter in Berkeley."

"I am planning to go to Cal too."

"What do you plan on majoring in, Anna?"

"I am thinking about zoology, or maybe chemistry. I'll see where my interests travel after I'm actually on campus. I've just been taking general prep courses at a 'J. C.' How do you like our little mountain resort, here in God's country, as they say?"

"I do. I was down at the stream today and I saw a large doe come down to drink. And the fish are so big."

"You've had a good start."

The food was hearty and filling. Anna had just brought him an oversized piece of pie.

"What fruit is in this pie?"

"Mom's special wild berry and pear."

"She sure can cook, Anna."

"Everyone thinks so. We are just so used to it. I guess we are spoiled. George says the good food and these mountains have restored his health. He was frail when he came to us after he had been studying to be a priest."

"Interesting, Anna."

"He's been a great help to Mom and Dad. Mom says he even helped deliver me with the midwife. Dad works away sometimes and it's great to have him here. Dad's helping to build the new high school in town. He and George built these cabins. They say someday they'll build a hotel here."

"I don't quite believe it. I think just more cabins and some indoor plumbing would be an undertaking. They might need an architect at some point in time." Anna excused herself to help George clear tables. By the time she got back to Don, he had finished his pie.

Anna and George were in the kitchen doing dishes. Don watched them for a while then saw Anna look towards him. He smiled and gave a small wave. Then he left to go to his cabin. He sat on the edge of the bed musing to himself about this pretty and friendly mountain girl. He could hear a pair of coyotes calling as it grew darker. They sounded quite close. His thoughts returned to Anna and her sweet smile. As he drifted off, he smelled a strange aroma. He recognized it as skunk. Even San Francisco still had a few.

When he awoke the next morning, he could hear voices talking and laughing. He dressed, went to the outhouse, and noticed a laundry tray with a mirror over it in a shed a few feet away. He would shave, but in cold water. Maybe a good lather would help. He entered his cabin and removed soap, a straight razor, and a strap from a small bag.

He returned to the laundry shed where a woman was rinsing undergarments. She blushed.

"I'll be out of your way in a couple of minutes. We came up for four days and have been here a week. We're thoroughly enjoying this country."

"Yes, it's beautiful and everyone is so friendly. It's really nice when everyone is so considerate. I've been here three days and slept most of the time. The food is sure great."

"I agree. But they give you too much."

"My name is Don White. I'm a student at U.C. Berkeley."

"I'm Kathy Sees from San Francisco. My husband Jim and I love to hike and he heard about this place from friends. While out hiking the other day, Jim found an old arrow in a clump of bushes while he was answering a call of nature."

"Really? I suppose there might have been some Indians here in these mountains."

"You forget about them except for stories of the Old West. We've hiked with Anna and George and felt safe to wander on our own, though they warned us of the possibility of rattle snakes and told us what to do or not do. George says they mostly move off if they hear you coming or hide in rocky spots."

"I guess some lucky deer or rabbit was happy about that stray arrow."

"You are right, Don. I'll tell my husband that. Nice meeting you and I'll see you around."

Don soon found out how cold the water was. It was hard to get much of a lather up, but he forced the stubby growth off with only two minor cuts. "Not bad under the circumstances," he said to himself. As he cleaned his razor, Anna and four guests came walking by.

"Hi, lazy bones," she called.

"Morning, Anna."

Anna and the guests headed towards the left as they left camp. Don wondered what hike they were taking. Noticing Anna's picnic basket, he guessed it was going to be a long one to the Petrified Forest area and an old Indian camping site where two very small streams fed into the stream which snaked through the resort.

Don went up to the main cabin for breakfast. Eva called from the kitchen, "Mr. White, are you enjoying your stay?"

"Yes, Eva, but call me Don."

"Yes, Donald. What would you like for breakfast?"

"Surprise me. Everything you serve is so good."

She served Don a stack of pancakes with two eggs on top, fresh fruit, bacon, fresh orange juice, and coffee. He brought his dishes over to the sink when finished and thanked Eva.

"See you at dinner," she said. As he left the dining room, he thought, "The poor woman must spend fifteen hours a day in that kitchen seven days a week throughout the whole season."

He was almost right. George and Anna cooked on Saturdays. Eva was driving now and would go to town or visit friends. Saturday off really helped her. After breakfast, Don walked around the grounds checking familiar sites and then hiked up to the crest of the hill above camp, where to the east he could see Mount St. Helena and the smaller mountains surrounding it. In the far distance he could see the tips of a mountain to the northeast of St. Helena. A few clouds were passing over the Napa Valley and a couple of birds were drifting on the air currents. He wasn't sure if they were eagles or buzzards. He sat down at the base of a large, old tree which was probably over one hundred years old. He saw a large buck with a full rack of horns crossing an open patch of lava. The buck wandered over to a bush and started to eat. Birds were flying from bush to bush in their search for seeds and insects. He heard their cries and songs and hoped no architect would find work in this area. God had already done everything. Don fell asleep where he sat on the ground amidst the beauty, peace, and aroma of the pine.

George and his hikers reached the foot of Fire Mountain. He described the large cave near the top of the mountain. "I am sorry we only hike to the cave when I carry a gun, but three years ago a bear had wandered down from Mt. St. Helena and was using it for her home and at times I know mountain lions have denned up there."

George would not shoot an animal unless there was a real danger. He would fire just to scare it off.

"We stayed a little long at the old hillside Indian encampment and I do want to show you my secret swimming hole." It was a warm day and they moved to where the stream went into the hillside near a path which cleared through the Manzanita bushes.

George said, "Wait a minute," and then entered the cave cautiously. There was no fresh sign. He returned to the hikers and led them to where the stream widened. When they heard Old Smarty hoot, several guests ducked or had a chill pass through them. Then George introduced them to the bird as he flew out of the tree and out of sight.

There were seven hikers counting George, five men and two women. "We'll give the married couples fifteen to twenty minutes while we men wait back at the mouth of the cave. Then I'll call. You folks can dress and the rest of us will take our swim."

The couples left their underclothing on and shrieked as they entered the cold water. The current slowed quite a bit at this time of the year, but the stream was still cold. A little later George called and told the couples they had a couple of minutes to dress. Then the men went for a quick swim except for one who sat it out. After the swim, George guided the party back to camp in time to clean up and go to dinner. On some Saturday nights, George would play his guitar and there would be a sing-along with some wine offered by Eva and Hans. A large fire usually burned in the fireplace because it usually became quite cool in the evenings.

A fun time was had by all! Many of the guests were becoming regulars. A certain intimacy was building among them and their hosts. Don came late to supper and Anna teased him saying, "You're early for breakfast."

"Anna, am I too late?"

"No, Don. I'll fix you a plate."

"Thanks, Anna. I fell asleep up on the hill under that large fir tree."

"Yes, that is a restful place. The aroma of that old tree is intoxicating."

While Anna was cleaning up in the dining area, she catered to Don as he ate. George had gone early to get his guitar for a sing-along. As he was tuning up near the fireplace, the first words of "Down in the Valley" left his lips in light refrain. Don finished eating and asked Anna if he could help wash or dry dishes for her.

"Don, this is not for the guests to do."

"Anna, please. It would give me a chance to talk with you."

"Ok, Don. You can dry."

Eva had retired early since she had worked late in the kitchen the night before, baking and starting to prepare a special dinner for Hans' birthday. There was going to be a big party for his fiftieth and all guests present would attend, along with friends and neighbors. As they worked in the kitchen, Don asked Anna about her life. She explained how she loved her home, the surrounding mountains, the animals, and even the steelhead in the stream.

"You spoke of taking college courses in zoology. Wouldn't working in a profession take you away from all this?"

"Yes, Don. Maybe for awhile, but I would come back and try to tie what I had learned into this area."

"That might work."

"Where do you plan to work, Don?"

"I think San Francisco will become a great city. There should be a lot of opportunities for me there."

"I would imagine. Don, do you have a fiancée?"

"No, Anna. Between work and school I don't have much time. I don't dance and I really don't have too much money to spend at present."

They finished the kitchen work and joined the other guests arriving to hear George. He sang many old favorites and some early American backwoods pieces he had picked up at a summer camp for children back in Wisconsin's lake country where he had worked one summer as a counselor.

After a while, Anna said, "Let's go for a walk."

"Sure, Anna."

They walked up to the old fir tree, and looking towards Mt. St. Helena they could see a fire burning on the south side of the mountain.

"Is that dangerous?" Don asked Anna.

"Not unless the winds pick up. A slow burn is good for the area is what the old timers say they learned from the Indians. They also say the Indians used to start slow burns. They create more feed for the deer and some of the smaller animals. That area is just about free of any settlers because it's very rocky and remote. In-season, hunters use it a lot. They've gotten some big bucks up in that area."

"Gee's, Anna. You know a lot about this mountain area."

"Just what everyone else that lives up here knows. I just know a few more secrets about our area because I've been here so long."

"Yes, all of seventeen years."

They watched the fire burning slowly in a southerly direction. The stars in the sky were quite bright. Don knew a little about the constellations and Anna listened to him with interest. He pointed to one in the northwest and Anna had a little trouble seeing it. While she was looking for it, he kissed her softly on the cheek.

"You tricked me."

"Yes, Anna. I wanted to do that since the first day we met."

"We better go back to the main house and listen to George."

"Yes, Anna. I didn't mean to scare you."

"You didn't scare me. You just surprised me."

When they returned to the songfest, some guests were leaving and Anna told Don she was going to bed. It had been a long day.

"Thank you for the late dinner, Anna."

"Thanks for the kitchen help."

"See you tomorrow. Anna, is there any chance for a hike?"

"Yes. I have to take a few supplies to our mountain friend, Oscar, who spends his life hiking. He came in from Tahoe late this year. He's camped down by the river cave. Dad picked up coffee and a few things for him. You can come along if you like. I'll call you so you can have an early breakfast with me before we leave."

"Sounds good, Anna. Goodnight."

Anna went to bed tired, but she did remember his kiss. It was sweet. He seemed so very nice.

The next morning Don awoke to Anna's voice calling, "Lazy bones, time to go."

"I'll be right there, Anna."

They had breakfast together. Eva fixed pancakes and a dish of regenerated dry fruit. They finished breakfast and Anna said she would be right back. She returned with a large backpack on her shoulders. Don said, "Give that to me."

"No, Don. It's heavy and I have been doing this for the last four years."

Overhearing their conversation, Eva told Don he could carry a lunch basket. Anna and Don hiked down to where Oscar was camped by the stream. When they arrived, he was sitting in the stream in the raw.

"Hi, Oscar," Anna hollered.

"Hi, Lipschun."

"Oscar, this is my friend, Don."

"Good morning, Donald."

"Good morning, Oscar. How's the water?"

"Refreshing. It keeps me young."

"I'll bet."

"Come on out, Oscar. I'll start some coffee. Mom sent a big lunch for all of us."

"I am coming."

Anna told Don to put the lunch down on a nearby rock and gather some kindling. Then she went down to the stream with Oscar's coffee pot and passed him on the way. He had his pants on and was pulling on his shirt as he walked. He was quite hairy.

"Oscar, I think you're the real Bigfoot."

"Maybe I am, Lipschun."

When the coffee was ready, Oscar took out his two tin cups and gave one to Anna and Don. Anna said, "No, Oscar. You take my cup."

"Lipschun, I'll use my dinner plate. It cools quicker."

"Okay, Oscar."

Anna unpacked the basket. Eva had sent roast beef sandwiches, some dried fruit turnovers, and a bottle of red wine. They talked, joked, and finished the wine. Anna brought the backpack to Oscar. He opened it, removed a ten pound bag of coffee, half a dozen pairs of hiking socks, spices, two well-wrapped bottles of brandy, and a hunting knife. Oscar had written Hans in the spring to buy him several of these items, but Hans had sent the brandy along as a surprise.

"Tell your dad 'Thank you' for me. I appreciate his generous gift." He handed Anna a small Bull Durham bag. "For your father. Gold dust from panning in the Sierras."

"I will, Oscar. We're going to the cave. I want to show Don."

"Donald, you'll enjoy it. I was there yesterday, Anna. No signs of bear or mountain cat."

"Thank you, Oscar. I won't have to throw a rock in."

"You better, Anna. You never know. Something might have arrived last night."

"You're right."

Anna kissed Oscar on the part of his cheek that was not covered with beard and then on his big rosy nose.

"Thank you, Lipschun, it's good to have seen you again. You get prettier every year."

"Thank you, Oscar."

Oscar walked over to Don who was putting the empty backpack into the picnic basket.

"Good to meet you, Don. If you ever want to take a long hike, come with me some year."

"No thank you, Oscar. I'd slow you down. Good to have met you. I'll remember you, Oscar."

As Anna and Don walked off, they turned and waved goodbye. Oscar waved back. They could hear him start yodeling. As they walked along, it continued for a couple of minutes. When they eventually reached the cave, Don exclaimed, "That water goes right in there."

Anna picked up a couple of rocks and threw them into the cave. They waited about three minutes and then entered. Don was glad he was with Anna. He would have been too nervous to enter alone.

They arrived at the place where the stream widened and Don looked up to the sky. Old Smarty hooted as if giving a greeting. It sent a chill through Don. Anna saw him buckle a little. "It's okay, Don. It's our friend, 'Old Smarty.' He was here the first time George and I entered this cave. As usual, she quickly removed her clothing. Don was quite surprised. She dove into the water, surfaced, swam a little up stream, and came back.

"Aren't you coming in, Don?"

"I guess."

"Come on. It's refreshing."

"I'll bet."

Don had never seen a girl of Anna's age in the nude. She was beautiful and full-bodied. He removed his clothes and as she watched him, his manhood seemed to leap from his body. Anna had seen other nude men, but never in such a state of arousal. He put his hands in front of himself. "I'm sorry, Anna. I can't help it."

It took a minute for her to find her voice. "You better come in."

He jumped in and came up splashing violently. "Anna, I can't swim. I can't."

She grabbed one of his hands, and swimming on her back, pulled him to the other side of the stream. Don was choking water as they walked up the bank and sat down. "Don, why didn't you say something?"

"I was just looking at you and listening. I guess I would have done anything you asked."

"Don, oh Don."

"Thank you for saving me."

"Thank God you didn't fight me."

They sat there like Adam and Eve for a while and Anna leaned over and kissed Don. "We have to get back across the stream. It's the only way out of here. I just want you to float on your back and I'll pull you across. Just arch your chest and keep your head back. It'll only take seconds."

"Okay, Anna. Thank you."

Don did as he was told and though he swallowed a little water, they climbed out of the stream and dressed. Then they took the shortcut back to camp and talked very little except for Anna pointing out a bush or animal they both saw. They arrived at Don's cabin and Anna said, "I'll see you at dinner. Soon I will teach you to swim."

"I leave in two days, Anna."

"You can learn the basics in half an hour. I've taught a lot of the guests' children and some of our adult foreign guests."

"In the raw?"

"Yes, as always. Here it's like a part of nature."

Don came late for dinner again.

Anna said, "Hi."

"I know I am late, but I wanted to help you in the kitchen again."

"That's sweet." She still had a vision of Don and his red hair at the cave. They did the dishes again and Anna said that when she got back from a scheduled morning hike, she would meet him about two and give him a swimming lesson. The next afternoon they went to the stream and Anna explained the basic fundamentals of swimming. She had him put his head under water a few times, take a mouthful of water, and slowly blow it out. She held his hands and explained to him how to kick and she pulled him along while he kicked and turned his head in and out of the water as he breathed. Then she let his arms go and after traveling a couple of feet, he was standing up wiping water out of his eyes.

"You let me go."

"Yes, to see if you would stroke on your own."

"You mean flail my arms."

"No. I mean to stroke one arm at a time as you pull through the water and turning your head to breathe every third pull of your arms."

Fifteen minutes later he was swimming. A few minutes more and he actually made it across the stream. She joined him, kissed him on the lips quickly, and said, "No more drowning."

"No more," he said. "I am going to learn to be good. They have some pools in San Francisco."

"That's a good idea, Don. You never know when you might really have to swim for your life."

She noticed Don's manhood rising again and she said, "We have to dress. I have to help Mom in the kitchen." They swam back across the stream and hiked back to camp.

"See you at dinner, Don."

"Yes, Anna."

Don went to his cabin, lay on the bed, and thought about the past few days. The place was beautiful and refreshing. And what a pretty young lady! That night he again ended up drying dishes.

Anna's mother commented, "You like this young man, Anna?"

"Yes, mother."

"Be careful. He's only here for the week and leaves soon."

"Yes, mother."

Later they hiked up to the big fir again. The fire to the south of Mt. St. Helena was out. Clouds covered the sky and there were no stars visible.

"I am going to miss you, Anna. Can we write?"

"That would be nice. We'll exchange addresses when I drive you to town to catch the bus."

"Okay. Yes, Anna. I'd like that. May I kiss you, Anna?"

"Yes."

He kissed her gently. He smelled nice. She felt his firm body against her breast.

"Thank you," he said.

"We better go. Morning will be here soon and we need a good night's sleep."

Half way back to camp he took her in his arms and kissed her deeply. She felt like a great warmth had entered her. He walked her to the house and kissed her on the cheek.

"See you tomorrow, Anna."

"Good night, Don."

Anna went to her room. She was warm. She climbed under her covers and thought of Don. He was a great-looking man with wild red hair everywhere. That kiss coming down the hill had ignited something in her. She tossed and turned, but couldn't lose the warmth she was feeling. She tossed off her blankets. The air was cool, but she wasn't. "He's leaving tomorrow." She got up, put her robe on, opened the window, and climbed out, praying all the guests had gone to bed. She reached Don's cabin. The door was unlatched. She moved to his bed, dropped her robe, and gently climbed into the big, double bed. He was snoring. She tenderly ran her fingers over his arm. He stirred a little and she whispered, "Don, Don."

"What, what?" He sat up.

"It's me, Anna."

"Anna, what…?"

She pressed a finger to his mouth. He kissed it. "I just want to be with you, Donald. Can we hold each other?"

"Yes, Yes, Anna."

He turned on his side and she felt his underwear against her thighs. His hardness slid between her legs.

"I am sorry, Anna. I have no control over that."

"I think I understand, Don. I see the male animals get large when they are with a female of their own species."

He kissed her lips and held her close.

"Anna, I have never been with a woman."

"And I have never been with a man, Don. That kiss on the way down from the fir tree made me so very warm. I couldn't sleep. I just wanted to be with you."

They kissed and kissed and then his kisses started to wander. The first kiss of her nipple seemed like a hot coal touching her. She squealed, "Oh Don. Don stop!"

And he did. "Anna, I just wanted to kiss all of you. I have seen all your beauty. I would love to kiss every bit of it."

"Don, I'm feeling some strange feelings. I think I better go back to my bed."

"Anna, I won't do anything to hurt you."

"I believe you, Don. I just wish we had more time." She jumped out of bed and put her robe on. She could feel moisture between her thighs. "Don, I love you."

She kissed his lips as he sat there.

"I'll see you at breakfast, Anna. Now I am the one who won't sleep."

She turned at the door and whispered, "I love you."

"I love you, Anna."

Eva had to call Anna in the morning. "Darling, it's time for work. See you in the kitchen."

"Yes, mother."

Eva had never seen her so excited. She knew it must be the young redhead. What had happened outside of a couple of walks together?

"Mother, can I cook Don's breakfast when he comes in? He's leaving today."

"Yes, I know. But when have you cooked breakfast?"

"When you and dad went away a couple of times, George let me."

"I guess. Don't serve anything if you burn it. Just start over."

"Yes, Mom."

Anna drove Don to the bus depot Sunday morning. They had agreed to write to each other. They talked and both were looking forward to Anna joining Don at Cal in February. Anna parked in the parking area behind the old Calistoga Hotel. Don said, "Thirty minutes 'til my bus departs."

"Thirty minutes too soon, Don."

"Anna, I do love you."

"And I you, Don." He slid over to Anna and put his arm around her as she turned to him. "I have to be careful, Don. This is a small town."

"Yes, I understand." He took her hand and held it to his lips. She leaned her head on his chest. After a little, he felt a tear fall on his hand. "Anna, don't cry. It's going to be okay."

"I hope so, Don. I never felt like this before."

"Nor I. I think it's the magic of where you live. It's like leaving the real world and stepping into an enchanting mountain garden."

"Don, it is magical when Fire Mountain glows and the hidden places of beauty are viewed. There are so many other places I want to show you."

"Anna, you've shown me the most beautiful sight of all, your enchanting beauty in all its glory."

"Don, you're sweet to say that." The bus pulled in and the new arrivals disembarked. Anna walked Don to the bus. Minutes later when the driver called, "All aboard," Anna reached up and Don took her in his arms, lifting her off her feet. They kissed deeply. As he set her down, she said, "I love you. Please write."

"I will, Anna." He kissed her again quickly and boarded. Anna watched the bus pull out, waving to Don where he sat. He waved back. She went to the car. Tears were coming from her eyes. She would miss him so! Someone rapped on the window. "Are you the driver to Fire Mountain?"

"Yes, are you Mr. North?"

"Yes."

"My mother told me to pick up you and your wife and child. I am Anna, Mr. North."

"Pleased to meet you, Anna. I am glad you reminded me. I'll get the wife and my daughter."

"Wait. I'll help you with your luggage."

"Mabel, this is Anna, our driver. Anna, this is my wife, Mabel. And Mary, this is Anna. Anna, Mary is thirteen, almost fourteen."

"Anna, pleased to meet you."

"Nice to meet you, Mary."

As they drove to the camp, Mr. North asked Anna, "Were you crying, dear, when I knocked on the windshield?"

"I was. I think I had something in my eye. It's fine now."

"I am sure you have to be sharp-eyed on this mountain road."

"Yes, you do, especially because of the animals that wander on these roads so often."

The summer passed in the usual way except that they were accommodating more and more guests. Hans and George would have to build more cabins this winter.

In late January, Eva and Anna went to Berkeley. Anna enrolled, and after a few days they found a home which Anna would share with two other female students. Eva and Anna returned to Calistoga and a week later Hans and Eva drove Anna to her place near Cal.

At first, "U.C." seemed a little bewildering to the country girl from the mountains. The campus was beautiful and her roommates were friendly, but the professors seemed negative to the female students, who were few in number. Also, most of the male students seemed "macho."

Anna had written to Don that she had a new address and would look for him on campus. After two weeks with no word from him, she rode the ferry to San Francisco. Taking a trolley, she went to the address he had given her. It was a rooming house on Page Street in the outer Haight District. She rang the bell and an older, Irish woman answered the door.

"You be looking for a room, missy?"

"No, just looking for a friend."

"And his name be, Mr. Don White?"

"Yes."

"The lad just came home from the hospital yesterday."

"Is he okay?"

"Yes, lass. He had a little touch of pneumonia again. Not as bad as last time. But we took him to the hospital when he didn't leave his room for two days. My husband checked on him because he rarely missed his evening meal. It's only a few blocks to St. Mary's hospital."

"Can I see him?"

"I guess that might be good for him. Just remember this is a respectable and God-fearing home."

"Don't worry, ma'am. I am a good girl."

She led Anna up two flights of stairs and down a hallway and then knocked on a door. Twice Anna heard Don's voice. "Yes, come in. The door is open."

"It's me, Mr. White. Molly. I be bringing you a friend. Leave the door open."

"Yes, Mrs. Reagan."

Anna entered a large room with a bed on one side and a small table and two chairs on the other. A window faced the wall of another building. Don looked quite pale.

"Anna, Anna," he exclaimed. She went to him and bending over the bed, kissed him.

Molly admonished, "Young lady, you keep one foot on the floor and this door stays open."

"Yes, Mrs. Reagan. We haven't seen each other in months and I see how frail poor Don is."

"Okay, dear."

Don interjected, "Pull up one of those chairs and let me look at you. You're the best thing I could have wished for. I love you."

"And I love you! You're so pale, Don."

"It's so good to see you, Anna."

"Don, I looked for you on campus."

"Yes, Anna. I missed the first two weeks of school. It will be hard to make it up, but I think I can. I am going to try and go in Monday."

"Are you up to it?"

"I think so. I won't go into work for a few more days until I feel stronger, but school should be okay."

"I hope so, Don." He did look drained by his illness. He swung his feet out of bed and onto the floor. Sitting on the side of the bed, Anna came into his arms. "Oh, Don, I've missed you so much."

"And I you, Anna." They kissed ever so tenderly and then deeply. Don had to take the first breath. His lungs were still weak. "I am sorry, dear."

Anna pulled away and sat down again. "I am still a little weak, Anna. You feel so wonderful in my arms." They talked for hours and Molly came with a tray and utensils for the two of them. "Mr. White, you won't have to come to the table and your friend can eat with you."

"Thank you, Mrs. Reagan."

Anna said, "How very considerate of you, Mrs. Reagan!"

"I think the two of you can start calling me Molly."

They echoed, "Thanks again, Molly." They enjoyed the simple fare and Don ate with interest for the first time in days. After eating and a few more kisses, Anna said, "Don, I better leave. It's starting to get dark and I want to get back to the house I am sharing in Berkeley."

"Yes, Anna. You're right. I know I'll be busy the first couple of days back, but after that I'll look for you at the library at noon each day."

Several days later they met at the library with smiles when they saw each other. They left their books on a table and went to a remote aisle, kissed, returned to their books, and quietly whispered endearments to each other. Don was returning to his restaurant job Friday. He'd look for Anna in the library each day. They did see each other occasionally. One Sunday they agreed to meet at the belltower on campus. Anna would bring a picnic basket. They met and hiked to a remote part of the campus on a hill overlooking the bay. Don had brought a blanket and a bottle of wine. "Wine. Just like at your folk's place."

"That's sweet of you, Don."

Don spread the blanket and they sat down with the basket and wine. Anna swung herself onto Don's lap and kissed him deeply. He did the same. Many kisses later, Don opened the wine bottle as Anna set out sandwiches, apples, and cookies. "The cookies are from Mom. She sends me a tin every two weeks. My roommates love them, but I saved these for you."

"Thank you, Anna."

They ate their lunch and finished the wine. "Let's walk a little, Don."

"Okay." They walked farther up the hillside and could see the hills of San Francisco and far down into San Mateo County. They returned to the blanket and lay down together. Anna rolled onto her side and kissed Don little, butterfly kisses all over his face. He laughed.

"What are you doing, Anna?"

"Thinking about what you said about kissing me all over my body. I want to do the same to you."

"Anna, I love you so. I want everything to be very special for us."

"Don, I do too." They kissed. In a little while the wind started to come up and Don said, "We better head for home." They gathered their things and Don walked Anna to her campus home. They kissed goodbye and said they would meet tomorrow at the library.

Don graduated in early June. He had asked Anna to attend the graduation ball with him at the Claremont Hotel. As they entered the hotel, Anna was thrilled. She had had her roommates help her find a dress for the ball. They followed the signs to the ballroom. Other young people were already seated and several of the professors and their wives were also attending. They were escorted to their table where some of Don's fellow classmates were seated with their dates. Introductions were made and small conversation followed.

Champagne and dinner were served and then the orchestra which had been playing softly paused and the director announced dancing was now permitted. Don and Anna both told each other they couldn't dance, but they waited until the floor was crowded and made a clumsy attempt together. They returned to their table and joined in more small talk with others when they returned from dancing. When they were alone again, Don said, "Anna, I have a surprise for you."

"What, Don darling?"

He took a key from his pocket and showed her. "It's to a lovely room upstairs, Anna."

"Don?" He put the key back in his pocket. She looked at him and smiled.

"Shall we go now, Anna?"

"Let's have another glass of champagne, Don, and in a little while say goodbye to some of the others."

"Yes, Anna."

Thirty minutes later they were taking the stairway to the room Don had reserved earlier in the week. He had arranged to have a bottle of chilled champagne and flowers in the room at about 10 p.m. As they entered the lighted room, Anna saw the most beautiful room she had ever seen. A vase of lovely, long-stem roses were on the table near the bed along with a silver bucket holding a champagne bottle and two crystal glasses.

"Oh, Don!" She kissed him deeply. He picked her up and carried her to the bed.

"I love you, Anna, and I want us to be married as soon as I can afford to support a wife."

"Oh, Donald." Tears come into her eyes.

"Don't cry."

"They're tears of happiness, my Donald." He kissed her and then knelt and placed his head on her lap. She stroked his red locks and raised his head to kiss him. Then she excused herself saying she must use the restroom. After a little, she returned as he had first seen her at the cave where the river ran. He kissed her and then rained kisses all over her neck and breasts. She kissed his forehead and head. Her body was warm and aroused.

"Excuse me too, darling." In just a couple of moments, he was coming back to the bed where Anna had crawled under the sheets. She saw he too was very aroused. He slid in with her and they turned to each other and kissed deeply. Then their hands began to roam and their breathing increased. Anna rolled onto her back, her thighs spreading. Don came between her legs and caressed her with his organ. Their mutual moisture helped his entry. A small groan escaped Anna's lips as he slid in deeper. He held back a little, but she pulled him to her more tightly and they kissed a lover's kiss. Eventually they were spent and lay side-by-side, holding each other and murmuring of their love for each other.

"Anna, would you like a glass of that nice, cold champagne?"

"Yes, my dearest."

They were thirsty and drank two glasses. Each used the restroom and returned to bed. "Can we do that again, Donald?"

"Yes, darling." It felt even better to Anna this time. Eventually they fell fast asleep. In the morning Anna woke first, used the restroom, showered, and looked at herself in the mirror for a long time. "Would anybody know?" She returned to bed. The covers had slipped off Don as he lay sleeping. As she listened to the sound of his breathing, she looked at the man she loved and thought, "How handsome he is!" And he loved her! She gently touched what had entered her body last night and he started to stir.

Don opened an eye and thought, "God, she is so beautiful! And she loves me."

Anna said, "Hi, sleepy bones."

"Hi, yourself. Have you been awake long?"

"About an hour. I used the restroom and showered."

"I wanted us to do that together."

"We can. Two showers won't hurt me." As they got out of the shower, they heard a knock on the door. A bellhop said, "Checkout is in thirty minutes."

"We'll have to hurry, Anna."

"Yes, Don."

"If I had the funds, we could stay another day and night."

"I understand, Don. It's been the most wonderful night of my life."

"Are you really okay with this, Anna?"

"Yes."

"I know you finish school next week and then it's back home to your parents. And I have to scour the City to try and find an opening for a young architect."

"Yes, Don. But we'll write and maybe you can come up for a few days."

"I'd like that, Anna. Of course, I'll write."

Don saw Anna home and returned to his room at Mrs. Reagan's.

Don spent days looking for work, but still reported for his job as a waiter. Their letters now became more intimate and more frequent. Anna was leading hikes and helping at the camp. Her parents and George were really glad to have her home. Rags was licking her hands the very day she returned.

Don was still having no luck finding employment, but was working extra days tutoring a few students in the afternoon. He was trying to save for a car and a week at the camp. He was aiming for the second week of September. By mid-August, Anna had noticed she had missed her last period. Apprehensive, she went to Mrs. O'Malley's home one afternoon after dropping off a guest at the bus depot in Calistoga. Mrs. O'Malley opened her door with her apron on. She was a very stout woman.

"Anna, good to see you."

"Hi, Mrs. O'Malley."

"Oh, start calling me Kate."

"Kate, can I talk to you in private?"

"Sure dear. Everyone's away from the house. You're just in time for some cupcakes. I've baked four dozen. And have a cup of tea."

"Okay, Kate."

"What's on your mind, dearie?"

"Kate, don't please breathe a word of this to my mom."

"You can trust me. Many's the secret I hold of the people in these mountains. I am like a priest, dear. I don't tell no one."

"Kate, can you get pregnant if you only have sex for the first time on one day?"

"Oh my god, honey. This is a secret you can't keep for too long if you are."

"I know. I've seen other women and I know they grow big."

"When did you do it, Anna?"

"About the 7th of June. I was always very regular and there's been nothing the 10th of this month or in July."

"Then you're probably caught, dearie. What do you want to do?"

"I want to tell the father first. I think I should."

"That is a good idea. Maybe I'll deliver yours just like I delivered you."

"I know you're the best in these mountains, Kate."

"Thank you, Anna."

That night Anna wrote to Don about what was happening. She was amazed it had happened the first night of their sex life, but the midwife told her sometimes that's how it happens. Don had just purchased an old car that weekend from a young man who was joining the navy and when he read Anna's letter, he immediately made arrangements to go to her. Hans was the first to see Don. "Hello, Mr. White. Nice surprise to see you."

"I've come up to see Anna. Did she tell you we were seeing each other at school?"

"She mentioned she saw you. She is out on a hike now. She should be back in an hour or two."

"Thank you, Hans."

"Go in the kitchen and say hello to Eva. She'll fix you something to eat." Don entered the kitchen. Eva was starting to prepare the night meal. "Hi, Mrs. Dobling."

"Hello, Donald. It's still Eva."

"Yes, Eva."

"Have a seat. I'll bring you a piece of my apple pie and a glass of milk."

"That would be nice, Eva."

"I know you and Anna have been writing."

"Yes. We have, and I saw her at school, often in the library." Don thanked Eva again for the food and wandered outside. He hiked up to the big pine above the camp. He looked at the magnificent view, sat down, and then fell asleep. When Anna returned to camp, her mother told her, "Don White was here to see you and he might stay a couple of days."

"Thank you, mother. I'll go see him. Then I'll be back to help you."

She scouted the camp, but didn't see him. Then she went up to the pine tree where he was sleeping. "God, he is so handsome. I hope the baby looks like him," she thought. She would have a boy because of her ruggedness. She knelt and kissed Don on the lips. He was startled for a second, but opening his eyes, found it was his love. They kissed and kissed again before the words of revelation came. Don said, "You're sure?"

"Yes, darling. You'll marry me?"

"Most certainly."

"What will we do? We don't have much time before I'll be showing."

"What about your parents?"

"I don't know what to tell them, but I've heard the story of how they met on the boat and were married the second day after they arrived in New York."

"Let's tell them after dinner tonight that we want to be married this Friday at the courthouse."

Hans and Eva were in a state of shock and Eva started to cry. So did Anna. "Mother, we were going to be married next year when Don already had had a job for six months. Don will return to the City and find work to support us and some weekends he'll come to be with me."

Hans said, "Enough of this crying. We have some wine and go to bed early and think about this until morning. Don, you sleep in the empty tent cabin. A little cold, but you be okay. Anna, you pray tonight and be sure this is what you want."

"Yes, father. Can I show Don to the empty cabin?"

"Yes, but you return to your bedroom."

"Yes, father."

The young couple left the room. "Eva, I know you're disappointed. I know you had hoped for a big wedding for Anna someday, but we know these things happen. I think he is a good young man."

Friday morning, Hans, Eva, Don, and Anna went to the courthouse in Santa Rosa and obtained a license. They found a justice of the peace to marry them for $10. Don barely had enough money. When the justice stopped the ceremony to ask for the ring to be put on the bride, Don gasped, "My God, Anna, it's been so quick I don't have one." The justice interjected, "This happens, son. Give one to her at Christmas."

"Yes," Anna said.

After the ceremony concluded, Hans took everyone to the Santa Rosa Hotel for a nice lunch. Eva was crying and smiling at the same time throughout most of the meal. Hans consoled her, "Don't cry, dear one. We'll have a grandchild soon."

She replied, "Thank you, Hans."

The newlyweds spent the night in Don's tent cabin. Even though it was cold that night, they didn't notice. On Sunday night, Don left for San Francisco because he had many things to take care of. "Anna, I'll see you at least by next Friday night. I love you so much. I am glad you are pregnant and we're together."

"So am I, my Donald. I love you so. I'll miss you so much."

"Me too, dear."

Seven months later, Mrs. O'Malley helped Anna deliver a baby girl. The birth was easy, and they named her "Alicia."

Chapter 8

Murder

Anna was reading the local Calistoga newspaper and noticed an ad on the last page. It read: "Home needed for young Indian boy. Approximately 14 to 15 years old. Speaks and understands some English. Contact Father C. Durkin at Our Lady of Perpetual Help Catholic Church, Calistoga."

Anna mentioned it to her mom. "Don't you think we could use someone to help with the chores and trail clearing?"

"Yes, Anna. We should talk to your dad when he comes home tonight."

As dinner ended, Anna spoke of the ad she had read in the paper. Hans and George thought it was worth looking into. Hans advised, "Anna, you and Don go to town and talk to the priest and the boy."

The next morning Anna and Don called at the priesthouse and talked to Father Durkin. He was a very amiable, older Irishman. "John's his name. He seems to be a good boy. He's out back chopping firewood. He's already cut enough for a year. He doesn't eat much and he's not too fond of bathing, but he doesn't smell." Father Durkin called John, "Come over here. I want you to meet these folks. John, this is Mr. and Mrs. White. They have a place up above town on the way to Santa Rosa."

"How you be, Mr. and Mrs. White?"

"Hello, John," they echoed extending their hands.

Don and Anna liked the looks of the boy and his meeting their gaze. Don asked John, "You want to work up at our place? It's a guest resort. People come from all over, stay a few days or weeks, and then go home. We feed them and show them around the place. They see animals, the hills, and streams. They fish, swim, and hike."

"What would I do?"

"Cut wood, clear trails, help in the kitchen, just whatever is needed. We are going uptown for supplies. We'll be back in a couple of hours. John, you and Father Durkin talk it over."

"Yes, Mr. White."

"Is that okay with you, Father?"

"Yes."

Goodbyes were exchanged. Don and Anna went to the post office and then stopped for coffee at the local creamery. They talked about the young Indian boy and what a help he could be at the resort. Anna said, "Don, if he wants to, we'll take him back with us." Don agreed. Then they went to the general store and purchased needed things for the resort. Don bought a bottle of whiskey. Anna was surprised.

Don said, "It's for the priest. I know Irishmen like a drink."

It was time to go back to the rectory. Father Durkin answered the door. They could see John seated on a bench near the door, a small bag beside him. He rose as they entered. Father Durkin said, "The boy wants to go and I don't blame him. It's too quiet here for a young boy." Don handed the priest a brown bag. "Something for you, father."

"Thank you, Mr. White, and you also, Mrs. White. Well, John, you be good for these nice folks. Do what they tell you."

"Yes Father, thank you for helping me."

"You were a good help, John. Come see me if you come to town."

"Yes, Father." Goodbyes were again exchanged. John followed Anna and Don to the old touring car. They talked to John during the 20-minute drive to the resort. Anna told John she would show him around for a few days so he could learn the lay of the land that the resort was on.

They got to the resort and Don showed John to one of the tent cabins. "John, this will be where you sleep and have some privacy. You'll eat at the house with the rest of us. Lunch is soon so you'll be meeting the others."

Anna came and knocked on the door, saying, "It's time to eat, John." He left the open curtain he had been looking out and joined Anna. A few guests had already left the dining room and they joined the others at table. John was introduced to Eva, Hans, and George. John was shy, but he seemed to enjoy the food.

In the days following, Anna showed John the steelhead stream and the cave at Fire Mountain. The stream also flowed into the passage that led to Mr. Smarty's hiding place and the old Indian ruins. John became very quiet as he looked at the old fire pits and hollows where the acorns had been pounded into meal. He finally said, "Anna, my people!"

"Maybe John?"

"No maybe, Anna. My mother's mother told me of this place and of the big cave and the many fish nearby." Anna then showed John the big fir overlooking the resort and across to Mt. St. Helena. "Anna, that is where I come from. There was much sickness and, when I was small, mother took me to some old people's house she had cleaned often. She asked them to take me because I would be of help to them soon. I learned the white man's talk and worked in the garden. And as I was bigger, I cut wood and mended fences. A couple of years after the old man died, his wife brought me to Father Charlie as she was going to go to San Francisco and live with her daughter."

"Hope you like it here, John."

"I do, Anna."

"Do you have a last name, John?"

"No last name. I have Indian name. It's mine."

"Oh, I think I understand, John."

Earlier they had stopped and eaten berries at the wild berry patch. John said, "Many raccoons come here."

"Yes, John. We share with them." They arrived home in time to hear the dinner bell. "You can wash up, John, and in about an hour we'll eat with the family. We consider George family and now you are part of our family."

"Thank you, Anna."

The next day John was put to work cutting wood. One late afternoon John was fishing in the stream and he heard a noise behind him. It was a young girl on a Pinto horse, riding bareback. She asked him, "Any luck?"

"Not yet, I am only trying to hook a big one. When I see the small ones coming for the bait, I pull it away. Where did you come from?"

"We have the place just over the hill in the canyon to the right. There's a small dam fed by one of the side creeks leading into this stream."

"Do you get any fish up that far?"

"A few, but most go up the bigger creek in the draw to the south of our place."

"How old is your horse?"

"He's eight. I got him when I turned twelve four years ago."

"He is a nice looking horse. What's his name?"

"He came with the name of Rex. I didn't try to change it."

"Could I ride him sometime?"

"Do you know how?"

"I rode a little at the peoples I lived with."

"You can try him as long as you stay in sight." She dismounted. John handed her his pole and swung up onto Rex. He rode Rex in a small circle staying close to the girl. It lifted John's spirit to be on horseback. His people had no horses when he lived with his mother.

The girl had been watching John closely and holding his pole when a seven pound steelhead jerked it right out of her hands. She yelled and John was quickly beside her and passed the horse's reins to her. Then he went into the water and recovered his pole.

John landed the well-hooked fish. "He's a large one," the girl exclaimed. "Thank you for bringing me the fish. What is your name?"

"Judy. And what is yours?"

"I am called John. Do you want the fish?"

"No thank you. If I brought it home, there would be too many questions. I am not supposed to ride off of our place. My dad says I might get lost in this area with so many canyons and draws."

"He could be right, Judy."

"Well, I better get on home. Goodbye, John."

"Goodbye Judy." Judy quickly mounted and rode away towards her home. John picked up the fish and his pole and headed to the main building.

Eva was in the kitchen when John walked in with the fish. "That's a good one, John. I'll fix it for breakfast in the morning."

"Yes, Eva."

"John, you can start a fire in the fireplace. Warm it up a little for the guests."

"Yes, Eva." That night as John lay in bed, he thought of the young girl and how friendly she was. He liked the horse too.

By the end of his first year at the resort, John had some better clothes, a hunting knife, and a few dollars. He had run into Judy a few times when she had strayed from her dad's place. Occasionally she would let him ride Rex and they would talk about little things pertaining to the area. Judy was friendly, but she rarely looked at him directly. He wondered what was bothering her.

One day as he followed the stream in search of fish, moving ever so quietly and carefully so as not to scare the fish, he heard noises. Judy was saying, "No dad. It's not right."

"You mind and you do what I say." John froze where he was and lowered his body position. After a little, he heard the man groaning. He quietly moved back downstream, wondering about what had taken place. Days later when he met Judy on a

trail he was widening, he thought she seemed sad.
But she was friendly to him and they made small
talk. Judy asked if he had been up to the blow hole
yet.

"No, I've heard about it from Anna, but she
hasn't taken me there yet."

"Put that hatchet down and swing up here with
me." She held her hand out to pull him up behind
her. "John, put your arms around me and sit close."

"Will he carry us both, Judy?"

"Yes."

This was the first time John had ever been close
to a white girl. Judy knew the trail and where it
forked. She took the right fork and twenty minutes
later she said, "It's here, John." They could hear the
light whistle of the wind as it came out of the earth.
She tied Rex's reins to a young madrone sapling.
They walked over to the hole. John put his hand
over it and the pressure of the wind moved his
hand upward.

"It's strange, Judy."

"Yes, John. A quirk of nature."

"Thank you for showing me this place."

"Sometimes in August it can be heard from
quite far off, making a louder whistle." She let John
mount first and came up behind him. John felt

strange about this closeness. They rode back to where John had been working on the trail. "Thanks again, Judy," he said as he eased off Rex.

"You're welcome, John. See you again." Then she rode off. He wondered if he should have mentioned what he heard the day he was fishing. As Judy rode home, she thought about how she had liked the feel of John close to her. He was a quiet one, but he seemed very gentle. Her thoughts drifted back to her home. Her mom was taking a bus to see her sick sister in Tucson the next day.

She had wanted to tell her what her father had been making her do these last three years, but his threat that he would kill Rex if she told had stopped her. With Mom gone for a couple of months, she knew it would be bad. She could always feel him looking at her. When they took Mom to Calistoga to get the Greyhound, she wished she was going with her. She had asked to and been told, "Your dad needs you to cook and look after him."

After the bus left, her father bought a couple of candy bars at the bus depot and said, "These are for my favorite girl, Judy." Her mom was about twice Judy's' size and to Frank Judy always looked so desirable. That evening after eating the dinner she prepared, Frank had a few sips from his jug and was smiling at her. "Well honey, it's you and me. I want you to start enjoying what I do to you. I am going to show you a few pleasantries tonight. You go in and bathe if you still want Rex to be alive in the morning."

"Yes, dad."

That night he was gentle with her for the first time. He kissed her on the lips for the first time and also other places. She hadn't liked the alcohol kiss on her lips, but the other kisses were making her feel strange. And when he finally entered her, she felt a stirring of a somewhat different kind. When she woke in the morning, he was gone, probably to his quicksilver mine. She got up, bathed again, straightened the house, went outside, and gave Rex a little grain. When he finished it, she brushed him, got her bridle, and mounted.

She rode Rex up a nearby hillside and as she reached the top of the hill she noticed that in her loins she felt a little like when her father was doing it to her. She wondered why she had never noticed this before. A few nights later when her father was in her, she had her first orgasm. He had encouraged her, "That's the way, honey," as he reached his own orgasm. He soon rolled off of her and was asleep.

She thought, "I know this isn't right." At school they had explained that families did not have sex together, just as most animals were not bred inside of their kin. The molesting continued in the house until her mom returned and then it was back outside in the open or in the barn.

On another occasion when she had run into John, she had him swing up behind her. It did feel exciting. She wondered if he felt anything. A few days later she was again riding with John and they had stopped to water Rex. As they were standing there, she kissed John briefly on the lips. "You are my real friend, John."

"Thank you, Judy." John had been surprised by the kiss—his first. Sadly Judy's father, who was out hunting, had picked them up in his scope.

"That little bitch. Kissing an Indian," he murmured. That night when he came in for dinner, he punched Judy in the face. "What was that for?" Tears were rolling down her cheeks. "You're messing with that Indian boy."

"No, dad. That was the first time I ever kissed him. And I think it was his first kiss. He didn't know what to do. You must have seen it, he didn't even know I was going to do it. And neither did I."

"Don't let it happen again."

That night when his wife had fallen asleep, Frank came into Judy's bedroom and was very rough with her.

John thought of the kiss all the way home—that night and for several days after. She must have felt sorry for him he thought. In the weeks which followed, whenever he sighted her, she would wave and ride off in another direction. He wondered why. She had always been so friendly. One day when out clearing trail, John came upon her watering Rex and it reminded him of their kiss.

"John, dad saw me kissing you. He was quite upset and hit me hard."

"Judy, I am sorry."

"No, it wasn't your fault. I did it because I like you and you've been my friend. I know he's bad tempered and if he sees us together, it wouldn't be good."

"I am not afraid, Judy."

"John, you really should be."

"Okay, if you say so, Judy."

"I am glad I ran into you, John. Now you know why I've been avoiding you."

"I understand now, Judy." She mounted Rex and rode away. John kneeled down, drank from the stream, and then moved over to a fallen tree. He knew he didn't belong in her life.

Months later during deer season, John was cutting the rest of the same tree he had been cutting the last time he had been seen by Frank. When he had seen the Indian, Frank had been out scouting for some meat. This time he was scouting just above the river looking for a deer who had come to water. He looked through his scope, checked an area, and moved down to the next stretch of stream. He picked the Indian up in his scope. He thought, "I've got him. No one will ever know. Just a hunting accident." He moved quietly to where he could not miss. He took the safety off and squeezed.

John heard the first shot as he bent to pick up his ax. The second tore into his back, passed through a lung, and exited out his breast plate. "It doesn't hurt," he thought as he fell to his knees and pitched forward to the ground. Blood trickled from his mouth. A young steelhead jumped nearby.

John was missed that night at dinner. Everyone asked one another if they had seen him.

Eva said, "He took a lunch and said he was going down and clear a fallen tree which might be a problem this winter when the stream would rise and cause it to possibly create a dam."

Anna said, "Maybe he's hurt or got snake bit."

Hans said, "We'll finish dinner and if he's not back by then, we'll take some lanterns and look for him."

Dinner finished, Hans, George, and Anna got the lanterns and headed for the stream. It was slow going in the dark, but an hour later they found John's body. Anna burst out crying. The men were also deeply moved. They all liked the young man. Hans turned the body over. They could see where the bullet had torn through John's breast. Hans said, "George, you and Anna go back to the house. George, call the sheriff. I'll build a fire and keep the varmints away from the boy's body."

"Yes, Hans. Come on, Anna." She was sobbing softly. He took Anna's hand and led her away.

Hans picked up some redwood, dry twigs, leaves, and other kindling. He struck a match and the fire ignited. He gathered a few larger pieces and added them to the fire. "I guess Indians are just not supposed to live here."

At two in the morning, Sheriff Lamberton arrived. Anna, her mother, and George were sitting at the table sipping coffee. Hellos were exchanged.

"Coffee, Sheriff?" Eva asked. "Yes, Eva. No use rushing. George told me the boy was quite dead." After some small talk was exchanged and his coffee finished, the sheriff said, "Well George, let's go see what we have."

Sheriff Lamberton saw the fire in the distance first. He was a large man, six foot four, an ex-football player who had attended college at U.C. Berkeley. Raised in the county, his election had been easy. His dad being a banker and mayor had helped. He was the youngest sheriff Calistoga ever had.

"Morning, Hans. Sad meeting! You touch or move him?"

"Yes, I turned him over and checked his pulse. I don't know why. I was sure he was dead."

Lamberton squatted and looked closer at the body. The front of John's shirt was heavily bloodied. He thought, "Deer rifle caused this," and then mentioned this to Hans and George. "He died pretty quick. Must have been a stray shot."

Hans replied, "It looks that way, Sheriff."

The sheriff was thinking, "Down there by the stream? It didn't seem quite right." He removed John's shirt with Hans' help and placed him in a sitting position. He could see where the bullet had entered under the left shoulder blade. Whoever fired this shot had been just up the hill a short ways. Had a deer come down to drink and paused because of the boy's presence? How could the shooter not have seen the boy? He wondered. "Hans, you can put that fire out. Make sure it's really out, the cover is so dry right now."

"Yes, Sheriff. I realize the danger."

"George, help me get this boy up on my shoulders. You lead out."

"Yes, Sheriff." When they arrived back at the main building, Lamberton put the body into the back seat of his vehicle. And pulled out a blanket that had been draped over the front seat to cover the body. The men were just finishing eating when Hans returned. "Fire out, Hans?" Lamberton asked.

"Yes. I moved the ashes and coals to where John had fallen. I let it burn there a little where his blood had seeped onto the ground. I didn't want it left for varmints."

"Good, you did the right thing."

Anna said she would build a rock mound at the spot in John's memory. The sheriff thanked Eva for breakfast and the men for their help. He said he would take the body to the funeral parlor and come back the next day to examine the area where the shot must have come from. "Keep your guests out of the area for a few days."

Hans answered, "Yes, Sheriff." Lamberton tipped his hat and left.

The family was quite saddened at the loss of John. They all liked the young man. Two days later the sheriff was back and followed the stream down to where Hans had built the fire. He looked at where the shot had to come from. With things so dry, there would be no tracks. He moved up to the area where the shooter must have been standing. Could a deer have been blocking out John? Possibly, he thought. The shooter had to see the boy. Or did he only have eyes for the animal? Was he blinded with buck fever? The sun could not have been a problem and who would want to kill the boy? A dry, broken bush was the only out-of-place thing from the shooter's position and an animal could have broken the bush. He could find no shell casing. Lamberton felt he would have to call it an accidental shooting, probably by an inexperienced hunter.

On occasion Judy looked for her friend John. A couple of months passed and one day she met Anna clearing trail. "Hi, Anna."

"Judy! How are you?"

"Fine. I thought John was the official trail clearer for you folks."

"Judy, didn't you hear? John was killed two months ago by an unknown deer hunter's bullet. At least that's what Sheriff Lamberton put in his report. There was a small article about it in *The Calistogan* the week after it happened."

Anna could see the tears come from Judy's eyes as she climbed down from Rex and fell to her knees. "I am sorry, Judy. I thought everyone knew."

"I didn't hear about it and we don't get the paper, Anna."

"Judy, I built a little monument where we found his body. Dad burned the ground where his blood had spilled. The night we found him, he had been cutting up a dead tree."

"Will you show me where?"

"Yes, Judy." Judy mounted and gave Anna a hand up. Anna directed her to the spot near the stream where she had built a four-foot high monument. The girls dismounted and Judy could see the effort Anna had made to make this monument out of river rock, lava, and petrified wood. "I wish I could have helped you, Anna. If I had only known!"

"I wish you had, Judy. It was a lot of work. Yes, you and Rex could have been a big help. I dragged the lava and petrified wood here on a small sled I made."

"Can I bring flowers here, Anna?"

"Yes, Judy. Anytime except maybe during deer season. We'd hate to have this happen again. Judy and Anna dismounted and went to the monument. Then Judy started to cry loudly and exclaimed, "No, no!" Anna was surprised at her grief. Judy wondered, "Did Frank do this? He might have." After a while, Judy regained her composure. "I'm sorry, Anna. I really liked John. We were friends."

"I didn't know, Judy, or I would have come and told you. Father Durkin said a mass for him. There were only a few of us there. He buried John in the cemetery in town at his expense. We all liked John and miss the quiet, young man. He was a very good worker."

The women remounted and Anna said, "You can take me home, Judy. I'll go back to the trail tomorrow." They rode making small talk. Darkness was coming on.

When Judy entered her home, she began to fix dinner. Frank came in with blood on his hands.

"Got a couple of rabbits for tomorrow night's dinner."

"Did you kill John?"

"What are you talking about? The Indian boy who was working at the resort? Of course not. This is the first time I heard he was dead. They work him too hard. No."

She looked at him, his long hair and face covered with his beard. She just couldn't tell. That night she refused to let him touch her. He had drunk more than usual at dinner. "Why not?"

"I feel bad about John and so does Anna."

"That nudist?"

"Yes. She's not a nudist. Just when she swims."

"I've seen her. Honey, you look just as good as she does when you're nude."

Dinner finished and dishes cleaned, Judy went for a walk. When she returned, Frank was slumped over the table, passed out from his jug of alcohol. Judy had a good night's sleep alone for the first time since her mother, Agnes, had gone to Arizona. But she awakened still wondering if Frank had killed John.

Chapter 9

Stella and George

For the first time Anna could remember, that winter they had four inches of snow at the resort. She had seen snow occasionally on Mt. St. Helena, but never in these lower hills. The past resort season had been very good. Everyone had worked hard to make the resort year successful. Last spring Hans, George, and Don had built a swimming pool using heavy redwood boards, overlapping the boards so that as the redwood became wet and swelled, the pool was watertight. A pipe from the stream ran to the pool and also to cold-water showers and nearby outhouses. The snow brought two weeks of rest to everyone and the men and woman had time to enjoy one another. George had gone to see his brother Sam and his family for a couple of days. On his way back, he stopped at a bar half way between Santa Rosa and the resort. It was about 9 p.m. On a

Monday night. A woman was behind the bar, which surprised George.

"Help you, mister?"

"Good evening. Yes I would like a glass of red."

"I'm sorry. I don't sell wine here. Booze or beer."

"Maybe a little whiskey and water."

"Sure." She was in her mid-forties and husky. "I am Stella. I own this little place. I also have a couple of rooms in back."

"My name is George. I work at the Fire Mountain Resort."

"I've seen the sign, how's it doing?"

"We had a good season this year."

"I get a few tourists on the way to the Petrified Forest and Lake County. Friday and Saturday nights are my best nights."

"How'd you come to this place, Stella?"

"I used to work over in St. Helena and I know the area. Old Gus who used to run this place was tired and he mentioned he'd like to sell it. I had some dollars set aside and we worked out a deal."

George started to say "Thank you" and leave, but she insisted he have one with her on the house. George then bought her one back and after a half a dozen drinks George was woozy.

"Honey, you better stay here. I don't want you driving those curves between here and your place. I am locking up now anyhow. There probably won't be anyone else tonight."

"I'll sleep in my car."

"George, it's too cold for that. You'll get pneumonia." She locked the front door of the bar and led George back to her apartment.

"I'll take that couch there."

"Honey, you can sleep with me. I won't bother you." George undressed and got into bed in his long johns. Stella eventually came to bed in a long, silk nightgown. George moved to the edge of the bed. "Don't worry, honey, I'm going to sleep."

When George awakened in the morning, Stella was asleep, but her hand was on his crotch. He was aroused and sticking out of his long johns. He was scared to move. He lay there and eventually Stella turned and moved her hand. He went to the bathroom, an in-house one, the first one he had ever used. Stella awakened and asked, "What's your name again?"

"George. Good morning, Stella."

"Morning, George. Give me a couple of minutes and I'll fix you breakfast."

"You don't have to do that."

"I'd like to, George. I rarely have overnight company and I get tired eating alone. You're the first one outside of family and a girl friend or two to stay over. It would be bad for business if I slept with the customers."

They had a nice breakfast. George told her of his life at the resort and his having studied for the priesthood. "My god! I slept with a priest."

"We didn't do anything, did we, Stella?"

"Oh George, you are the best man I ever had. You are so big." George turned crimson.

"Did I do something?"

"Honey, I am only teasing you. You were a perfect gentleman. You fell asleep quickly."

"I've never been in bed with a woman before."

"I can understand. All that religion."

"At the resort I see people happy together and the owners' daughter has always swam in the nude. A pretty creature, but I try to look away."

"George, it's part of the beauty God made, like the forest and streams, flowers, the stars. It's okay to look, George."

"I don't know, Stella. It might be sinful at my age."

"Age has nothing to do with it, George."

"Stella, you are a fine looking woman and you've been very nice to me."

"Thank you, George." She walked George to his car and kissed him on the lips. You come back, George, even just to say hello."

"I will, Stella."

George drove home not believing what had happened. Three nights later after many thoughts of Stella, George drove to her place. She had a couple of customers, ranchers talking cow prices and drinking beer. George went to the other end of the bar. Stella smiled and brought him whiskey and water. "Good to see you, George."

"I missed you already, Stella."

"I've been thinking of you too, George. These guys should be out of here soon. They get up early." She left his money on the bar and went about her duties. When the ranchers left, she came around the bar and kissed him on the lips. "I'll have a couple with you." An hour later they were going back to her apartment.

Hans and the women had noticed George borrowing one of the vehicles every Sunday night and returning Monday morning in time to work on whatever the ongoing project was.

"He's got a girl friend," Eva said.

"Do you think so, Mom?"

Hans spoke, "I think he's just going to see his brother's family."

That afternoon Hans and George were working on a new cabin. Hans asked George, "How's Sam and his family?"

"Fine, I guess. I haven't seen them for a couple of months."

"I thought you were seeing them every Sunday night."

"No, Hans. I have a friend, Stella. She owns the 'Bend in the Road' Tavern. You've passed by it on your way to Santa Rosa."

"A woman owning a bar? Isn't that kind of unusual, George?"

"I am sure it is, Hans, but that's how it is. She's a nice lady and I really like her a lot."

"You must be staying over night—the man who was almost a priest."

"I know, Hans. I've seen how happy you and Eva are, and Don and Anna, and so many of the couples that come here. I think maybe that's how life should be. The early apostles were married men."

"I think some of them were, George. You thinking of getting married?"

"Yes. I haven't asked her yet. Just trying to work up the courage."

"I think you will, George. I'd hate to lose you."

"I think of that too, Hans. I owe you people so much and we are like family. Stella's place is only fifteen minutes away. I am sure I could still help you, Hans."

"Well, we'll see what happens and maybe we can work something out."

That night Hans told Eva she was right. "George not only has a girl friend. He's thinking of marriage."

"Really? That's serious, Hans."

"He said he's seen how happy we and the children are."

"I am sure it's his first experience with sex, I hope she's a nice person. And speaking of sex, Hans." He kissed her deeply and his hands slid between her thighs and the tediousness of the day left them as they consumed each other.

Eva told Anna about George in the kitchen that morning. "Oh mother, how exciting! At times I thought I had seen George dreamily looking at you and dad. I thought he had a crush on you, Mom."

"Not the priest man."

"Why not? You're a pretty lady and he's human. I know sometimes when I swam, he'd look at me and turn away. But I'd notice a bulge in his pants when he would turn back as I finished dressing."

"It's good he loved you as a daughter or something might have happened."

"Not George."

"Anna, sometimes men do lose control."

* * *

"Stella, I want to be with you always, you are so dear to me, and beautiful. I would ask you to marry me, but I have no money except the occasional $20.00 Hans gives me. I don't know what kind of work I could do to make a living. I just want to be where you are. I don't want people to think poorly of you seeing me parked here overnight all the time."

Stella had come to enjoy George so much—his sweetness, consideration, and sincerity. And she could see the love in his eyes. They seemed to sparkle every time he touched her or looked at her.

"George, I'd be proud to marry you. Let's think this thing through. We could manage on what I make here. The place is paid for. I'd definitely feel safer at night with your presence. You already have been a help fixing things for me. You could still help Hans and Eva. We could grow old together."

"Are you sure, Stella? You make it sound so nice."

"It will be, George. Let's plan on it soon."

That evening at dinner, George told the family that Stella and he were planning to be married soon. "Oh, George," Anna said; Eva exclaimed, "George! I am so happy for you."

Hans and Don added their congratulations. Hans went to the kitchen and returned with a bottle of wine. "A toast is in order." Anna and Eva went to the kitchen and returned with glasses and Hans soon retrieved another bottle.

CHAPTER 10

FIRE

It was mid-September and it had been a dry year. Anna had had another daughter, whom she and Don named Michelle. The resort season had been successful and the twilight Sunday dinners, "Open to the public," were bringing in the locals and a few people from the bay area. Fried chicken, dressing, hot rolls and honey, vegetables, salad, homemade pie, and wine were served.

The Sunday diners could also take advantage of the pool and hiking. Some of these people were also making reservations for weekends and next summer. The resort was now open from May 1st to November 1st. Hans and George knew they would have to build more cabins.

Anna had led a group of ladies out of the stream cave where Mr. Smarty lived in his old, hidden tree. She and a couple of the ladies had gone swimming *sans* clothes. A couple of nonswimmers teased the "nudists." As the group started to head back to the resort, Anna thought she smelled smoke. She looked down the canyon to the right, but trees and the canyon's curve blocked her view. Maybe someone was clearing stumps.

Later that afternoon Eva had received a call from the new fire tower on Mt. St. Helena. The lookout told her that a fire had gotten out of control in Franz Valley and was headed up the canyon toward the resort and the wind was starting to get gusty. When Anna came in, her mother told her about the lookout's call. "Yes Mom, I thought I smelled smoke when I came out of the stream cave."

"Go tell your dad and George. They're working on the new cabin."

"Yes, Mom." Anna told the two men and they hurried back to the dining room. One of the local volunteer firemen had just entered the dining room. Hellos were exchanged by all. "Hans, the fire lookout alerted us and asked us to take a closer look. As I drove in, about three miles from your place, I started to get some small particles of ash on my windshield."

"I'll use your phone to alert the local crew."

An hour later Ted and his crew were going down the canyon with axes, saws, buckets, and old moving blankets. The smoke was starting to get heavier. Hans said, "We'll have to have the guests leave."

"What about their bills?" Anna asked.

"We have their addresses and will work something out." As the last guest left, Ted and his men were coming up to the resort.

"Hans, you'll have to get your family out of here. Going to try and start a back-fire. It's our only chance. This wind is really getting stronger."

"You really think it's necessary, Ted?"

"Hans, I do. We may all have to leave if this doesn't work."

"Anna, you and your mother grab whatever is important."

"Where will we go, dad?" George spoke up. "Go over to Stella's place on Petrified Road. Tell her what's happening and wait there."

"Yes," Hans said. "That should be safe." After goodbyes and kisses, the women left. Two hours later Ted was telling Hans and George to leave. He and his crew would follow them out. Minutes later, with his crew, Ted showed up where Hans and George had been waiting—that is, where the ranch road ran into Petrified Road. The men were crowded onto one fire truck because an older truck had not started. Hans asked, "You got your whole crew?"

"Yes, thank God. Old Rolly just made it. I told him he's too old to do this anymore. Now maybe he'll believe me. I think if the wind will only let up some, we might hold it here. As Ted spoke, more crews were coming in from Calistoga and Santa Rosa. "Hans and George, you can help reinforce us too; we'll need every man."

"Yes Ted," they answered. By 9:30 the next morning the fire was contained along Petrified Road. Ted told Hans, "You and George go ahead and leave. Check on your women and get some rest. That ground is too hot to go back in there for a couple of days. I fear the worst, Hans."

"Yes, everything was wood. I am sure it burned like kindling."

"You'll have to rebuild, Hans. I enjoyed some of your Sunday dinners with the wife."

"Thank you, Ted. If we do, I owe you some Sunday dinners."

"Sounds good, Hans. See you and George in a couple of days when I come back to make my report." They thanked Ted and went to Stella's place. As they came through the door, they were greeted by the women, with expressions of relief and joy. Stella opened up bottles of cold beer. "I know you're tired, but I'm sure you're also dehydrated." They downed several beers as they told of the night fighting fires and the probable loss of the resort. They also told of all the wild game that came out of the area and crossed Petrified Road, showing little fear of the men and their equipment. Even a cougar with a pair of cubs crossed their path. Fire crews contained the fire two miles east of the resort over the next two days. Eva and Anna commented on how gracious Stella was. After feeding the men, they both slept for the next twelve hours.

The women listened to the radio for news about the fire. There was a brief report on the local station stating that approximately six and one half square miles had burned. That evening when the men awoke they were fed again. Some of the bar patrons had brought in some beds, clothing, and food; the outpouring of assistance by neighbors was overwhelming. The extra beds were set up on Stella's rear porch and sheets divided the porch into two halves with an alley way to the rear yard. Hans and his extended family mingled with locals in the bar. Some they knew and others they came to know.

Wednesday morning Ted came by just after Stella had put together breakfast for everyone. He had coffee and then told everyone it was safe to go back to the resort area, but it had been decimated. Following Ted back in their vehicles to the resort area, Hans and his family saw that everything along the ranch road was black. It had burned down to a point where some of the old lava beds were now exposed. The women and even Hans were in tears. Ted pulled up where the dining room had been. Nothing but charcoal, wood, and ashes, remained. Blackened sinks lay exposed. The women were now crying openly. They could see that most of the area around Fire Mountain had escaped the flames. The fire had stayed mostly to the east side of the steelhead stream.

"Next season will be lost," Hans said. "We can never rebuild in time with winter coming on."

George offered, "Hans, we could go with some tent cabins again."

Ted said, "That's the spirit. You promised me dinner, Hans." Anna said she was going to look around along the stream and the caves. She'd make a forced march of the area. Don suggested, "I'll go with you, Anna."

"I can do it, Don."

"No, I want to go with you." Hans interjected, "We'll pick up some supplies and clothes in town. We'll take the children with us and meet you back at Stella's this evening."

"Okay, Dad."

Anna and Don hiked down to the steelhead stream. The stream was murky with ash along the banks. The current had kept the stream livable for the steelhead. They could see several near the bottom. They soon passed the swimming pool on the west side and the marker for John. It was ok. As they passed on the east side of the stream, the stones were black, but a single flower lay on top of the stones. Anna noticed horse tracks leading back up the canyon. Judy must have been here. She was surprised she had come back that soon on horseback. They continued on down the stream opposite Fire Mountain and could see that the fire had not crossed the stream. They soon entered the stream cave and when they reached Mr. Smarty's area, they could see that the big, old tree was quite fire damaged. Anna wondered out loud to Don if the old bird had made it out. "I am sure he flew some place, Anna. The advantage of wings."

"I hope you are right."

Don said, "Let's check the ground around the tree."

"Okay." They stripped and swam across the stream. They picked their way around some burnt, fallen branches and could see no signs of Mr. Smarty. As they returned to the water, Don grabbed Anna's arm and kissed her. They sank to the ground. It had been days since they had been intimate. Later as they walked back to the resort, they could see that the fire had wiped out the berry patch. Anna said, "I wonder if we could replant it, Don."

"I don't know, honey. We'll have to talk to a nurseryman."

They reached the deserted dining room area and left for Stella's. As they passed Judy's place, she was riding up to the road. They stopped to talk with her. "When I saw the flower on John's marker, I knew you were okay and somewhere near."

"You're right, Anna. It's terrible what the fire did to your place."

"Yes, Judy."

"Are you going to rebuild?"

"Dad expects to. How did *you* make out?"

"With the sheet metal roof we had on our place and the fact the goats had eaten everything around the house for a hundred feet or more, we didn't lose anything. When it got so terribly hot, we went into the dam, Rex and me."

"I am happy for you, Judy. It looks like we're living in a field. Everything is so black. We'll see you, Judy."

"Where are you staying?"

"For now we are at Stella's place on Petrified Road on the way to Santa Rosa."

"Okay, I'll be seeing you folks."

After goodbyes were exchanged, Anna and Don headed for Stella's. As they neared Stella's, Don said, "Let's run into Santa Rosa and pick up a little bit of clothing."

"Yes, Don."

They arrived in Santa Rosa, went to Montgomery Wards, and purchased a few items. Then Don drove to a drafting shop and explained how they had been burned out. He was able to purchase some drafting apparatus on credit. Anna asked, "What's the paper for, Don?"

"Remember I'm an architect, Anna. I have some thoughts I want to put on paper."

That night after dinner as they all sat around a table in the bar talking, Anna said, "Dad, I was wondering. The pool is in good condition and we were talking to an old gentleman clerking at Montgomery Wards and we told him that we lived in the fire area. When we mentioned the fire, he said not to worry. The Indians used to burn all the time and come spring they would see a lot of green vegetation and some of the burned oaks would start to come back. Maybe we could run this coming season with tents and a large lean-to for a dining room. Some of the guests liked the rustic, tent cabins."

"That's something to think about, Anna. What do you think, Eva?"

"I can cook anywhere I have a stove."

"George, Don, what do you think?"

"Yes, if we worked some through the winter and hit it real hard during the spring. Maybe a shortened season when the weather is best."

"Yes. Maybe mid-June to mid-September. Anna said I can write to quite a few of the guests whose addresses we have that I took with us when we learned we had to leave. Some might be interested in an explanation of what happened due to the fire."

Later that evening, Stella was talking to George. "George, you're going to have to enclose that porch. It will start getting cold."

"You're right, Stella. We'll have to do something about heat too, I'm sure." She snuggled up to him and said, "We'll give Hans and Eva our room and I am sure Anna and Don can survive."

"I don't know if they would take it. I know Eva has always been very private about her bedroom at the resort and often calls it her special world." George's hand became familiar and she took a deep breath.

The last few days Don had been drawing sketches on a table in the bar after dinners that Anna and Eva were cooking so that Stella could serve drinks. Business had picked up with her house guests, people who were coming to see Hans' family, and several other fire victims who were now using her restaurant as a common meeting place. On Saturday, Don unrolled several large sheets of papers. Hans, Eva, George, Stella, and Anna were gathered around. They saw what looked like a long, chalet-type building sitting on the ridge above where the resort had been. The building had a front side with large windows.

"What is it?" Hans asked.

Don turned the sheet and showed a floor plan of 48 units with a large, main room in the middle. A large, central hallway extended from each end of the building to the main room. Twenty-four of the units looked toward Fire Mountain, twenty-four looked toward Mt. St. Helena, and a swimming pool was on each side of the building. A driveway ran under the main room where the old road had come in. Hans said, "Under the building?"

"Yes, Hans. The ridge rises to the left and right. The units are at ground level along the ridge and tie into the main room where the old road had divided this ridge. We have to use that road entry and the main room will be approximately 15 feet off the roadbed."

"How could we ever build all this?"

"One, by following my plans, and two, by hiring some additional help."

"There's not enough savings for something this big."

"I know. But we should be able to get a bank loan for its construction."

"We never have had a loan on this property and I really don't like the idea."

"Hans, it means a better resort. You'll get better income and we'll have a building that will never burn again. Why not? It's built out of cement with a fireproof roof."

"My god! What's it going to cost?"

"That I'll have to figure out."

"Don, what about the big, old fir tree?"

"It's gone, Anna."

Lying in bed that night, Hans talked with Eva. "I don't know about those plans of Don's. I know Anna will go along with anything he proposed and all this was to be hers and Don's someday."

"I guess it's what is called progress, Hans." She kissed him on the cheek and said, "I am going to sleep, Hans. I am quite tired today."

"Are you okay, Eva?"

"Yes, Hans. Being out of my own home, I am just out of sorts. Good night, dear."

Anna lay in bed with Don just after making love. "I think your plan scared dad."

"I know it's a big step, Anna, but it's practical and we intend to be here for a long time."

The next week Don was in Santa Rosa numerous times getting blueprints made and prices on materials delivered to the resort area. The cement work would require quite a bit of help. There would also be a lot of glazing work with the number of large windows in the units and it occurred to him that he should add balconies and cut the window size a little. A month later Don had preliminary cost figures and was in the Bank of America branch in Calistoga inquiring about a loan. Bank appraisers said the bank could loan no more than 50% of Don's estimated cost of $180,000.00. The bank had never been in the resort business and they were always inclined to look at the dark side of things even though Hans and Eva had approximately twenty thousand on deposit in their branch.

Don called for another discussion one evening after dinner. Anna and George seemed to understand the undertaking. Hans said, "Don, I've always built with wood. I don't know about this cement construction."

"Hans, wood burns and there can always be forest fires. What we'll build will last 100 years or more."

"Where do we get the additional funds? We're $70,000 short and we need funds 'til we start to operate again." Stella had come over to the table and was looking at the plans.

"Don," she said, "You have a bar drawn here in a corner near the front window. I was listening to your conversation about finances and looking at these plans. You'll need someone to operate the bar. I know you all had your rules about running the resort, but supposing I sold this place? I think it will bring about $30,000.00 and I have another 28,000.00."

Hans said, "Stella, you already have been big help."

"Well, it would save George driving back and forth and you could pay us back interest free. I could work the bar on a percentage basis."

Don interjected, "Stella, that's kind and it makes sense."

Hans said, "This is all coming too fast for me. Let's think about it for a couple of days."

"Fine," Don said.

Stella offered, "Let's have a drink and relax a little."

Several drinks later Don and Anna were dancing to radio music and Eva eventually pulled Hans up for a couple of dances. As the customers thinned, Stella came out and danced with George while Don went behind the bar to help for a few minutes. The next morning, as Eva woke, she looked at Hans who was awake.

"What are you thinking?"

"About Don's plans. I'd just thought we would rebuild what we had. He is right about the possibility of fire. I know and I don't mean to be a dunderhead about this, but the financing worries me. Stella's offer is sincere, I am sure, and it would make sense to have her run the bar. She truly loves George and he is so happy with her. It's nice to have them around."

"What if you wrote your mom and Fritz? Send them copies of the blue prints. I am sure Fritz would understand them and your mom would appreciate the frontal beauty of the first page."

"That's an interesting idea, Eva. We could offer to pay some interest on the loan. Don't tell the children yet until I write a sensible letter and get a copy of the plans. Their financial situation may have changed after the war. The last letter we received from your mother said they were living in Switzerland."

"Yes, that had been Fritz' idea when the war looked inevitable. He's a brilliant man."

Two months later they received a letter from Fritz. It read: "I will finance your entire project at 2% less than your local bank and your mother and I will have the use of a unit for 30 days each year."

Hans was smiling as he handed the letter to Eva. Tears came to her eyes.

That night after dinner, Hans called all to the table. "Your financing problems no longer exist. I'll read this letter aloud."

Don was dumbfounded, Anna was smiling, and only Stella looked sad. "I can't help?" she asked.

"Stella, we would still like you to come and live at the resort with George and operate the bar."

"You would?"

"Yes. Eva and I talked about it after reading the letter this afternoon. And we'd really like you with us."

"Thank you, Hans. And you too, Eva."

One of the owners of the blueprint company had talked about the resort project with Don and, at the time, Don mentioned the financing could be a problem. Mr. Hanford had suggested getting a hold of Jim Bond in Napa. He was a state probation officer who placed delinquent youths and about-to-be paroled convicts into work programs. He knew of several contractors and ranchers who had used this labor force. They received room and board and maybe a small allowance if they worked satisfactorily. If they didn't, a call to Jim and they were removed the next day. "That's a good idea, Mr. Hanford. Thanks."

"You're welcome, Don."

Don talked to Hans and George about the idea and, with the three of them supervising, they felt safe. However, the women would have to be consulted. Eva thought everyone deserved another chance and Anna favored any idea Don had. So Don did go and meet Jim Bond. It was a very cordial meeting. Don explained the set up to Jim—how the resort operated when it was open and how he would need men to help build this large undertaking. Jim said, "Let me know about two weeks before you are going to start. They'll need a place to sleep and three meals a day."

"For a while we'll put up a lean-to and we'll bring meals to them until we have an operating kitchen. I want to get the family living back at the resort as soon as possible. We intend to tent it this summer. We don't expect too many guests this year so we will really be busy building. Thank you for your help on this project, Jim."

"Thank you. This helps me too, Don."

Don returned to Stella's and told everyone of his talk with the probation officer and what a nice fellow he was.

CHAPTER 11

THE NEW RESORT

To everyone's amazement, that spring in the middle of April Marta and Fritz arrived at the resort. The men were building their tent city for the coming summer. Hans had tears in his eyes as they stepped out of a chauffeured touring car. Hellos and introductions were exchanged among all. Fritz said, "I've brought the funds and a little more. We've taken lodging at Nance's Hot Springs for two weeks. Then we'll tour California for several days and then come by and say goodbye. Then we'll return to Europe and continue to reside in Lucerne."

"Marta and Fritz, I am overwhelmed. I am sorry we can't put you up. We're crowded up at Georges' wife's place about eight miles from here. Nothing is ready yet for anyone to stay here."

"I can see it's going to be primitive this year. Hans, is the fishing still good?"

"Yes."

Marta said, "I want to see Anna and Eva, and my grandchild or grandchildren."

"I'll lead you to where they are."

George and Don said they would keep working. All said their goodbyes. Hans got in his vehicle and led them to Stella's place. At Stella's, Eva and Anna wondered at Hans' arriving in his car with the chauffeured touring car pulling up alongside of him. Then they saw their European relatives getting out. They rushed out to greet them. Kisses and hugs and "How good you look" were exchanged.

"Come in! Come in!" Anna said. They went in and met Stella. She asked what she might serve and apologized she did not have wine. "A beer, drink, or soft drink?" Then the grandchildren met Marta and Fritz. They had lost their shyness at the tavern from being there so long and had gotten used to strangers. Fritz and Marta told the women they were staying at Nance's in Calistoga for a short time. They would return from Europe for an extended stay when the new resort building was completed.

Stella disappeared and eventually she came out with a tray of pickles, peppers, sardines, pigs-feet, and liverwurst and salami sandwiches. Fritz said, "A feast! Thank you, my dear. And another beer, please." Marta was holding her grandchildren on her lap with an ecstatic smile.

After Hans had eaten, he said, "I am going back to help at the resort. We have so much to do." Fritz spoke up. "Hans, I'd like to take everyone to dinner this evening at the Calistoga Hotel. Would you ladies like that?" Eva and Anna quickly answered yes. Fritz said, "You too, Stella."

"I can't, Fritz. I have to run this place."

"No one to replace you?"

"No, I never even thought about that, Fritz."

"What about the grandchildren?"

"I can call in Sally Fector. She sometimes cleans and helps out on holidays. I am sure she would be available, or her sister, to watch the children."

Hans returned to the resort and told George and Don of Fritz's offer of dinner that evening. George said he'd stay with Stella. "I think it's really a family thing, Hans."

"George you are family. You're the brother I never had."

"Thank you, Hans. But I'll stay with Stella."

Work completed for the day, the men returned to Stella's. Sally was already there to watch the children. Eva and Anna were both ready to go. Don and Hans cleaned up and the four left for Calistoga. They arrived at the hotel where Fritz had a table reserved for them. They all enjoyed as sumptuous a dinner as the hotel was capable of preparing. The local wines were a great surprise to Fritz and Marta. They said they had tasted few wines in Europe as good. Maybe several French wines had more aging.

Fritz said, "On our next trip here, Hans, I'll have to inquire about the availability of vineyard investing."

"Fritz, we have a very dear Italian gentleman in St. Helena that has quite a bit of acreage in vineyards. You'll have to speak with him. I'll introduce you."

"Thank you, Hans. I'll take you up on that."

Don said, "There is talk of prohibition in the near future. If it happens, Donald, it won't last. People will drink always. And, if it happens, that's when I'll buy. The vineyard's price will fall. We can age the red wines for many years and develop some really good wine." Don interjected, "That's an interesting outlook, Fritz."

Everyone enjoyed the dinner and Fritz and Marta beamed at the thank-yous. They all walked to the hot springs where Fritz and Marta were staying. They had never been inside, but were led into Fritz and Marta's spacious suite.

Goodbyes were said and Hans and family returned to Stella's. After the children were sleeping and Stella had let Sally go home, George and Stella insisted that everyone tell them about the evening with Marta and Fritz.

They told them about the nice dinner and wished they were there. They said Marta and Fritz were leaving in a couple of days for Carmel. Then to Big Sur and then to Los Angeles. They would return to Calistoga for three more days and then go home to Europe.

The men continued to work on the temporary, tent city for the coming season and Anna helped much of the time. A few days later, after a previous visit, Jim Bond arrived with two teenage men. Hans walked over to greet him and Jim said, "Men, this is Hans. He's your boss. You do as he says and you can stay for three months. If he has a problem with one of you, he'll contact me and you'll be back in the detention home."

"Hello, men, I am glad you're here. We have a lot of work to do in a short time so you can be a big help. The work is not too hard. Just lots of it."

"Hans, the tall one is Keith and the redhead is Ray."

"Glad to make your acquaintance." The new dining area had just been completed and there was already a working bathhouse. Jim brought two sleeping bags out of his vehicle and the young men removed cots from the trunk.

Hans said, "You'll sleep in this building until we get a tent finished for you. We'll bring your meals to you. As you can see, there was a big fire here last September. No fires inside this building or anywhere near it."

"Yes, sir," they both answered.

"I'll go and pick up your dinner later and we'll share our lunches with you. We have water canteens with us and there's a stream down below where you can fill the canteen. Take turns doing it. I don't know if any rattlers have moved back into the area yet, but be watchful. Make yourselves hiking sticks after we leave this evening. They're handy to move a snake out of the way if needed." Hans then thanked Jim for the men and introduced him to George.

In the next month they finished their tent city and three more bathhouses with cold showers. But flush toilets were something new. Anna, Hans, and

Eva traveled to Santa Rosa to Montgomery Wards and ordered a large business stove, grill, kitchenware, metal beds, mattresses, bedding for twenty-four tent cabins, tables, chairs, and some fishing equipment for themselves and guests. By May 25th, they had received requests for reservations for 75% of the tent cabins. They were really encouraged because all they had hoped for was to break even and continue their contact with customers. The two young men were a little slow to learn, but they were polite and good eaters. Ray seemed to like the resort and Keith talked a lot about missing his home in Oakland.

That summer Anna and Eva ran the resort while the men labored at implementing Dons' plan for the new resort building. The summer was hotter than usual and the mixing of concrete by hand was time-consuming. The pours were early morning or late afternoon to miss the heat of the day. Jim Bond had brought another man to Hans—Tony, an older convict. He had killed a man in his younger days when he had been drinking. Jim assured Hans he was safe. The prison chaplain and warden had vouched for him and Tony had sworn to never drink again. Hans said, "We'll keep an eye on him, Jim, we do drink a little here. I am really shorthanded on this project. Anyone who can use a shovel or push a wheelbarrow is useful. Tony moved in with the two young men Jim had brought up earlier. He was a little rough with the young men, but when they asked why he had been in the "joint," he explained his crime and they accepted his ways. The season was successful, but Eva and Anna were overworked so the last part of the season one of Mrs. O'Malley's girls had been hired to wait table and help Eva. She even took over Anna's chores of clean linen changes each week. A young cousin of Don's had come to the resort to watch the children for the summer since Anna was constantly leading hikes.

At summer's end, the men had completed almost half of the new building. They would continue to work through the fall and winter, weather permitting. Everyone was now living in some of the new units and the main dining hall and leisure room was completed. The building was finished in late May and they were ready for guests by the first of June. An extensive advertising campaign in several Bay Area papers was bringing a rush of reservations. Moreover, the guests of the last few years had been telling of the wonder of Fire Mountain and the overall beauty of the area. The trees were green again and, for the most part, brush was back. Friends wanting to see the place were now driving up for the Sunday dinners. Keith had returned to his parent's home in Oakland and Ray had asked to stay on at the resort when his time was up. Hans, Eva, Anna, and George all thought this was a good idea since the young man was a willing worker. Tony was still working since he had another year to do on his probation. He was now helping Eva in the kitchen. Stella had sold her place and had taken over running the bar. She had also started Saturday night dances and guests and local people were attending. Hans and Ray were the general handymen. Don was doing part-time architectural work in Santa Rosa. George was back leading hikes and overnight campouts with Anna. Since Anna was now doing a lot of the paperwork pertaining to the resort, the hikes were an escape for her. Sally Fector was now watching the children full-time during the resort season. Still they knew next season they would need additional help and they felt they should add a dozen more units onto the existing building which wouldn't be ready until the following year. They also agreed there should be a full-time dishwasher and at least two more waitresses.

CHAPTER 12

THE DEERHUNTER

Anna had run into Sheriff Lamberton on one of her shopping trips to town. As he helped carry supplies out to her vehicle and she was thanking him, he said, "Call me Roy now."

"If you want."

"Yes, please. Anna, I wanted to ask you something."

"Yes, Sheriff, I mean Roy."

"Anna, my 15-year-old son has been giving me a little trouble here in town; he is forever at the pool hall or cutting school. I know you've been using a few of Jim Bonds' boys up at the resort and Jim tells me they come from your place changed for the better."

"Roy, I don't think we've done anything special. Everyone is friendly and it's a beautiful peaceful place."

"Whatever, Anna. Jim says it works."

"Roy, we were just talking the other night about hiring a dishwasher and light chore person. He'd live in one of the units with another young man and an older con who's one of the nicest gents to come to the place. He's polite, a willing worker, and he attends mass here every Sunday at 6 a.m."

"I'll have to tell my wife about this, I've only been thinking about this idea."

"You do that, Roy, and we can work something out. I'd like to help, I haven't forgotten your kindness in helping when John was killed."

"Anna, that was just doing my job."

"Roy, I have seen the tenderness you extended to my family and how you helped with everything. I'll mention it to Hans and the others."

"Do."

"If Jim Bond calls, we can say we don't need anyone else for the present."

Lamberton's son, Owen, came to work that season. He was a tall, lanky youngster with black hair and blue eyes. You could tell he was going to be big like his father. He mixed well with his two roommates. During time off, the three of them would go out to a nearby, abandoned mine site and shoot the twenty-two Ray had purchased from Sears Roebucks. Owen quickly became the best shot. He asked Hans if he could accompany him on one of his deer hunts. Hans was still supplying the table with deer meat in the off season. After watching Hans bring down deer on a couple of hunts, Owen asked if he could go along the next time and take a shot. Hans asked, "What have you learned from me, Owen?"

"Not to miss, to be very quiet, to get well away from the resort area."

"That's correct. Next time you go by yourself."

"Really?"

"Yes, and good hunting."

A week later Owen left the resort early in the morning. He hiked down to the cave stream area and farther down the canyon and to the east he crossed a ridge and sat down looking over a small creek that fed into a basin of water. He could see trails leading away from both sides of the water. He sat down at the base of a large fir and waited. A couple of raccoons came down to wash, and left. Soon a doe with a fawn came to water. Hans had taken bucks or does when he hunted. Owen didn't want to leave the fawn motherless even though he was good size. He also felt his first kill should be a buck.

Hours later a large buck appeared, sniffing the air as he came and pausing and looking. Owen was motionless against the base of the tree, but he felt like the buck was looking right at him. The buck continued his careful trip to the basin for his drink. As he started to lock him into his sights, Owen thought he'd let him finish his drink before he fired. His thirst quenched, the buck turned and started back on his trail. Owen squeezed the trigger. He heard the shot about the same time it entered the buck's heart. The animal dropped to its knees, tried to rise, got one leg up, and rolled to its right.

Owen waited a little as Hans had always done when he had made a kill. Then Owen moved to the downed animal, saw that it was dead, and cut its throat to let it bleed out. Then he field-dressed it as Hans had done and carried the intestines off the trail. After he moved the buck a couple of yards off the trail, he scattered dry leaves over the place where the buck had lain. He placed his rifle on a nearby stump, went to the animal, hoisted it on to his shoulders, went to the stump, and picked up his rifle. He'd have a long carry back to the resort, but the pride of his first kill gave him increased vigor.

After several stops along the way for water, he arrived back at the resort. He laid the buck down in the utility shed where Hans always dressed the deer he brought in. Hans, George, and Don were eating lunch. Smiling, Owen said, "Hans, I got one in the shed."

"Owen, wash up and have something to eat. We'll go look right after lunch." Owen did as he was told and ate voraciously. After lunch, he led the men to the shed. They all commented on what a large animal it was. Hans said, "That was a hard carry, Owen. Where did you get him?" Owen explained. "That's a good spot, Owen, but it's a long ways back."

"It didn't seem too far, Hans."

"You did well, Owen. You're the official hunter from now on." Owen was bursting with pride.

"Finish dressing him and hang him in the bay tree as I've always done."

"Yes, Hans."

Several years later as Owen became a superior hunter, knowing where deer would be on certain days or nights, he would amaze the guests and tell them where they could see deer. Moreover, Hans was lending Owen out to vineyard owners that were having problems with deer herds depleting their vineyards. The damage was severe. Hans had talked to Sheriff Roy about the vintners' deer problem and the lack of cooperation by the local game warden. Lamberton had said, "The vintners are the bread and butter of this valley. If there's a problem, I'll talk to him forcefully and make him see the light or the warden can ask for a transfer to another county."

Owen was replaced by another of Jim Bond's parolees in the kitchen. He now was using a five-cell flashlight to eradicate the deer, but it took a couple of years before he really made a dent in their population. The vintners were now smiling at his arrival and many daughters asked to accompany this good-looking youth in his hunts. Owen was sharing his kills with others in the county whom his dad suggested needed a little meat.

When Sheriff Lamberton would pull up, at first people would be a little apprehensive. But on his second visit, they'd be inviting him in for coffee, pie, cookies, or cider. One bright, moonlit night, a deer had just come out of the brush into the vineyard and Owen was raising his rifle to shoot when a blur was on the deer, biting into its neck. It was the first time Owen had seen a mountain lion make a live kill. He lowered his gun and watched.

The lion dragged the deer into the brush. He could wait a little longer for another deer to appear, but he thought nothing else would probably show. An hour later he was right, and left. That vintner said he hadn't seen a deer in several weeks thanks to Owen, but Owen thought to himself, "I've got a partner working your place."

One day at the resort Anna was talking to Owen about his calling and said, "What will you do when all the deer herds have thinned out?"

"I'd like to be a long-haul truck driver and see the country."

"You are a very good driver for a young man, Owen. I hope you get your wish. If not, you'll always be welcome here."

"Thank you, Anna."

Chapter 13

Lance

They had just started to add the new guest rooms and Don had laid out the stakes for a new pool near the main building. Jim Bond had been up the week before and talked to Hans about a young, 24-year-old man he had to place. "This is Mr. Nice guy, but he's just coming out of San Quentin after doing two years for bad checks. The D.A. in Napa had dropped a bigamy charge against him since he had picked up the sentence for checks. Hans, this guy could talk you out of this place if you gave him half a chance."

"Why should I consider taking him?"

"He's like a piece of steel and he'll work all day. A little praise and he eats it up. He's sinfully handsome and you'll have to watch your woman. My wife met him at the office one day and she thought he was some kind of god. She said, "That boy is too pretty.""

"Well Jim, we've had good luck with your men so far. Let's give him a try." Jim brought Lance up early Monday morning. He went to the dining room where Anna said the men were already working on the new wing.

"Jim, you and your friend have some coffee and breakfast."

"We ate as we left town, Anna, but another cup of coffee sounds good. Anna, this is Lance. He's the new man I've brought up to work. Lance, this is Mrs. White."

Lance nodded his head and said, "Pleased to meet you, ma'am."

"Lance, you can call me Anna, as everyone does."

"Yes, Anna."

She thought she had seen someone who looked like him at the cinema. She caught herself looking a little too long. "I am sorry, Jim. I'll get that coffee." Anna returned with the coffee and the men drank it while they talked about the weather. Jim mentioned he'd been hearing about Owen and how pleased the vintners were.

"He's a busy man, Jim."

"Thanks for the coffee, Anna," Lance echoed Jim. Jim led Lance to where the men were working.

He introduced him to Hans and the crew and told Lance he could leave his suitcase in the main dinning room with Anna or her mother.

"Fine, Jim." Lance took off his shirt and Hans put him to mixing concrete. Six shovels of gravel, two of sand, and three of cement. "Be exact, Lance. It's important we have a good even pour."

"Yes, sir."

"'Hans' will do, Lance."

The others were surprised at how quick the concrete was coming. The wheelbarrow man was hard pressed to keep it moving. "Slack up, lad. We got all day and a lot more days. I'll spell you once in a while. Take a break."

"I'll take you up on that," Ray said. By the end of the day, Hans and Don had noticed Lance was a relentless worker. When they started to work on the pool site, the concrete had to be carried up a grade to a place where they would mix it and then make their pour. Everyone would carry a sack of cement to the site, but Lance would carry two, smiling at the labor. His roommates thought he was a fabricator of tales, but to their amazement, every once in a while something would be true.

Don and Anna's adolescent daughters were "gaga" over him. The resort season started and you could see the female guests catch their breath the first time they'd see Lance. Anna mentioned it to Hans. "I'll have to keep him busy and work him late to keep him out of the way." Hans even went so far as to lend Lance and Ray to ranchers hauling hay or bringing in crops. Lance would come in some nights after working out in the hay fields and hike down to the stream where he would bathe before coming back up to his living quarters to shave and then go to the kitchen and eat.

Often affluent guests would send their families up for a couple weeks or a month and return to the City to work during the week. Then they would return on weekends unless some unforeseen problem would arise. Several women would notice the pattern of Lance's routine and accidentally wander down to the stream looking for a lost hat or scarf they had left behind. They'd gaze at this six foot two, golden blonde with the green eyes and soft flaming lips. He was an Adonis, his upper torso tanned and his lower loins pale. As men often fall for the beauty of a young woman, these women, sometimes lonely and not seeing their husbands for eight or nine days, would "melt." Some he could have taken right there, but he didn't want Anna, Hans, George, or anyone connected to the resort to find a reason to return him to Jim Bond. Lance would suggest a meeting after dark at their cabin or they would take a short walk to a hidden spot where he slept out on warm nights. His beauty and gift of gab would make them forget their good sense. He was the supreme lover, giving them whatever they desired and convincing them they were the most beautiful, fascinating women he had ever been with. At times he had a problem with too many "hitting on" him at the same time. He'd have them go to different locations and ask Tony or Ray to walk by the area and say Lance had been called to town. Then they would talk to these ladies or get whatever they could. Once in a while, a woman still in ecstasy from the long night would slip and talk to others about Lance and you could see the frowns on the unlucky ones. But if their turn came again, they'd forget about being stood up.

The summer passed and Anna received a couple of letters from guests who said they would not be coming back next year. She wondered why and thought they might want a change. Newer and better cars were giving people the opportunity to travel farther.

The following summer there were many reservations and Anna hired a couple of more waitresses. Ray had fallen in love with one of the young girls, a college student from Berkeley. She enjoyed her off duty hours with Ray, swimming, hiking, and watching a movie in town. A kiss on the cheek and that was it. She knew she had no future with this young man whose prospects were so limited. One evening when Ray had gone home for a couple of days, she wandered down to the stream and saw Lance swimming. "How's the water?"

"Nice, Connie. This is the best time of year to swim in this water. Come on in."

"I don't have my suit with me."

"Neither do I. I'll turn my back and you can sneak in."

"Can I trust you?"

"Of course, Connie. We both work here." She was just hot enough to do it. And she had appreciated Lance's looks, but felt he'd never look twice. Lance swam to the other side of the stream so she felt more comfortable. She started to backstroke up the stream. Suddenly she knew she had swum into someone. He held her shoulders gently and leaned down and kissed her. She accepted his kiss.

He said, "I'll race you to the turn."

She took the challenge and won by half a stroke. "You're good," he said, taking her into his arms. He kissed her gently and Connie felt his hand come to rest between her thighs. "I've been watching you, Connie. I don't know what you see in Ray, you're a smart girl."

"We're just friends, Lance." She was thrilled he had been watching her.

"I love the way you move, Connie. You are so graceful."

"Thank you, Lance. That's sweet of you to say." She felt him getting more personal. "Doesn't it feel nice, Connie?"

"Yes, too nice."

"You ever do it in the water, Connie?"

"No."

"Lets."

He brought her closer to him. She had a few experiences at Berkeley so she joined in their coupling. Never had a man been in her so long. She thought she was going to faint. "Hold me, Lance." He kissed her fervently. When he led her back to her clothing, she was so spent he had to help her dress. A couple of days later when she saw him in the dining room, he was nice, but distant. Ray had returned, but she just couldn't start back with him.

The summer passed slowly for Connie after that. She did get drunk with a young guest one night, but he was not Lance. Would anyone ever be?

One late summer evening Lance and Owen were showing a couple of male guests one of the trails that led to a good hunting area. The guests planned to return during deer season. As they walked down the trail, a buck jumped out just in front of them and, like a leopard, Lance had caught and bull-dogged him to the ground. The guest and Owen were astonished. "My god!" Alan said to his friend John. "I don't believe it." Owen was shaking his head. What couldn't this guy do? "Owen, use your knife and cut his throat."

"Let him go Lance, it's not deer season."

"You kidding me?"

"No. You don't want our guest to think we take deer out of season." Lance realized Owen was right. "Okay Blitzen, I'll let you go. Say hello to Santa." He stepped away from the buck. It staggered up and went into the brush. Alan asked Lance, "You do that often?"

"No. He was just surprised for a second and I was on him quickly." Later back at the main dining room bar, John and Alan were telling Stella and a couple of other guests what had happened. Some thought it was a tale and accused them of having one too many. Stella said, "I've heard he did it one day in a neighbor's freshly disked orchard. That boy is quick in a lot of ways."

Owen was back at the bunkhouse, with Lance saying, "Okay, super stud. That was quite a trick, you had those two guys talking to themselves."

"Just surprise, Owen. It's like grabbing a steelhead out of the stream in shallow water. We're animals too."

"I know you are, Lance."

"Come on, I am not so bad, except with women." Lance was the only man Owen had ever seen get involved with women who were on their honeymoon. Unknown to Eva and Hans, during the off season Lance would hike the six miles into Calistoga and get involved with some of the local women. Married or unmarried, it didn't matter to him. He eventually tied in with an older waitress who had a car. He explained to his bunkmates that it was a little hard pumping all night, walking six miles back to the resort, getting an hour's sleep, and returning to work in the morning.

She was a decent enough looking older gal of forty, but had a hard look. Lance said when his parole was up he would marry her and get the car. Eventually he did. Sometimes he would drop by on a date with some young thing from town while Shirlee worked. The following summer he dropped by alone several times and eventually met the daughter of one of the guests, a beautiful girl attending Stanford. Lance returned every night that Ellen's family stayed at the resort. She was madly in love with him.

After Ellen had returned to San Francisco with her parents, he came to the resort one night having a drink and looking for a woman. Owen said, "I thought you were in love with Ellen, you old, married man."

"I like Ellen and she loves me. Shirlee gave me the wheels and now it's in my name."

"What's she think about you catting around?"

"I am careful and I'm just up here seeing my old friends." After several trips to the Stanford campus to see Ellen, an engagement followed. Ellen told her parents she was pregnant to speed up a wedding date and a wedding soon followed. The priest thought Lance was a fallen-away Catholic, but he knew the family and Ellen begged for his cooperation.

Following the wedding, they left for a month's trip to Europe. Lance had told his wife, Shirlee, that he was going to ship out for a while so he would leave the car with her and catch a bus to San Francisco. Shirlee didn't like the idea, but Lance said he'd make a lot of money and after a little while she wouldn't have to work anymore. He stayed with his brother in San Francisco until the wedding. Ellen and her parents had believed his story that he was an aspiring screen writer and a couple of months after the wedding, would be working in Hollywood. He had only been at the resort working to rebuild his health following a back injury.

The boat trip to Europe opened Ellen's eyes a little. Lance was a heavy drinker and wanted to be the star in almost every conversation. Exhausted after intimacy, she would fall asleep, waking in the morning to find Lance not in bed. At first she thought he had gone to breakfast or a walk around the decks. Sometimes he arrived with a tray of breakfast for her. Other times he'd look at her and, after going for a shower, come out and say, "I was drinking with the crew. I am going to get some rest. You go up on deck and get some sun, Ellen."

"Can't I lie here with you, Lance?"

"Yes. But let me get some sleep." As he slept, she could smell the aroma of alcohol on his breath. Some days she would join him in bed and when he started to get aroused, she couldn't get enough of him. He came to know this.

In Europe it was much the same as aboard ship. They rarely fell asleep together. Lance was having the time of his life. Two days before they were scheduled to return to America, Lance did not return to their room. At two in the afternoon Ellen talked to the hotel manager who said if Lance wasn't present by 7 p.m., he would contact an officer at the police department for his advice. Seven came and Ellen talked to the manager who then called the police department. An hour later an officer from the Paris detective squad was knocking on Ellen's door. She had dozed off and the knock startled her. She hoped it was Lance and he had lost his key, but she opened the door to a short, bearded man in glasses who had the biggest brown eyes she had ever seen.

"Madame, I am Detective George Salet of the Paris Police Department," he announced as he extended his credentials to her.

"Thank you for coming. Your English is very good," she said in French.

"You are well-versed in my language, Madame Biglow." Ellen explained that her husband was missing. "Has this happened before, Madame Biglow?"

"We are on our honeymoon. Some evenings he would stay out drinking with the crew, but always came home by morning."

"Do you have a picture of him?"

"Not with me, Detective Salet, but I can describe him and what he was wearing."

"That would help. I will check the local hospitals or maybe the jails too. He may have fallen asleep and was picked up by our night porters. You are very beautiful, Mrs. Biglow. I am sure there is some explanation."

When their departure time came three days later, after talking several times to her parents and Detective Salet, Ellen was persuaded to return home. Detective Salet said he would stay on top of his search and asked that she forward a picture of Lance to him as soon as possible.

Two weeks later Detective Salet had a picture of Lance. "Handsome man," he thought. "No wonder the poor Mrs. Biglow is so anxious to find him." Ellen had told the detective that her father promised a reward if he could gather any information. Salet pinned the picture on the wall above his desk. A few fellow officers asked him if it was his new love. He cursed and assured them he only liked women.

Several weeks later Salet recognized Lance with a beautiful, German starlet. He had tried to contact him at several hotels, but he only stayed for a day or two so he lost his trail. The same happened today; Lance left before Salet could confront him. Eventually Lance went underground and lived with an older woman who was a chef. He ultimately learned to cook well enough to work in several top stateside restaurants.

CHAPTER 14

RANDY

Don noticed the weather-beaten man standing at the side of the road with his thumb raised and holding a small sack. Don pulled over and asked, "Where are you going?" He replied, "Anywhere I can find work."

"What do you do?"

"I am a Jack of all trades and a steady worker."

"I notice you have a Southern drawl."

"Yes, I'm from Florida and raised in Alabama, Georgia, and Tennessee. Been on my own since I was twelve. My name is Randy Parker."

"Pleased to meet you, Randy. I am Don White. I operate a resort with my wife and her parents. Randy, we don't pay too much, but we feed real good and there's not too much pressure if you would like to give us a try."

"Well Don, I could sure use a good meal and a bed for a change."

Don turned on to Petrified Road, which led to Santa Rosa. They climbed the mountain for the next few miles and turned on to a private road leading to ranches and ending at the resort ten minutes later. Randy was surprised at the modern building nesting on the ridge as they passed under it. "Quite a place you have here, Don."

"Yes, we really enjoy it here and the surrounding beauty."

Randy looked toward the pool. He could see guests in bathing suits in and near the pool, swimming and sunbathing. As Don pulled to a stop, he told Randy to follow him. They entered the building and Don led to a table near the kitchen. "Sit down and I'll see you get something to eat." Don went into the kitchen where Anna was at table kneading dough.

"Hi, Anna. My dear, I picked up a man on the way home. I think he's quite hungry and he says he's a good steady worker."

"I hope so, Don." She kissed him on the lips.

"Can you rustle up something for him to eat? I am a little hungry myself, dear." Don returned to Randy. "Sit down, the wife will fix you something to eat."

"Thank you, Don."

"What actually have you done, Randy?"

"Well, I worked the shrimp boats, oil fields, mines, and lumber camps, pearl dived, tended bar, and worked a lot of labor jobs."

"Well, we don't have most of what you mentioned, but we'll keep you busy if you decide to stay. Do you drive, Randy?"

"Yes. Cars, trucks, and tractors."

"We always need someone who can hop in a car and run errands or take guests to town." Anna placed a large tray of roast beef sandwiches on the table. She asked Randy what he would like to drink. "I am sorry," Don exclaimed. "Randy, this is Anna, my wife. Anna, this is Randy." Hellos were exchanged.

"A cup of coffee would be nice, Anna." She returned with coffee for the men. "Thank you, ma'am."

"Randy, call me Anna."

"Yes, ma'am. I mean Anna."

Anna checked back later. The sandwiches were gone. She brought a fresh-baked apple pie to the table. You could see Randy's eyes light up. Several more cups of coffee and after eating half the pie, Randy pushed away from the table. "I didn't mean to be a pig, Don, but I was really starved."

"That's okay, Randy. I will show you to the bunkhouse." Don led Randy out of the dining room and along a path to the left of the main building to an area on the other side of some large, bay trees. The bunkhouse was a long, low building. Randy could see the grapevines crawling up the support post of the porch. "Do they produce grapes, Don?"

"Yes, but the help eat 'em as soon as they're ripe. God bless 'em." Randy could see quite a few doors off the porch. He wondered how many employees Don had, but didn't ask. Don opened a door and led Randy in. There were two single beds and a large old bureau with a mirror. A door led out the back of the room. Don said, "The toilet and shower are in back. We place a high demand on cleanliness here, Randy. We all come in a lot of contact with the guests."

"You'll start tomorrow, Randy. Look around the place. Get familiarized and someone will help you learn the layout of the surrounding countryside. Take a rest or do what you want. If you don't feel comfortable, I'll run you back into town tomorrow. Dinner for the help is after the guests eat. Come back to the dining room, eat, and meet your fellow employees."

"Yes, Don. Maybe I'll take a little nap."

"Suit yourself, Randy. See you later."

"Thanks again for picking me up, Don." Don smiled and was out the door. He returned to the dining area where Eva was cleaning up in the kitchen. "Well Donald, what did you bring us?"

"I am not sure, Eva. He seems pleasing enough. We'll see how he works out."

Randy removed several articles from his grip, placed them in an empty drawer, and laid a brush on top of the bureau. He knew he was grimy. He went out to the shower area. There were four toilets and showers, each partitioned into small rooms. He noticed one shower had a partial bar of Lifeboy. He entered that compartment, stripped, used the shower, and, while showering, washed his underwear and socks. Finished, he put his pants on and returned to his room. He hung the wet clothing on a hanger fashioned from a cord, lay down, and fell asleep.

He woke to a knock on the door. "Dinner time, buddy."

"I'll be out in a minute." He dressed, opened the door, and a tall, young man extended a hand. "I'm Owen."

"Pleased to meet you, Owen. I am Randy."

"Where you from?"

"Florida and all over."

"I'm local. Someday I want to see all over."

"It's a big country, Owen."

Owen drew a pack of cigarettes from a rolled up, t-shirt sleeve. He offered Randy one. Randy took it and placed it behind his ear.

"You want another for now?"

"No. I smoke 'em as a treat, Owen. When I've got the money, I buy a sack of Bull Durham and roll three or four a day."

"Yeah, these things do cost. I use a pack a day." Owen led Randy to a large table and introduced him to everyone.

Randy said, "Nice meeting you all. I'll eventually learn your names."

The next morning after a large breakfast, Hans spoke to Randy. "Just follow me around or help with what I am doing."

"Yes, sir."

"You can call me Hans. Everyone does."

Anna, Eva, and Stella were still sitting at the morning meal sipping coffee. Stella asked, "What do you think of the new man?" Anna said, "He's different and not bad looking with that curly, blond hair. He looks short, but I noticed him walking in with Owen, he was only a couple of inches shorter so he must be close to six feet."

"His blue eyes are pale like a Norwegian's," Eva offered. Anna mentioned his Southern twang. "Yes, but it's kind of musical," Stella said. Ray came in and started clearing dishes. He had been helping Eva in the kitchen.

Hans and Randy drove down to the stream in an old Mac truck flat bed with a wheelbarrow, a couple of yards of manure, and a couple of shovels on its bed. Hans had planted flowers near the sulfur baths and liked to give them a feeding a couple of times a year. Randy looked at the clear, running water under the bridge.

"Hans, any fish in there?"

"Yes, Randy. We get a nice run of steelhead and a few trout."

"What are steelhead?"

"They're a west coast sea-going trout, they come up here to spawn like salmon, only they don't die. Then they return to the sea."

"Do you catch them?"

"Occasionally we take a few here. They're good eating." Hans then told Randy how to feed the manure to the flowers and they cleaned up the area of twigs and a few unwanted weeds. Telling Randy to follow him, they walked along the stream until they came to John's memorial.

"Who was this for?" Randy asked.

"He was a nice young man that worked for us who was accidentally shot by a deer hunter. The hunter probably never knew he killed someone."

"Sad," Randy said.

"Yes, we all really took it hard." On the way back to the truck, Randy noticed a large fish in the stream. "Is that one of those steelheads, Hans?"

"Yes, Randy. He's probably headed up to the spawning area."

That afternoon Hans went into town for supplies. As he was finishing shopping, he asked Randy if he needed anything. "If you got me a pack of Bull Durham and a pack of Gillette razor blades, I'd work it off."

"Sure, Randy." Hans ordered the clerk to add six packs of Bull Durham and some Gillette blades to the resort's order. Ten minutes later they were loading things onto the truck that now had side boards in place. They returned to the resort and Hans told Randy to unload. Ray would tell him where to place things.

Anna made it a point to take Randy along on her hikes so that he really came to know the area completely. The first time he accompanied her to the stream cave with two sets of hikers who were old clients who had been to the cave before and joined in the nude dips. After the long hike, Randy excused himself and said he would wait at the cave entrance. Anna thought he was a little old to be so shy since they all were about the same age. Sitting at the dinner table that night, she mentioned, "Your friend, Randy, left as we all started to strip for a quick skinny dip to Mr. Smarty's Island." Several chuckled and some smiled. It was a way of life they had come to accept.

Owen said, "Don't be shy, Randy. We all have the same plumbing."

Randy turned quite red and replied, "I guess I am shy, but I can learn."

"That's the spirit," Don said. Randy was working out quite well and seemed to have a natural knack for electrical work. Don had drawn a plan for extensive outdoor lighting and Randy had taken on the project. Don was very satisfied with his work. That summer at the outdoor fireplace where they had an amateur hour every Wednesday night for the guests and any of the help who wanted to participate, several of the help who had heard Randy singing or humming persuaded him to participate. He was the last to perform, singing "Big Rock Candy Mountain," made famous by Burl Ives. The children and the adults loved it and demanded an encore. He then sang "Down In The Valley" and continued on for over an hour with western ballads and songs from the Smokey Mountains and some yodeling. People clapped and many had tears in their eyes. Anna had come to the site to see why the amateur hour had lasted so long and caught his last few songs. Later in bed she was telling Don how wonderfully Randy sang. As Don kissed her, he said, "Honey, I am glad to hear it. It will be nice for the guests if we can get Randy to do it on a regular basis." As they joined, they still felt the importance of their finding each other.

The next morning, Owen knocked on Randy's door. "Come on, Burl. Let's eat and get to work." Owen had been helping Randy with the outside lighting work, digging the pole holes, setting them in place, and then passing wires and insulators to him. Randy hollered, "Just a minute, deer hunter. I'll be right out."

Later that day as they were setting poles down by the sulfur baths and it was really hot, Owen said, "Let's take a dip in the stream."

"Okay, Owen. I guess I might as well get used to it." They walked over to the stream, pulled their boots off, and dropped their shirts and pants to the ground. Randy quickly dived in. Owen followed and challenged Randy to a race to a log sitting half in and out of the water about 100 feet upstream. No one had ever beaten Owen in a race, but they hit the log at the same time.

Owen was amazed. "You're fast, Randy."

"I don't know. Never did too much swimming 'til I joined the Navy and then was stationed in Hawaii. Nice duty. Yeah, it was all right! Friendly Kanaka women over there, and went to some great luaus. I made a bad dive off of a cliff one day and was in a coma for three weeks. They discharged me early since I had a lot of problems with headaches for a long time. They finally went away after I was out for a year. Come on, I'll race you back."

"Okay." Owen beat Randy by several feet and was out of the water before him. As Randy came out, he couldn't help notice Randy's manhood. It reached to his knee. He was fairly endowed himself, but this guy was hung like a stud.

"Yeah, it's long."

"What happens when it gets hard?"

"I usually pass out it takes so much blood."

"You're kidding?"

"Yeah. I am like anyone else, Owen."

"How the hell do woman handle it?"

"Patiently, I take my time."

"I can see why you didn't want to strip with Anna and the guests."

"It's a little embarrassing, but it's just part of me." They went back to work.

The next Saturday night at the weekly dance, a couple of lingerie models had come to the resort during the week and were attending the dance, enjoying the evening, and sipping the punch. One named Helen was seen to walk out with Randy. When they returned several hours later, she was walking a little tenderly. Randy said he had been a little quick with her, but it had been over a year since he had been with a woman and she was pretty high.

The next morning at a late breakfast, Helen was asking the waitress where Randy was. "He's around somewhere, wherever the boss placed him today."

Helen later found Randy as he was leaving to take a couple of guests to the Greyhound terminal in Calistoga. "Can I ride along?"

"Sure. I have no one coming back. Just have to gas this vehicle up and have the rest of the day off."

Helen climbed in. One of the guest's children asked Randy to sing "Big Rock Candy Mountain" and he obliged. Helen said, "Sing another," and he did 'til they reached town. After unloading the guests and helping with their baggage, he and Helen drove to the gas station on the edge of town. Randy checked the oil and water while a young man pumped gas. Randy signed for the gas and they left town. Helen slid over and dropped her hand onto him.

Randy made a slight swerve in the road and said, "Warn me, girl. When I am driving, I don't want to cause an accident."

"Next time, Randy." Half way up the mountain he pulled off the road behind some trees. She said, "Easy now" as they came together.

"I am sorry about last night. But it had been a long time."

It took several stops to get back to the resort. "Eat with me tonight and I'll introduce you to my friend."

"I can't eat with the guests, but I can have a drink with you at the bar after dinner."

For the rest of the summer and the next, Helen came up to see Randy about every other week. When the second summer ended, Helen told Randy she was moving to New York for a job with a high profile lingerie company. She would miss him. Randy had enjoyed her company, but he never thought it was love. He just didn't feel love. He liked people, especially the kids at the resort, but he didn't know how to love—at least not yet.

Toward the end of summer on his way back from town in the resort Pontiac, Randy was forced off the road by someone who kept going. He climbed out of the car with his nose bleeding and his shoulder aching. He hiked back a quarter mile to a rancher's house for help. The rancher said he would drive Randy to the St. Helena Sanitarium while his wife would go to the resort on her horse to let them know what had happened. He was bypassing Calistoga Hospital since he knew Doc Massey was away deer hunting.

The Seventh Day Adventists ran the sanitarium's hospital. They also had a training school for nurses. Along with learning to be a nurse, the students got plenty of bible education. They wore no make up, and unattractive uniforms, attended a lot of prayer meetings, and were allowed no movies or dancing. It was a stern life for these young women and they were expected to marry within their religion.

Randy was a little rummy when they led him into their hospital. Hours later he was informed that, indeed, his nose was broken and he also had a broken collar bone. Don arrived to find him in a hospital bed. His eyes were blackened and he was in traction.

"How do you feel, Randy?"

"Okay, boss."

"Any pain?"

"Not bad."

"Anyone you want to know about this?"

"No."

"Want me to bring you some Bull Durham?"

"No smoking here, Don."

"That's right. Seventh Day people. Okay, Randy. I'll be back in a couple of days to see how you're doing."

"Thanks for coming."

That night at dinner Don told everyone how Randy was doing. Anna said, "I'll go with you when you go back to see him."

"Yes, dear. That would be good."

That day at the hospital a couple of the young nurses were talking about the good-looking young man in Room 27. A supervisor heard them and admonished them, "He's not one of us." Then she instructed a trainee to handle his bathroom needs for the next few hours. During the next few days, the trainee became smitten with Randy, but she was careful to keep her thoughts to herself.

Randy had never had anyone so attentive to him. She was a little thin, but a pretty blond almost as tall as he was. She brought him a bible one evening, kissed him quickly on the cheek, and was gone. He opened the cover and a small flower fell into his lap. A little piece of paper said, "I love you." He smiled. He was sure she didn't mean it and thought he still didn't know what love was yet. Anna and Don came in a little after and found him smiling.

"Well, someone is feeling good," Anna said.

"Hi, Anna, Don. Thanks for coming." Anna took a small package of cookies out of her jacket pocket. "Thank you, Anna."

"How are they treating you, Randy?"

"Really nice, but the food is plain and skimpy."

"Any news when you're getting out?"

"Next Monday morning, maybe."

"I'll call and make sure you're getting discharged. If you are, I'll pick you up."

"Good, Don."

They talked about the resort and the crew. Randy said to say hello to everyone. "We will." Then Don and Anna left. The next morning when Barbara came in (he had learned her name on her second day of caring for him), he had saved half of Eva's cookies for her. She turned red and thanked him profusely. Later she ate them in the bathroom and was surprised at how good they were.

After Barbara helped him to the bathroom that afternoon, Randy pushed the door closed before she had a chance to get out. Then he kissed her tenderly on the lips. When their lips parted, she said, "I love you, Randy," and hurried out. As she was straightening the bed, the supervisor came in. She noticed Barbara's red face and said, "It's not a sin to fix a man's bed, dear."

"Yes, Mrs. Hallet." Randy came out of the bathroom and said, "Good afternoon, Mrs. Hallet."

"Yes, it is. Are you feeling better?"

"Yes."

"The doctor said he would release you Monday morning about 11 a.m."

"Can you call my boss at the resort and tell him to pick me up?"

"It'll be arranged."

"Thank you, Mrs. Hallet." When she left the room, Randy said, "Barbara, will you marry me?" Barbara got dizzy for a minute and leaned on the bed. "How can I leave this place? It's so regimented."

"You said you loved me."

"I do. I can't tell anyone. They would try and stop me. Maybe lock me up in my room in the dormitory."

"I'll think of something."

"You must."

"How old are you, dear?"

"I'll be nineteen next week, Randy." He kissed her again. She pulled away quickly. "Randy, I must not be caught or we won't have a chance."

"Yes, dear one. We'll wait for more of these wonderful kisses."

By Monday morning they had a plan. Randy was released in a wheelchair and Barbara pushed him to a waiting car. Don and Anna had come to pick him up. As he climbed into the car, the girl in white got in and, as Anna started to inquire, Randy said, "Don, please hurry away. I'll tell you what's going on as you drive."

As they looked back at the wheelchair, they told Don and Anna of their love. Anna asked, "How old are you, Barbara?"

"Nineteen, next week."

"Are you sure about this, Randy and Barbara?"

"Yes, we are. We know we were meant for each other," Randy said. Barbara nodded in agreement and said, "I am sure the school will be calling the sheriff's office, Anna."

"You want a quick vacation with your love?"

"Yes."

"I'll stop in Calistoga at the bank. We'll tell Sheriff Lamberton what's going on and he can get word to the resort." Don stopped at the bank, withdrew funds, and stopped at the sheriff's office after picking up a quart of Jack Daniels. They were lucky enough to catch Sheriff Lamberton in and told him what was going on.

"They'll be quite upset, Don."

"I am sure they will."

"What are you going to do?"

Randy told them the plan. Everyone loved it.

Randy, Barbara, Don, and Anna arrived in Reno at 5 p.m. They checked into a reasonably-priced hotel and got two rooms. Don said, "We'll eat, have a little champagne, and you two can practice for the wedding tomorrow."

After they had a nice dinner, Barbara said it was the first time she had ever eaten in a restaurant and the first time for steak and champagne. After two glasses, she was feeling strange.

Dinner completed, Don handed Randy the key to his and Barbara's room. They thanked Anna and Don over and over. Then Don put some money into Randy's shirt pocket. "Have breakfast in the morning just in case we sleep in a little."

"Yes, boss."

"Come on, Anna. Let's look around a little." They played a few machines with no luck and then found a place to dance. After a few dances, Anna said, "Husband, I am feeling horny."

"I like that talk." Don picked up a bottle of champagne on the way to their room. It was still great when they made love and Anna got carried away a little. Don said, "I know why I married you. 'Cause you are so great."

"I love you, too."

When they came down in the morning, the young ones were eating breakfast. Barbara was smiling and Randy looked quite content. Anna asked, "Is the wedding still on?"

"It sure is!" Barbara gushed. "Yes," said Randy. After Anna and Don had eaten, they all went to the courthouse, got the license, and found a little wedding chapel to do the honors. The minister asked if there was a ring and Randy went white. "I am sorry. I forgot. This has been sudden."

The minister said, "Step in the other room," where he had a few gold bands.

Randy said, "I don't have much on me."

Don interjected, "Randy, I'll advance whatever you need."

The transaction completed, they began the ceremony. Finally the minister proclaimed, "Barbara and Randy, you are now Mr. and Mrs. Parker."

Anna exclaimed, "Congratulations!"

Don announced, "We'll go back to the hotel, have a little more champagne, and you young'ns can relax together. We'll meet for dinner about 8 p.m. Sound good?"

Everyone agreed. After sharing the champagne, Anna and Don drove over to Virginia City, picked up a few souvenirs for everyone at the resort, and got back to the hotel a few minutes before eight. They freshened up in their room and then knocked on Barbara and Randy's door.

After a few minutes, Randy came to the door in a towel. "We are just starting to dress. We'll meet you downstairs."

"Okay, Randy, I'll get a table." Barbara was walking a little gingerly as they came to the table.

"You okay, dear?" Anna asked.

"Yes, Anna."

Later when they went to the restroom Barbara confided, "It hurt a little at first, but Randy was so tender and I so wanted to please him."

"It gets easier and better, Barbara. After a few times."

"I do hope so. I love him so much."

"Try and drink a little more tonight. It makes things easier."

"Yes, Anna."

They had Napa Valley wine with dinner— several bottles. Then they danced a little to a western group playing at the hotel. Don talked to the bandleader and, with a ten-dollar bill, convinced him to let Randy sing a song. Then he had to talk Randy into it. Anna and Barbara begged him to go along. The musicians were surprised at the young man's voice, and after a couple of songs those in attendance clapped and congratulated him.

The bandleader announced, "He has a nice voice. He should do something with it."

Don replied, "We told him, but he says it's only for fun and he doesn't want to be a singer." The next day, they left for the resort.

The day following their arrival, the nursing supervisor, two Adventist religious, and Barbara's uncle showed up in a huff. "Where is our daughter?" they asked. "Barbara Wilson!"

Anna met them as they entered the dining room. "We have a Barbara Parker—a newly married young lady. She works here with her husband. My husband and I stood up for her. The young man is a good person—hard working, clean, and a God-fearing Southern Baptist."

"We'd like to see her."

"I'll send someone to find her."

She called Ray from the kitchen.

"Yes, Anna."

"Go and find Randy. I think he's by the outdoor fireplace installing lights. I'll go and get Barbara."

Anna found Barbara making up a bedroom in one of the units and told her what was going on. She started to tremble a little.

"Honey, you hold my hand. We'll wait a few minutes to give Ray a chance to get Randy there before us. Then you take his hand and don't let go. It will give you strength."

"Yes, Anna."

They entered the dining room and Anna walked Barbara over to Randy. The Adventists were dumbfounded. This girl had on a little rouge and a light lipstick. "Barbara, you look like a whore," her uncle said. Randy raised his fist, but Anna pushed him back.

"Mister, we don't talk like that in this home."

Don had come into the room looking very formidable. "What's going on?"

Anna replied, "These people are upset. They are too blind to see God brought this young couple together."

"You kidnapped her."

"My wife and I picked Randy and Barbara up in broad daylight. We drove to Calistoga, told the sheriff what was going on, and drove them to Reno where they were legally married."

"We want to see a license."

"You have my word. Drive to Reno. You can check the public records. God works in strange ways. Here people accept what he has orchestrated. It's surely His will."

They grumbled and left. That night there was a big wedding party for Barbara and Randy. Guests and help were all invited, the champagne flowed like water, and the hangovers were many. The next morning, Stella said she had never poured so many drinks.

CHAPTER 15

RETURN HOME

The season at the resort had just ended and the last of the rental funds had arrived from the past season's guest who occasionally had been extended credit. There was a good surplus of funds for the first time. The business was growing, and setting the daily rates to just below other resorts in the area had brought occupancy to almost 94% for the past season.

Anna talked to Don and asked if he had any further improvements in mind. "Not really, Anna, just maintaining what we have now is right."

"Don, we have a decent savings account and the new checking account is flush. I was thinking about surprising Mom and Dad with a paid trip to Europe so they could see their families. Mom has never seen hers. Dad's comes here every year."

"That's a nice idea, dear one, but they'll think there's probably not enough money or it will cost too much."

"I know, but we'll have to convince them."

The next morning at breakfast as Hans was about to leave to work on one of his self-made chores, Anna said, "Stay a minute, Dad. Don and I have an idea."

"It was Anna's idea and a great one. I think she thought of something wonderful and deserving for you two." As Anna explained her idea to her parents, they looked at each other and Eva burst into tears. Hans put his arm around her.

"That's something to think about. It's good that we obtained our citizenship several years ago, but we'd have to obtain passports."

"Yes," Don said. "That doesn't take too long."

"What about my work here, and Eva's in the kitchen?"

Anna said, "If you left in late spring when the weather is starting to turn nice, you could spend two weeks traveling each way and a month in Europe. You could go to Mom's home first, then see some of Europe, then stay with Marta and Fritz."

"You can make it sound so easy."

"It can be, Dad, with the help of a good travel agent in Santa Rosa."

Eva was still in tears, but started to smile. "Hans, if we could do this, my happiness would be complete."

"Let's talk of it tonight, Eva. I have things to do. Thank you Anna and Don for thinking of us."

"I know we can take care of things in your absence, Dad." Don had gone to the kitchen and brought Eva another cup of coffee.

"What about the work it takes to run this place, children?"

Don spoke up and said, "We have a good crew here now, Eva. George, Stella, Ray, Owen, Randy, and Barbara."

"Barbara told me she's with child."

Anna replied, "Oh, that's wonderful!"

Don said, "Randy must be proud."

Eva responded, "She hasn't told Randy yet."

"She better," Anna said. "That secret doesn't keep too long."

"She is this weekend; she told me. Yes, the people that work with us are capable, but it still seems we are always so busy during the season."

Don said, "Ray has learned so much from you, Eva, and we can get someone else to do his job. I can pick up Han's chores now that everything is completed."

"Well, I'll talk to Hans tonight."

"Good, Mom." Don kissed Anna and left the dining room.

He ran into Randy and said, "Randy, you're getting a raise of twenty dollars a month."

"Thanks, boss."

"You got that old Pontiac back together yet?"

"Almost. A trip to the wrecking yard in Santa Rosa for a few body parts and it will look as good as new."

"When you're through fixing it up, we'll take it to the motor vehicle department and transfer it to your name."

"You really mean that, Don?"

Anna and I talked about it last night and we agreed you should have it, as it played such an important part of your life and Barbara's. How's that wiring coming down around the sulfur baths?"

"I've got it ready to go. Just have to run a line from up here to down there."

"You and Owen go down to the lumber yard with the old flat bed and pick up however many poles you think you need."

"Okay, Don. We may have to make several trips. Those poles are heavy."

"Whatever it takes. Have 'em put it on the resort's account."

"Yes, sir."

Nothing was said the next morning, and after breakfast Anna asked her mother if she and Hans had talked about the trip.

"Yes, Anna. I am very excited about it. Your dad is slower to answer, but I am sure he'll come around."

"I hope so, Mom."

"What are you doing today?"

"I've got a group going to the mountain cave and Mr. Smarty's home."

"It makes a long day, Anna."

"Yes, but I enjoy it and it keeps me fit."

"Are you and Don thinking of having more children?"

"We've kind of thought about it and haven't done anything to avoid it. I am happy with our family now…maybe that's enough."

"I never got pregnant again after you were born, Anna."

"Did you want another child?"

"I think Hans would have liked a son, but he's so proud of you I don't think he missed having a son. And you were such a Tomboy!"

"I really was, thanks to George and Dad."

Anna led her hike that day and after crossing the stream and hiking up to the cave next to the rock that reflected the moon on bright nights, the clouds that had drifted in as they hiked up to the cave let loose a heavy downpour. Anna told the other hikers to make themselves comfortable and she would gather some wood so they could build a fire and wait out the weather. One of the ladies offered to help and they left the cave to gather wood.

They were back in ten minutes with kindling and some small branches that were dry. Anna quickly got a fire going. Then she and Ruth, her helper, removed their shirts to let them dry near the fire. Anna removed the lunches Eva had packed from her backpack for a group picnic on the hike.

After eating and drinking some wine, Anna said, "Well ladies, how about a little songfest? I think the rain should let up in the next couple of hours and we can hike home dry."

With songs and jokes, the cave had never rung with so much laughter. Wood was gathered again and the rain finally stopped.

The party hiked back to the resort as dusk was falling. They had an adventure to pass around in conversation at the dinner table. Hans told Anna, "Honey, I was about to come looking for you just as you entered."

"When the rain let up, I hurried along. I knew you'd be worrying."

"You never know, Anna, what can happen even here in our little world."

Later, Don had remarked to Anna that he had asked Owen and Randy if they had seen her coming up the trail. "They had seen you going and thought you had come back along the old berry patch trail."

"The rain held us up, but we had a good time in the cave singing and telling jokes."

"Not bad ones, I hope?"

"Oh Donald, you know me."

The next morning at breakfast, Hans said, "We're going to Europe. Eva and I will go to the travel agent in Santa Rosa today and make arrangements."

Anna was beaming the May Monday morning Don and she drove Hans and Eva to the train depot in Oakland for their trip. Eva couldn't stop bursting into tears. Goodbyes were said and Anna and Don waved until the train pulled out. Then Don said, "Anna, we don't have to hurry home."

"I know. The season hasn't really started yet. What are you thinking?"

"Let's go up to Cal and wander around."

After looking around the school, they went to lunch at Spengler's in lower Berkeley. After lunch, Don drove to the City by taking the ferry over the bay. They got a room at the Basque Hotel in North Beach. Then they walked through Chinatown and purchased souvenirs for the girls. They rode the cable car down to the Fisherman's Wharf where they nibbled on hand-held shrimp cocktails cooked near the fishing boats. They could see that even this early in the year tourists were finding their way to San Francisco's famous wharf and peering through mounted 10-cent telescopes looking out to the infamous Alcatraz Prison. They rode the cable back to Broadway and Powell and returned to their hotel room. Anna turned the radio on. Bing Crosby was singing a love song.

"He's one of my favorites, Don."

"I'll take Randy over any of them, honey."

"He is very good. He's been a blessing for the resort and such a sweet man. Barbara is so deeply in love with him and thankful for everything that has happened."

"Yes, they are a nice couple, Anna. Shall we take a nap, honey?"

"I know you just want to get me into that pretty bed."

"I sure do."

"I'll see the bathroom first."

Anna returned in the raw. Don smiled. "You do know how to make me happy."

"Don, there's a shower in there. Shall we use it together?"

"After you darling."

The shower was a treat.

Later they had a wonderful Chinese dinner at the Golden Palace. Returning to their hotel, they stopped in its bar for a couple of after-dinner drinks and then went to bed. A couple of kisses and they fell asleep. The next morning they returned to the resort taking the Sausalito Ferry out of San

Francisco and driving up the Redwood Highway to Santa Rosa and up Markwest Springs Road to the resort.

Barbara had spent the night with their daughters, so seeing Don and Anna, she said, "We didn't hear from you and there's really no room in our room."

"You did the right thing, Barbara," Anna said, "and thank you so very much. We knew someone would watch them for us."

"I had to talk Stella into letting me do it."

"Either one of you would have been fine."

Two weeks later they received a card from Anna's parents showing the Statue of Liberty. It had been mailed from New York. The season at the resort had started off heavily for so early in the year and they were just a little short of help. Anna received permission from the Calistoga Creamery owner to place a notice that Fire Mountain Resort was looking for help and needed two girls to help wait on tables and make some linen changes. Those hired would receive room and board, a small salary, and tips.

After a few days, a dozen young girls had applied. Anna hired two high school juniors who were close friends, hoping if they worked out they would be back for the next summer. The girls would share a room in the employee's row. They were instructed no men in their room and any socializing was to be out in the open. The same rule had applied to the men. The exception had been Barbara and Randy.

Hiring these girls gave Anna more time to catch up on paper work, which was consuming more and more of her time. She missed the hikes she had led so often in the past, but reservations, payroll, licenses, insurance, and many other new duties were falling to her. Since the number of guests was increasing, 100% capacity was becoming the norm. The in-house joke was that the beds never got cold. Randy was handling the campfire parties and they were thoroughly enjoyed. Locals were coming to hear his singing, and after, joining guests at the bar which Stella was running in the dining area.

Don and Anna received a clipping from Paris that Lance was living with a renowned woman chef who would be opening a cooking school to teach 5-star dining and kitchen skills to future chefs. The woman looked twenty years older than Lance, but they were both smiling. Don commented, "That smooth-talking bastard always lands on his feet. The missing man turns up."

Anna said, "I am sure the legal work must have been taken care of for him to risk that picture."

"The rogue must have mailed this to us. I don't know who else would have. When he gets all he wants from her, he'll leave. I'd hang this on the bulletin board, but some of the woman guests that still come here might be offended at the sight of him."

"Don, memories can work two ways."

"True, but why upset anyone."

"You're right, honey."

After Mrs. O'Malley helped in birthing Barbara's baby daughter, she was having a drink with Stella and said, "Well deary, it seems the men in these parts only sire little girls. This is the fourth one I've delivered here."

Stella knew whom she was referring to. "If I wasn't so old and had run into George sooner, I might have needed your services."

"I guess I've birthed close to two hundred babies here in these mountains, Stella."

"They all swear by you, Kate. The men are happy too."

"I take an extra stitch for them."

Stella laughed. "Have another."

"All right, deary."

Late August Eva and Hans returned home. They looked rested and had thoroughly enjoyed their trip. Eva said she had a young brother who would be coming to work at the resort next summer. Eva's brother, Gus, was studying English as one of his courses. They had brought home a few souvenirs for Don, Anna, and the girls. As Hans and Eva noticed in the next few days, everything had gone well without their presence. They knew Anna had carried the brunt of the operation of the resort. They were proud of their daughter.

"Hans, we'll have more time together if Anna runs things. And maybe we can see more of this wonderful country we adopted."

"Yes, Eva. We'll still be involved, but Anna and Don and the good people they have working here are making things run so smoothly."

"Hans, can we hike to the Fire Mountain cave in a couple of days and just camp there and relax?"

"If you want, dear. That's a nice idea."

They told Anna of their plan and she thought it was a cute idea. Three days later Eva left one morning with a bedroll, some supplies, and camping equipment. Hans took along a fishing pole. They took their time hiking to Fire Mountain. The cave was always fairly clean, but Eva brushed it out with some branches while Hans was gathering firewood. Food was hung from a nearby branch protruding into the cave. When Hans hiked back down to fish where he had left his pole by the stream, Eva gathered a few rocks to build a fireplace and then hiked up to the top of Fire Mountain, something she had never done before. Maybe no one had. The west side of the mountain was a sheer drop of 800 feet or more. She looked down into a small valley surrounded by other mountains. A small creek divided the valley, evidently flowing down to their stream through a small grove of Madrone trees.

She could see a good-sized buck walking to the creek. A couple of buzzards glided below her. She was entranced looking into this small world. Eventually as she turned to leave, she noticed an almost light blue colored animal moving on a rocky ledge to her right. Then it was joined by a black and a couple of brown animals. She realized they were goats. She had never seen or heard that goats were in this area. She'd have to tell Hans and

Anna. When she returned to the cave, she rolled out the bedroll, placed the firewood in the homemade fireplace, and then hiked down to where Hans was fishing.

"Hi, my darling," she called. He turned and put his finger to his lips reminding her to be quiet. She knew he was right.

CHAPTER 16

SADNESS

Quite unusually, there had been snow on the ground in late April. Not a lot, but a couple of inches, and Mount St. Helena had a white cover half way down its sides. It was rumored it had as much as four feet near the summit. There were quite a few auto wrecks with the locals not being used to driving in snow.

Eva loved to look at Mount St. Helena. It reminded her of home. She was looking forward to her youngest brother's arrival in June. She and Hans had enjoyed the winter and early spring when they had taken a trip to Baja. They had swum in the warm waters and enjoyed the beauty of the desert. The people were shy, but friendly.

One morning Hans woke up and looked over at Eva. She looked so very still. He touched her cheek. She was too cold. He shook her and no response. "My god! Eva, Eva." He knew she was gone and took her into his arms. The tears ran down his cheeks. He held her long and lovingly and eventually lay her down. Then he dressed and went to Anna's office. She looked up. "What's wrong, Dad?"

"It's your mother, dear. She's gone."

"Gone where?"

"I woke up and she was just lying there like asleep. I touched and shook her and she had no life."

"Oh, Dad." She was in tears too. Later in the day the coroner arrived and agreed she had just gone to sleep. God had called her home. Everyone teared on hearing Eva was gone. She was to be buried on the resort grounds.

Anna had called Father Durkin and asked him to come up and say a few words even though none of the family was practicing any religion. "I'd be glad to, Mrs. White. I haven't forgotten how you helped with John."

"Yes, father, and we lost him so painfully too." After the ceremony conducted by the good priest, and his assurances Eva had gone on to be with her heavenly father, the resort crew, friends, and neighbors gathered in the bar area and talked about the wonderful woman they would all miss.

The next morning Hans told Anna he was going to the cave for a few days. "Okay, Dad. Be careful, I know the stream is high right now."

"I know."

"Take an extra blanket."

"I will."

Hans grieved at the cave, remembering all of Eva and his precious time together. He lay there and time passed. It was a couple of days before he was hungry and ate. Later one day he hiked to the top and looked for the goats Eva had told him about. He saw them grazing near the little creek and wondered where they had come from. He thought, "They must have come off of some abandoned homestead."

When Hans returned to the resort, he found Anna pouring over paperwork. She rose and they put their arms around each other. "Did it help?"

"Yes, I found the goats your mom told me about. She mentioned them one day to me and I forgot about them. We'll call them Eva's goats. Something else to show the guests."

"That's a good idea, Dad."

The season began in May with a high occupancy rate. Financially things could not have been better. In mid-July Marta and Fritz arrived from Europe with Sofie and Karl for a month's stay, with side trips to San Francisco and San Diego. Marta so enjoyed her granddaughters that she gifted Anna and the daughters with exquisite, diamond earrings. Anna said, "We'll have to keep them in the safe."

"Oh, wear them," Marta exclaimed.

Fritz and Marta were again generous when leaving and insisted Anna, Don, and the girls come to Vienna for a Christmas holiday.

About noon one Monday morning in mid-August, Sheriff Lamberton came through the door, went to the bar, and asked Stella where Anna was. Stella replied, "She's in the office, sheriff."

Lamberton went to Anna's office and saw her doing paperwork. "Anna."

"Yes, Roy. You startled me."

"Anna there's been a bad accident."

"No!"

"Don is dead." She dropped her pen and the tears flowed.

"Anna, Anna," Lamberton said as he put his arms around her after she rose from the chair.

"No, no, no!"

"I am sorry. I didn't mean to say it so poorly."

"How?"

"A logging truck. The chain snapped just as they were passing side-by side."

"What about your son, Owen?"

"He jumped clear. A broken leg and arm and some bruises."

"I'm sorry, Roy."

"The boy will be all right. My wife's at the hospital in Santa Rosa with him."

Anna sat in the chair again. There were reservations to be confirmed. Then she spoke. "Thank you. I have to do this."

"Yes, Anna, call me for anything."

"Yes." He left, and she worked for a couple of hours before putting her pen down and crying loudly. Stella came to the door. "What's wrong, deary?" Anna put her hands to her face and continued to sob. Stella came to her, putting her hand on Anna's shoulder. "Deary, what's wrong?"

"Don's been killed. Some logs spilled onto him and Owen...Owen jumped clear. Roy says he's okay. A couple of broken bones."

"No, Anna! I can't believe it. I saw him and young Owen leave this morning."

Don was buried near Eva. Father Durkin had again come to the resort and given a sermon. Along with Hans and George, he eulogized Don.

Friends, neighbors, and some of the local businessmen attended. Anna held her grief to herself. Mothering her daughters and running the resort was filling the emotional void.

Weeks later, she hiked to the stream cave alone and broke down, remembering their discovery of each other in this special place. She swam across the stream to Mr. Smarty's Island and looked for him, but he was probably out hunting. She lay down and closed her eyes and thought of Don. She missed him. Tears came. There were so many memories! She returned to the resort and entered the dining area. Stella said, "Honey, I was starting to worry about you."

"I'm okay, Stella. Took a long hike and shed some tears."

"They help, honey. How about a glass of wine?"

"Yes, a glass of red, please."

CHAPTER 17

HORSES

One evening when Anna entered the dining area, she saw Judy at the bar talking with Stella. "Stella, pour Judy whatever she's drinking."

"Yes, Anna."

"Thank you, Anna."

"Judy, I've been meaning to come over and talk to you."

"Yes, Anna."

"The customers have been asking where they could ride horses. I've been sending them down to Boothe Park. They're unhappy with the riding trails down in the valley along the highway."

"I don't blame them, Anna."

"How many horses do you have, Judy?"

"Just two. My old horse, Rex, and a gelding I bought last month because the price was so reasonable."

"Judy, if I advanced the funds for a riding string, would you be interested in operating it? I know you're a good rider and a sensible person."

"Thank you, Anna. That's an interesting idea."

"Think about it, Judy…and get back to me."

"I will. How are you holding up, Anna?"

"It's rough, but I'm busy and I'm spending more time with the girls."

"I'll make a point of teaching them to ride."

"That's a good thought. I always noticed when I was in high school the girls that rode were more competent and physically excelled."

They had a couple of more glasses of wine and included Stella in their conversation. Eventually George came in to see Stella, and Judy and Anna left.

Several days later Judy came to Anna's office. "Hi, Judy."

"Anna, I think I'll need at least a dozen horses."

"Why so many?"

"I think there should be two rides a day. A morning ride and an afternoon ride. Horses have physical problems like us and they're seldom all sound at the same time. I'll need a lot of saddles, bridles, and other horse gear. Also I'll have to hire a groom. Caring for the horses and cleaning the tack is very important. It adds to the life of the leather."

"Judy, I'll give you whatever you need. I need to keep the guests happy and I want you to make some money."

"Anna, I'm just about self-sufficient at my place. Dad died of an apparent heart attack and Mom moved to Arizona to live with her sister."

In the coming months Judy gathered a riding string. She was able to pick up a lot of good, used riding equipment and she placed an ad for a groom in the Santa Rosa Press Democrat. There were numerous people who showed up seeking employment, but she explained the pay was basically room and board and a small salary.

After careful consideration, Judy hired a young Latino, Alfonso. His English was fair and he seemed quite gentle. The horses seemed to take to him right off. The opening of the resort season at Fire Mountain with numerous signs posted and information on the preseason fliers got the horseback riding off to a good start. Sometimes guests were wanting to ride twice a day.

Judy and Alfonso worked long hours that season. There were even some moonlight rides. Judy was able to give Alfonso a large bonus. He was most grateful and suggested bringing his girl friend from Mexico to marry. She could do the cooking, care for the house, do the laundry, and whatever else was needed. Judy thought it was a good idea since things had been badly neglected around the house and they had lived on sandwiches all summer. "Can you get her up here safely?"

"Maybe. I'll go for her and we'll marry at home."

The next Friday morning Judy drove Alfonso to the Greyhound Depot in Santa Rosa for a bus trip to San Diego. Three weeks later, Alfonso and Rosita were in a horse trailer destined for Bay Meadows Race Track in San Mateo. When they arrived, they then took a bus to Calistoga. A call to Judy and she was picking them up a half hour later.

Alfonso greeted Judy and introduced his new wife. Judy hugged her and led them to the truck. "She doesn't speak English yet, Senora, but she will learn."

"I am sure she will, Alfonso."

They arrived at Judy's place. She had decorated the kitchen and her parent's bedroom and provided new bedding. Alfonso, who had been sleeping in the tack room, said, "Senora, you didn't have to do this."

"I wanted to, Alfonso. We're going to be family."

"Thank you, thank you," Rosita said, bowing with happiness.

"Tomorrow night we'll have a party at Anna's place. I'll cook tonight. You and Rosita relax. Show her around and get settled."

"Yes, Senora. Judy called Anna and made arrangements for the party. Anna said it would be great fun for the crew at the resort. They all knew Alfonso from the summer and he was well-regarded with his polite manners and ready smile.

There were seven late guests staying at the resort—three couples and a single gentleman in his thirties. George and Randy played some music after the dinner, and a few drinks later everyone was dancing. A gentleman asked Anna to dance. She started to decline, but then thought better of it. He quickly told her to call him Jack since she had used his last name.

Jack was a good dancer and he held Anna gracefully, but with firm direction. "And what do you do, Jack, when you're not on holiday?"

"I'm a pilot at Pan Am Airlines."

"Oh, all those pretty ladies!"

"They're hand-picked, Anna, and I don't believe in mixing with fellow employees."

"That's a strict rule."

"Yes, but I abide by it."

After a couple of dances, Jack guided Anna to the bar. "I'd like to buy champagne for everyone for this occasion. They seem like such a sweet, young couple…if that's okay with you, Anna?"

"Are you sure? You really don't have to."

"I am sure."

Anna said, "Stella, do you have enough chilled champagne for everyone?"

"Yes, Anna. I have a case in the walk-in box and a couple of bottles here in the cooler with the white wine."

Stella set up a line of champagne glasses and opened four bottles, letting the corks fly to the ceiling. Everyone toasted Alfonso and Rosita. Anna and Jack danced some more and Stella continued to pour champagne. Anna finally said, "Jack, let's sit a few out."

Randy was singing "La Goldendrina" and everyone left the floor to Alfonso and Rosita. He followed with "La Paloma" and all clapped at the end of each dance. The newlywed couple radiated love and happiness.

"Anna, one of the guests was telling me about the hikes you used to lead to Fire Mountain and a cave with running water. I thought the name of the resort might have referred to one of the old volcanoes in Lake County."

"No, Jack. We have our very own Fire Mountain. My dad first noticed it here on a hike and camping trip. That's how he came to name the place."

"I'd like to see those places, Anna."

"It's a little late in the year. Kind of cold to be hiking."

"I wouldn't mind."

"Maybe George or Randy could take you."

"The guests said the stories you told as you hiked was what had really made the hikes great for them."

"Yes, I do love the places we see. How many more days are you here, Jack?"

"I'm paid through Sunday, but I could stay a few extra days. I'm not due for a flight 'til next Friday."

"Okay. Let's plan on Tuesday morning."

"Yes, Anna. I'll look forward to it."

The partyers were thinning out. Judy, Alfonso, and Rosita thanked Anna again and again for a wonderful party. Driving back to Judy's, Alfonso passed out. Judy and Rosita helped Alfonso to bed.

Judy smiled at Rosita and spread her hands. "He's all yours, Rosita."

For the first time, that morning Alfonso was late coming to the barn. The horses were whinnying and he had a good hangover. He mused to himself, "That sweet drink must have did it to me."

Chapter 18

New Romance

Anna and Jack left early morning. A heavy cloudcover had come in during the night. "Jack, we might run into a little rain."

"A little rain won't hurt us."

They hiked down the trail to the stream and crossed over on the small wooden bridge George had built with branches and twine. As they worked their way up to the cave, a blast of thunder rolled through the canyon bringing with it drops of rain. "Jack, we better pick up some wood and kindling."

"Okay Anna, you get the kindling." Anna picked up small dry twigs just starting to get damp and continued to the cave. Jack followed a few minutes later, dragging some branches. "Will this do, Anna?"

"Drop it and bring in all you can before you get too wet. We might have to spend the night." Jack moved quickly and made several more trips, bringing in heavier branches. Anna had the fire started halfway back into the cave. "How come so far back?"

"We'll trap a little more heat back behind the fire. Take that coat off and dry it near the fire."

"A little wet doesn't matter, Anna."

"It may if we spend the night here." Lightning was flashing in the area and thunder could still be heard. The rain was steady and fairly heavy. "That stream will rise if this keeps up, Jack."

"Will we be able to recross it?"

"We may have to hike a little further up this side of the canyon to where the steelhead cross at the ripples, but we'll get back okay. Let's hope the rain lets up before dark or we're here all night."

The fire was now starting to put out some real heat. Anna took her jacket off. She opened the large knapsack, spread another cloth, and started to put out the items she had packed for a picnic. A couple of medium-sized barbecue steaks, a loaf of homemade wheat bread, some dried apricots, cookies, a bottle of Cabernet, a small coffee pot, coffee, a couple of large kitchen forks, and a couple of steak knives. She had brought enough to feed both them and her animal and bird friends. Jack watched in awe as she opened the knapsack and removed the items. "Quite a bit there for a picnic, Anna."

"Not really. If we spend the night, we'll eat half for lunch, and the other half for dinner if we're still here." Anna then hung a steak on one of the large forks and held it near the fire. "How do you like it, Jack?"

"However you fix it, Anna. I've been eating good here all week at the resort."

"Here, you hold this for awhile. Nature calls." She ducked out of the cave and was back a few minutes later, pretty wet. "How's that steak doing?"

"I think it's about done medium."

Anna removed her wet blouse and pants, placing them near the fire. Jack's eyes roamed over the well-shaped figure. "I'll have to sleep in them, that rain is quite heavy now. I doubt if it will let up."

She reached into the knapsack and removed two tin plates. Then she cut several slices of bread and Jack placed the steak on a plate. She cut it in two, giving Jack the larger portion. He offered it back to her, but she said, "No, you'll need it to keep warm." Anna then opened the wine bottle and poured some into each of the coffee cups. Jack proposed a toast to the "Queen of the Mountain Cave."

"Thank you, sir. Your health." They ate slowly, talking about the weather and Jack asking her about the cave and whether she thought the Indians or wild animals had used it.

"Probably, years ago, a mountain lion or bear might have used it, but not recently. Maybe a mountain lion in a storm like this, but they're getting scarce too. The ranchers have pretty well finished them off. And tell me of yourself, Mr. Jack Collins? I know you're a pilot with Pan Am. But what else?"

"That damn near sums it up, Anna. I was raised down in San Mateo. From the time I was twelve, I wanted to fly. Spent after school and weekends at the San Francisco Airport. It was small then. West of 101 in those days. I'd pester anyone who flew for a ride. When I was thirteen, there was a guy flying two or three people for a twenty-minute ride for ten dollars each. For five dollars he'd let me go up if he had a vacant seat. By the time I was fifteen, I was helping him service his plane and washing his car. Then he started teaching me to fly. I got my first license when I was seventeen. A year later I was taking flights up for him. My dad was a pretty well-to-do doctor in Burlingame and he paid for advanced flight school. I received my commercial license at twenty-one. Took a job flying up in Alaska with a commercial line and really learned about bad weather."

"I'll bet it was terrible," Anna exclaimed.

"Yes, at times. So when Pan Am was looking for pilots to fly out of San Francisco Airport, I came back down and started to do the flight to Hawaii."

"That's where you got that tan. How are those hula girls?"

"Anna, sad to say, they're looked down upon by the locals. The tourists love them. I game-fished with some or attended a few dances on my layovers."

"A good-looking guy like you? A pilot? There must be something else in your life."

"I had a few dates, Anna, but I wasn't looking to get involved. I have my own private plane, a Piper Cub. I bought it a couple of years ago and spend my local time flying and servicing it. That's partly why I am up here. To make some changes in my life and to see a little more of life than the clouds and sunny sky."

Anna poured some more wine. "I thought you were quite a womanizer the way you whisked me out on the dance floor and took such a firm hold. You also have a pleasantly soft voice for a man."

"Thank you, Anna. No, I'm not a ladies' man. I really admire women and the tough road their life offers from the painful periods that my mother had to the hardships in birthing and the husbands that manhandle them. I was an only child and I am sure I've been spoiled by my parents. I got an allowance and a car for my seventeenth birthday. I had it easy and never really felt the need for relationships. I guess I've been a flying hermit."

Anna laughed and poured some more wine. When he asked for even more, she said, "We better save it for later when we have our evening repast."

Jack suddenly said, "Excuse me, Anna." He left the cave, returning a little later than Anna had expected. She had started to become a bit nervous about him getting lost. He was dragging some large branches which were wet, but could burn as soon as the bark dried.

He said, "I'll get some more. It may be a long night." Anna asked him many questions about flying and he promised he would take her up one day.

She replied, "I'll hold you to that."

"If I say it, Anna, I'll do it."

"We'll see."

Anna told him of her life in the Fire Mountain area, growing up close to nature and loving it. She told him about Don and their love as young lovers and his tragic death two years ago. The first weeks were hard and she missed him, but running the resort and looking after their daughters and the support of everyone working at the resort had eased her hurt.

"Do you expect to marry again, Anna?"

"I really don't know or think about it, I am so busy here."

"Anna, you're a lovely woman and you seem so very sincere. Could we be friends and get to know each other?"

"That would be nice, Jack." She leaned over and kissed him on the lips softly, but quickly.

"Thank you," he said.

"Do you like to sing?"

"Yes. I sing all the time when I am flying."

"We have a weekly amateur hour during the height of the season and Randy sings so beautifully. All the guests just love his singing and we have sing-alongs."

"I am sure you can out-sing me, Anna. My repertoire is small and I'm only good to about half way through each song."

"Okay, I'll start." They sang for a couple of hours and then Anna put her clothing back on and said, "Yours needs to dry some more."

The fire was keeping them quite warm. It was getting dark and Anna said, "We have to try and eat everything for body warmth. With full bellies, we should sleep better."

"Okay, Anna. You're the wise one here."

They took their time eating and, when the steak was done cooking, Jack asked, "Should I get more wood?"

"No, it's too dark. I think we have enough 'til we fall asleep. The warmth of the ashes will help for a while. At daylight we'll make a break for the resort." When they finished eating, Anna started to sing and Jack joined in. They finished the wine and were in a happy mood.

Jack inquired, "Do you like jokes?"

"If they're not too dirty." He told her different jokes for almost an hour. "Where did you learn so many jokes?"

"The crew and the mechanics always have a new one and I have a pretty retentive memory."

"I'll say you do. I've heard a few over the years, but I can't remember them the next day."

The fire was dying as the last strands of wood burned. Jack put his dry clothes back on and Anna then said, "Jack, come over and lay here with these warm ashes to your back."

"Okay. How about you?"

"My backside will be against your frontside. Can I trust you to be a gentleman?"

"We already proved that when you were in your panties and bra."

"That's true." As she knelt down to get in a sleeping position, she turned and kissed him deeply on the lips. "That's for being such good company today, sir."

"Thank you again. I am going to come back up here and pray to be on a hike with you and hope for rain."

When Jack awoke, he could smell coffee. Anna had a small fire going. "Anna, didn't you sleep?"

"Yes, 'til about half an hour ago."

"You should have woken me."

"No chance! I haven't seen a beautiful man sleeping for a long time."

"Thank you. The coffee smells great."

"It's raining lightly. I think we can make it back to the resort without drowning, although the stream will be high even at the low point." They drank their coffee and Jack asked to be excused for a moment. When he returned, Anna had the knapsack packed and they left in the drizzle. She guided them back up the left side of the stream to John's monument and told him quickly about John.

"Poor kid. Never had a chance at life."

"Yes, it was very sad."

They crossed at the ripples. Jack lifted Anna up despite her protest and waded through the water. They arrived at the resort wet, but well.

"Take a hot shower, Jack, and I'll meet you back here in an hour for breakfast and some hot brandies."

"Sounds good, Anna." Anna checked the office. No messages.

Her dad was just coming into the dining room. "Did you sleep at the cave?"

"Yes."

"Everything went good?"

"Yes, Dad. He was a perfect gentleman."

"Too bad. You need another man in your life, Anna."

"Yes, Dad." She went to her room, showered, and put a dress on to check on her daughters. They were still sleeping. Then she went to the kitchen. Ray had just come in to start cooking. "Morning, Anna."

"How are things going?"

"Good. Everything is so easy in the off-season."

"Yes, Ray. But it's been a good year."

"Yes, it has, Anna."

Jack walked in looking refreshed and clean-shaven. He *was* a good-looking man. "I'll buy you a drink, stranger."

"I'd be glad to pay, ma'am."

"How do you feel?"

"Great! I can't believe we slept so well."

"I bet you say that to all the girls."

He laughed. "Anna, you're teasing."

"Hot water and brandy still?"

"Yes, it sounds good."

Ray announced breakfast was ready. They moved to a table and found themselves to be quite hungry, talking little 'til they had eaten, and then lingered over coffee.

Randy came in and asked, "How was the hike, Anna?"

"We camped at the Fire Mountain cave when that storm came through."

"Good place to be in a storm."

Jack said, "It sure was, Randy. Anna was teaching me some of your songs as we passed the time."

"You'll have to make an amateur hour during the regular season."

"I'd like that."

"Well, Jack, I have to get the daughters dressed for school and finish what I have to do in the office."

"I understand, Anna. It's been fun the last twenty-four hours. See you for a cocktail this evening?"

"Maybe after the dinner hour for an after-dinner drink."

"Looking forward to it, Anna. See you then." Anna got the girls off to school, returned to her office, read the mail, posted some income for the week, and wrote a couple of bills. She then answered correspondence. By the time she was through, the girls were home from school. They greeted their mother with kisses and hugs.

"How did school go today, girls?" They told what they did in class that day and talked of a school play they would be in together. Anna had held Michelle back when she was sick and the two girls had started first grade together. Each class at the Calistoga School put on a play at Christmas time.

Anna had seen Jack eating dinner with another couple. They had smiled at each other. After the family had eaten and she had put the girls to bed, she returned to the dining room and saw Jack talking with Stella at the bar. She walked over and said, "I am ready for that drink, sir."

"Anna, whatever you would like."

"A glass of Chablis, please."

"Yes, and you, Jack? Another of the same?"

"I'll join Anna with a glass of the same. I see you were busy all day, Anna."

"Yes, a few things I had to catch up on. It's good to stay on top of everything. The profit margin is close in this business. How was your day?"

"I read some, took a nap, and didn't wake up until I heard the dinner bell."

"Good. You were shorted on your sleep last night."

They talked for a while and Jack mentioned he was leaving in the morning. "I know. I'll see you in the morning." Then she kissed him on the cheek and said good night.

He had a couple of more glasses with Stella and asked her a few discreet questions about Anna.

Stella was careful with her answers. Not that she had to be, but let him learn of Anna on his own. If he was interested, he would come back.

The next morning after breakfast, Jack went in to the office to pay his bill. Anna greeted him and said, "I'm going to be sorry to see you leave. Hope you do come and stay with us again."

"I'm going to be in Calistoga next Wednesday. Would you please meet me for lunch?" She was surprised. "I, I guess I could. How about the lobby of the Calistoga Hotel, about 10 a.m.?"

"Yes, but a little early for lunch. I want to take you someplace special for lunch."

"Okay, I'll see you there." She walked Jack to his car and he quickly kissed her on the lips. She liked that man. "And me, an old, widow lady with two kids," she mused.

The days passed quickly. She asked Randy's wife to keep an eye on the girls for her on Wednesday and wore a nice dress, hosiery, and heels, which she rarely wore. Jack was waiting as she walked toward the hotel. He wore a brown leather jacket, corduroy pants, and half boots. Sun glasses covered his eyes, but he removed them as she approached. "Hi, pretty lady. Hungry?"

"Not quite."

"Good." He took her arm and led her down the street toward Pacheteau's. She thought, "There's rooms and a hot mineral sulfur pool there. Massages and mudbaths, but no lunch."

As they came to the small field where there was a hangar and a couple of planes she had often seen, he led her onto the field and she exclaimed, "Oh, no!"

"Yes, lunch is in Carmel, Anna."

"Jack, I've never flown."

"Not too many people have yet, Anna. It's safer than a car or bus." They reached his two-seat Piper Cub. Jack helped her in, handed her a jacket like his, and sun glasses. "Jack, I'm scared."

"Don't be. I want you to get used to flying." He started the engine and it purred. He taxied onto the runway and they were soon airborne. He flew down the valley following the Silverado Trail and then flew over Vallejo and out to the coast. "Jack, it is so beautiful. I feel like I'm floating. Almost." He leaned over and kissed her cheek. He pointed out Santa Cruz and Capitola. They could see the many rows of artichokes in the fields and several orchards. "No vineyards that I can see, Jack."

"Maybe someday. How do you like flying?"

"It seems wonderful."

"It is, Anna, and I get paid to do it." Soon they were landing in Monterey. They took a cab to Carmel where they found a quaint little restaurant. Some wine and talk…the time flew by.

"Would you like to spend the night here, Anna?"

"Jack, Jack! Nobody knows I am gone or even with you. I told Stella I had a luncheon date and I'd be home late afternoon."

"Could you call and let Stella know you ran in to San Francisco and would be home tomorrow?"

"I could, I'd like to, but this is moving awfully fast, Jack."

"I don't mean to rush you, Anna, and if you can't, I'd understand. I find you so wonderful and delightful I haven't been able to put you out of my mind since I left you at the resort. Flying to Hawaii I was wishing you were with me. The next morning when I was walking on the beach, I wanted you there to see it in all its beauty. That afternoon sitting at the Royal Hawaiian Bar having a couple of Mai Tais, I was wishing I was being served by Stella and you would come walking in."

"Jack, that's so sweet. God, I have nothing with me for overnight."

"We can get whatever you need, Anna."

"Jack, this is serious for me."

"I know you're a very good person, Anna. And I have never been so consumed with this feeling before for a woman. I go back to the precious moments in the cave and your sweet kisses. Anna, you've captured me."

"Jack, that is so sweet."

"We'll get a room at the hotel and you can call Stella."

"You make it sound so easy, Jack."

"I know what I am asking is a lot. I want you, Anna. I want to hold and caress you."

"Jack, yes. I'll make the call." He asked for the check and they left. As they walked down the street, in the middle of the block there was a drug store. Toothbrushes and paste were purchased. They walked on down to the hotel overlooking the ocean. Jack talked to the clerk saying they flew in for lunch and decided to spend the night.

"Please sign the register. Thank you, Mr. Collins. What kind of a room would you and the misses like?"

"Something with a view of the ocean, a large double bed, and a couple of bottles of cold champagne."

A bellboy led them to their room, asking, "No luggage?" Jack replied, "It's at the airport." Anna exclaimed, "Jack, this is beautiful! And so large!"

"It's really beautiful now that you're in it, Anna." She came to him and kissed him deeply. "

Wow! You've awakened my instincts, Jack. I am glad. I'll sure try." They kissed passionately. "Excuse me, Jack. I need the bathroom."

"Yes, Anna." She was back shortly. He was gazing out to the ocean. "It's so big, Jack."

"I know, Anna. When I am flying over it, it seems to go on forever. Then we land on a little island surrounded by it."

There was a knock on the door. The bellboy brought in two ice buckets with champagne and glasses. "If you need more ice, just ring."

"Thank you," he said as Jack slipped him a tip.

Jack opened a bottle, poured, presented a glass to Anna, and raised the other in toast, "To my dream come true."

"I hope I am, Jack."

Two glasses of champagne and numerous kisses later, their clothes were sliding off.

Anna pulled the blankets down and they climbed into bed. They slipped into each other's arms and their kisses became deeper and hungrier.

Their hands were becoming more intimate and Jack's lips were finding other desirable parts of Anna's body. She was ready to beg him to enter her. He kissed her lips and eased into her. She thought she was going to melt. For a few seconds she just absorbed him. Then she started to move. His tongue was in her mouth and she was spreading her legs and accepting him as deeply as she could. She started to come and call his name, "Jack! Jack! Oh, Jack!" Then he reached orgasm too. Eventually they lay there spent.

"Jack, it's been a couple of years, I always enjoyed sex."

"Lucky me, Anna."

She touched him gently and started to caress him. "You're getting serious again, Jack."

"He wants to return to that wonderful place again, Anna."

As she slid over on top of him, she inserted him into herself. She gently began to ride him. It felt wonderful. In a little while, she was calling his name again and he was starting to moan, "Anna, Anna."

They finished the first bottle of champagne and then showered together, kissing again. Then Jack ordered dinner sent to the room. When the food arrived, Anna hid in the bathroom 'til Jack called, "You can come out now, sweet."

They ate watching the sun set. "Jack, this is the most beautiful day of my life."

"Really, Anna?"

"Yes."

"Then I hope we have many more."

"And so do I." They fell asleep in each other's arms. Jack awakened to Anna holding his manhood. He kissed her and slid between her legs. Again it was wonderful for both of them.

"Well, pretty lady, I guess we have to leave this wonderful place."

"Can we come back again, Jack?"

"Yes, Anna. We will. Our secret hideaway." They cabbed back to the airport and an hour and a half later were landing in Calistoga.

"Can you come to the resort, Jack?"

"I could for a night, but the following day I have to fly."

"How are we going to explain my arrival?"

"I ran into you in San Francisco and flew up to Calistoga and picked you up." They drove to the resort to have a drink.

"I'll see where I can put you for the night."

"Fine, Anna."

Anna talked briefly to Stella. "Don't let Jack buy any drinks. Put them on my tab, please."

"Your tab, Anna?"

"Yes, it's time, Stella." Anna checked the office. There were a few things to do. The girls would be home shortly. Barbara came in and said the girls had been fine. Judy had given them a riding lesson. They had eaten dinner and she had helped them with their homework. "Thank you, Barbara."

Anna returned to Jack. "Come. I'll take you to your room." She led him into a room looking into the canyon, closed the door, and turned to meet his lips searching for hers. It turned passionate and he quickly led her to the bed. He soon entered her and after reaching their climaxes, she kissed him deeply and said, "I have to run. The girls are due any minute and I have to greet them, especially after yesterday."

"I understand. I'll see you at dinner."

"You'll eat with the family and help, if that's okay with you?"

"Yes, Anna. It would be great." She kissed him again and said, "I better get out of here. Love you."

"For sure?"

"Yes."

Family and employees were surprised to find Jack eating with them. He was so friendly. The man who flew to Hawaii every week received many questions and he answered all. Hans knew something special was happening. Anna glowed at dinner that night. After she put the girls to bed, she joined Jack at Stella's bar. They talked and danced to the new jukebox. "I'll check the girls and come to your room in a little."

"Lucky me, sweet lady." Twenty minutes later Anna was slipping into bed and right on top of him. "You woke me and now you can forget about sleeping tonight." As she left the room at daylight, she said, "Get some sleep and when you wake up, I'll drive you to the airport after I feed you."

"Was tonight real?"

"It's what your in for if you come back."

"I'll be back again and again. Anna, I love you."

"That's a big statement, Jack. It's me and kids too."

Jack awakened a little after noon. He found Anna working in the office. "No rest?"

"No, I found energy in the happiness you gave me these past two days. I'll sleep tonight. What would you like to eat?"

"Whatever you give me, Anna."

"Sit at a table. I'll be right there." She went to the kitchen and had Ray cook rack-of-lamb, medium with a big salad and warm homemade bread. She sat with Jack and had a little salad and a glass of wine.

"I'll miss you," she said.

"Me too," he answered. A little later she drove him to the airport, walked to the plane with him, took off a light, blue scarf, and put it around his neck. "Lunch next Tuesday?"

"Yes. I expect to be away for two days."

"Okay."

As they flew out of Calistoga on Tuesday, Jack made a left turn as they flew over Napa. "No Carmel?"

"No."

"Where are we going?"

"A surprise."

"Good." As they passed over the Sacramento River, Anna inquired, "Reno?"

"Yes."

"I like Reno."

"Good. We'll have fun."

They checked into Harrah's bridal suite. "My god, Jack, the bridal suite!"

"Yes."

They got to the room and Jack took a small package out of his jacket pocket. "Open it."

Anna exclaimed, "My god, Jack! It must be the biggest green diamond in the world."

"It's an emerald, Anna." He dropped to his knees. "Will you marry me, Anna?"

"Jack, Jack. On a luncheon date? I am honored. What will my dad and the girls think?"

"They'll be surprised, but I think they like me."

"You're a nice man. How could they not like you? Jack, this is so beautiful. I am overwhelmed. I feel so strongly about you, Jack. I just know it's right for us."

"Then let's get a license and do it today."

"Jack, not today. At least let me get a nice dress and we'll do it tomorrow."

"Thank you, Anna. You'll be mine forever."

"And you'll be mine too." That afternoon Anna found a nice, pale blue, chiffon dress. "It's the color of the clouds you fly in. And the color of the scarf you gave me." That night they attended a show. Myron Cohen was the featured entertainer. They had a lot of laughs, a great dinner, and danced 'til the "wee hours" of the morning. They fell asleep in each other's arms. When they awoke, they showered and Anna put on her wedding dress.

Then they went to the licensing bureau, found a chapel, and were married. Jack slid a platinum ring with small emeralds onto her finger. It matched the engagement ring. They returned to their suite where clothes were shed and champagne led to marital bliss. Hunger finally pulled them out of bed.

They had a late dinner, more champagne, went dancing again, and returned to bed. When they flew back to Calistoga the next day, the winds were bumpy crossing the mountains and Jack really had to "fly the plane." Anna was nervous, but Jack explained that over mountains "These things happen." Back in Calistoga Anna went to the ladies' shop and picked up new dresses for the girls. When they arrived at the ranch, Hans was watering some plants. Anna led Jack to Hans. "Dad, this is your new son-in-law." Hans' mouth dropped open. Then he hugged her and shook hands with Jack.

"She a good one, Jack."

"I've found that out, Hans."

"Where will you live?"

"Don't worry, Hans. She lives here and I will too. I'll fly back and forth to San Francisco for my flights and I hope to become part of this special place."

"Anna, I am so happy for you. And you too, Jack."

Anna had previously told Stella and Randy's wife, who were already planning a party for that evening. When she saw the girls, she gave them their new dresses. "It's not our birthday, Mom."

"I know, but I am so excited I have a new husband. Jack and I were married yesterday."

"He's our new daddy?"

"No. But I am sure you'll come to love him like I do. He's a very special man. But Don was your daddy and Hans is your granddaddy."

"I love your mother, girls, and I am sure we'll become good friends."

Stella called to Alicia and Michelle, "Girls, I want you to go over to Judy's and invite her to the party tonight. And we want Alfonso and his wife to come too."

The party was a roaring success and Anna told her daughters they could sleep in and miss school. That night, in the same room Anna had "attacked" Jack, they spent the night together, only now she could fall asleep in his arms at the end of lovemaking. They were spent again, consumed by their love and desire. The following week Anna flew with Jack to Hawaii.

CHAPTER 19

FAMILY

Anna and Jack were growing deeper in love as each day passed. The resort was going smoothly and the girls were in awe of their new stepdad when they were told by classmates that that was what he was. Anna and Jack had come in from a short hike and were having a glass of wine with Stella. A couple of Stella's friends had just come in and she had moved down the bar to carry on a conversation with them.

Jack spoke, "Anna. I was thinking it would be nice to take the girls to Oahu for the Christmas holidays."

"That would be nice, Jack, but Christmas is a big day here at the resort. We've always spent it with the help and their families who are invited up to stay for a day or two and enjoy a big Christmas dinner."

"That's quite special, Anna. I didn't realize what was custom here."

"I know, Jack, and I would have told you in time. Maybe we could leave the day or two after. The girls would be thrilled I am sure. And I would like to see more of the island."

"Then I'll go ahead and take a week off for Christmas and New Year's. I have a lot of vacation time built up. The next trip out, I'll make the hotel reservations."

"Jack, that will be wonderful. Should I go ahead and tell the girls?"

"Yes, Anna."

The second day after Christmas, the four of them flew to Oahu. The girls loved the big plane. The "stews," who knew Jack, were meeting his family for the first time and really catering to all. One named Mary, remarked in the plane's galley to another named Vickie, "How'd we ever let this guy get away?"

"I don't know, but it seems like a great family. I guess that's the answer. We didn't have any kids."

"He does seem quite enamored of his wife."

"I noticed."

The pilot who had flown with Jack in the past came back to meet his family.

Jack introduced Bruce to Anna and the girls. "Who's the copilot?"

"Mike Duggan."

"Good guy."

"Yeah, but a terror in the clubs."

"He still dating that half-white hula dancer?"

"Yeah, I hear he performs with her in the comic hulas."

"Tell him to wear dark glasses or something. Pan Am might frown on that if it hit the papers."

Mary spoke up, "Jack, you and your family could see the hula dancers tomorrow morning at the Kodak show at the beach. They put it on for the tourists and naturally they buy film."

Michelle was entranced, staring out the window at the large white clouds hanging in the sky and the blue water below. She asked, "Is this where the rain comes from, Jack?"

"Some of it, Michelle. Well, I think I'll go back up front. I'm sure Mike wants to come back and meet the family." Fifteen minutes later Mike was being introduced.

The girls asked, "Are you a hula dancer?"

"Oh, oh. Someone's been talking. Don't tell anyone. It's a little true."

"Can we see you?"

"That's up to your mom and Jack."

"Can we?" they both exclaimed to Anna and Jack. "We'll see," Jack said.

"Jack, the wife and I are throwing a little hukilau Saturday night with a lot of her family. We would love to have you and your family attend. These Hawaiian parties, the more the better."

"We'll see if we can work it in. I hope so."

"Nice meeting you, Anna, and you, girls." Goodbyes said, Mike returned to the copilot's seat to eat.

"Jack, do you think it would be all right?"

"Yes, Anna. He's an upright guy." They landed at the Honolulu airport. Everyone was laden with leis. They cabbed to the Royal Hawaiian and checked in with the concierge, whom Jack knew. Introductions given, bellboys helped take them to their connecting rooms. The rooms were lovely, but the balconies impressed the girls the most. "Can we swim in the morning, Mom?"

Jack said, "Girls, this sun is not like at home. It burns. Quite a few people end up in the hospital. We'll get up early, swim, lay on the beach for a little while, come in and have breakfast, and then tour the island. Late afternoon we'll swim again and watch the Kanaka boys surfing on their big boards." The girls were excited. It was the first time they had ever been so formally served. They loved the coconut ice cream with pineapple sauce over it.

That night as Jack joined Anna in bed, she said, "I am still not pregnant, dear one."

"You missed last month."

"It happens sometimes."

"Well, just holding you is wonderful. Glad we came?"

"Very."

The days were fun and nights beautiful. They had run into Bruce in the hotel lobby and he mentioned he and his date were going to Mike's hukilau party and they agreed to go with him. He had rented a chauffeured touring car for his layover. He evidently was trying to make an impression on his date.

At six sharp, Bruce and Annette met them at the hotel. After introductions and a cocktail, they were on their way to Nankuli Beach. When they arrived, they saw fire torches burning in a large circle and in its center a long row of fire coals. After lots of introductions, they were seated on the ground near the coals. Singing was starting, backed by ukulele and a couple of guitars. Soon the coals had died out and, in a little while, women began serving plates of hot fish, yams, bananas, and poi.

Trays of papaya, mangos, and pineapple were also served. The girls loved the fruit and, just as they were finishing, they heard some loud drumming. Several women came up from the beach. They could be seen donning sarongs as they came dancing in front of the guests. A little later they were joined by a male dancer giving them leis and dancing with them. Then the drumbeat became faster and louder and only one female dancer was left with the male dancer. It must have been some type of mating ritual dance since it seemed very personal. The drums stopped, the dancers left, and ukuleles and guitars started up again. Mike and his wife began doing some comical dances. Then he and his wife were pulling up those new to the hukilau dance to show them how to do it. Everyone had a fun time. The girls said the kids in Calistoga would never believe their stories.

When it was time to leave the island they were asking Jack when they could come back. He replied, "Whenever your mom says or maybe during the summer you could occasionally come over with me when your mom is busy at the resort."

Anna and Jack brought back chocolate-covered macadamia nuts, fresh pineapples, and paper leis for all at the resort. The girls told of the hukilau and tried to show what they remembered of the dance. Eventually Jack was flying the resort employees to the island as a reward for their loyalty.

The coming season opened with solid bookings. Judy had the horse string going day and night. She was good with the guests and patient with her instructions. She'd come over for an evening and swim occasionally, drawing looks at her comeliness. Sometimes she had a glass of wine after a swim and a couple of dances with a single guy, but she always left them at the door.

Anna asked, "How come you leave so quickly, Cinderella?"

Judy laughed and said, "I am waiting for a flyboy like yours."

"Good luck, but remember he's mine."

"I know, Anna. I guess I'm just hard to please."

The girls did go to Hawaii with Jack a couple of times that summer, and Anna and they were planning to leave the day after Christmas like last year, only this year they were going to stay longer.

Chapter 20

The Long Flight

Around mid-September, the season had slowed enough to where Anna could take a few of the hikes with the guests and guide them to her favorite places. She associated the mountain cave with memories of Jack. The water cave reminded her of Don. She still missed him, but she was happy with Jack. Two different men and she had grown richer for knowing each. Her complete giving of herself endeared her to each man to the point they felt fulfilled.

Anna noticed the leaves falling earlier than usual. Winter would come in early this year. One time she took a hike by herself, just ambling around looking at each wild flower, bush, tree, birds, and small animals as they accidentally presented themselves to her. She ended up at John's monument just as Judy came riding up. They exchanged hellos and Judy dismounted, tying the horse to a Madrone tree.

"How did you come to be here, Anna?"

"I was just wandering and enjoying nature. Just wanted some alone time."

"Would you like me to ride on?"

"God no, Judy. I am ready for some company. What brings you here?"

"I really miss him, Anna. He was my friend."

"He was a pleasant young man. So dependable and helpful. He could always be counted on to do whatever we asked, or he'd do it sometimes even before we asked."

Judy took a small bouquet of wild flowers and put them at the foot of the monument.

"That's sweet, Judy."

"I miss him, and I think Dad killed him."

"Judy, what a horrible thing to say."

"He was a horrible man, Anna. I should not have said that to you, but I just needed to get it out, especially in this place."

"Why do you think that, Judy?"

"Dad accused us of being lovers. I did kiss John one day and he may have been out hunting and picked it up with his rifle scope."

"A kiss, Judy?"

"It's a long, sad story, Anna. Forgive me for dropping it here. Just forget what I said."

"Yes, Judy. You're one of my dearest friends."

"Thank you, Anna."

"Well, I'll head back, Judy."

"You want a ride back? This guy can carry double."

"Okay. I'll buy you a drink. We'll see what tale Stella can beguile us with."

"That's a good start to the evening." Judy gave Anna a hand and swung her up behind her.

Twenty minutes later they were enjoying a glass of wine with Stella. When a couple who were dressed quite classy drove up in a foreign car, Stella commented, "I think they're famous or something. I wonder how they found us?"

Anna replied, "Maybe they came in off the sign on the road."

"They said something about continuing to Clear Lake up in Lake County. They must have gotten anxious," Stella said.

The women smiled. Stella and Anna had been there often. Later that evening the newlywed gentleman came in asking for a bottle of champagne and some sandwiches. Anna was back at the bar and said she would make some. "It's too bad you missed the dinner hour."

"Yes it is. But it slipped by on us. I'll be back in about ten minutes."

"Fine." The gentleman took the champagne to his room and returned half an hour later.

"I was just going to bring them to you in a few more minutes, but I really didn't want to disturb you."

"Sorry. Could we have another bottle of champagne, please?"

As Stella opened the cooler for another bottle, Anna said, "That one's on me, Stella."

"Thank you. That's very kind of you."

"Enjoy the evening."

"Anna, they are probably here only this once."

"I know you're right, Stella. But newlyweds hit a soft spot." Stella smiled. "I am going to turn in, Stella."

"See you tomorrow, deary."

Thanksgiving came and it was raining hard. George built a big fire in the dining room fireplace and everyone had a fun day. The only sad note for Anna was that Jack was laying over in Hawaii. When he arrived Monday evening, Anna had saved some turkey and pie for him. She clung to him from the moment he entered the door. That first night she showed she had really missed him. "Anna, you are really something special. I hear other guys talking and it seems the love- making gets scarce after a while. But you turn me on so that each time is so very special."

"Because I love you and you're sexy." He smiled and kissed her deeply.

A week later when Jack was again laying over in Hawaii and had hiked down the beach until he was almost opposite Diamond Head, he thought he heard some distant thunder. As he turned to go back up the beach, he could see smoke rising in the Pearl Harbor area. Hearing planes approaching, he looked back to Diamond Head and saw bombers swinging out over the ocean and slightly away from the beach. Then they began swinging in towards Pearl. He recognized the planes as Japanese. He broke into a run for the hotel. As he arrived, there was sheer confusion. Some officers were still coming out of rooms, pulling clothes on, and looking rough from a hard night. They were jumping into cabs trying to get to Pearl or whatever base was their duty station. False rumors about the "Japs" landing and atrocities taking place were rampant. He went to the bar and listened to the broadcasters' reports. Pearl seemed to be one big fireball, with explosions following explosions. Several Japanese planes had crashed or been shot down.

The following day Jack was summoned to fly a complement of officers back to the West Coast, refuel, and take them to Washington. He flew into Moffitt Field south of San Francisco near the farm community of San Jose. He had been told they would lay over for about six hours. He would sleep in officer's quarters and eat with them. Could he get to a phone? They would work something out. He was not to give his location. He agreed and an hour later was able to reach Anna. "I'm okay, I love you, I miss you," he said.

"Where are you, Jack?"

"I can't say, dear Anna. I'll be home as soon as possible."

"Please call again when you can."

"I will. I love you!"

"I love you and need you here."

"I want to be there, my darling. I have to go now."

"Do you have my scarf on?"

"Yes, Anna."

"I miss you, sweetheart." He hung up. She held the phone to her breast and shed a tear. Then she walked into the dining room. The girls were doing homework. She told them she had heard from Jack. They were excited and asked many questions that she couldn't answer. Stella was replacing liquor from the storage room that had been depleted at Saturday night's Christmas party for the Lions Club. "I heard from Jack, Stella."

"Is he okay?"

"He sounded tired, but I think he's okay."

"When's he coming home?"

"I don't know and he couldn't say or where he was."

"Anna, they'll use him in this war that's starting."

"I know you're right, Stella. He's a great pilot."

Two weeks later to the day, Jack came in on a bus and called Anna from the Calistoga Hotel's lobby. Anna immediately drove to town to pick him up. He was unshaven and very tired. She rushed into his arms. They embraced and kissed. "Honey, I am spent." He fell asleep as they left town, his head on her shoulder. When they reached the resort, she gently woke him from a deep sleep. The girls ran to greet him. He kissed each and hugged them. They went into the dining area and several of the employees greeted him. Stella asked, "What can I get you, Jack?"

"A glass of red wine, please."

Anna asked, "Can I fix you something to eat?"

"No dear. I'll drink this wine and go to bed. I hate to duck out on you folks, but I am just exhausted." Anna led Jack to the bedroom and helped him undress. She kissed him as each piece of clothing came off.

"Honey, I'm sorry to let you down, but let me get a little rest." She kissed him deeply and said, "Get in bed. I'll just hold you 'til you fall asleep."

"Fine, honey." He was gone in half a minute. She lay there holding him for a good half hour. After leaving the bed and covering him, Anna came back later that evening and lay on her side looking at Jack for the longest time before turning the night light out. When she woke in the morning, he was still sleeping. She left the room, saw the girls off to school, did some work in the office, and returned to their room where she undressed and lay next to him. He stirred and she kissed him. He started to wake up. "Honey, honey."

"Yes, Jack."

"Oh honey, I've longed for this."

"Me too, darling." He took her into his arms. She soon was guiding him "home." After several orgasms and much tenderness, he said, "Wife, I'm starving."

"Yes, my man. What would you like?"

"The whole kitchen." She slipped a robe on and said, "I'll get cooking, dear one." When she entered the kitchen, Ray was there baking the cookies that everyone loved. "I've got a hungry man, Ray."

"What's he want, Anna?"

"I'll get it."

"No, Anna, tell me what to cook. You spend every minute with him. I know he must have to do something for the war effort."

"Thank you, Ray. I haven't talked with him hardly at all yet. Ham, scrambled eggs, and toast. And maybe some of those canned apricots."

"Okay." Anna returned to the bedroom just as Jack was getting out of bed. "Ray's cooking."

"I'll take a quick shower."

"I'd take one with you, but we'd miss breakfast."

He laughed, "You're right, honey."

Anna dressed in Levi's and a pullover sweater. When Jack came back into the room, she flirted, "You're a handsome man, my love."

"You're prejudiced."

"No, I see the women look at you. When do you have to go back and what are you going back to?"

"I have to be back at Moffitt Field in two more days. I've been flying an admiral and a general involved in war plans. I am not supposed to say anything about what I am doing."

"I won't ask. I just hope I get to see you."

"Me too, darling." They went to the dining room. Ray had set a table near the window looking into the canyon. On it he had placed a large candle and a bottle of champagne in a bucket. After Jack sat down, Anna said, "I'll be right back."

"Okay."

She went to the kitchen and thanked Ray. When she returned to the table, Jack was opening the champagne. "Breakfast will be in a minute." Jack poured the champagne and handed a glass to Anna. "Here's hoping it's a quick war, honey."

"I'll drink to that, my love."

After Ray wheeled in the breakfast, Jack ate ravenously while Anna ate little and just watched her man. "Oh Jack, I've missed you so very much."

"I think of you and the girls constantly, Anna."

After breakfast, they walked down to the steelhead stream, hand-in-hand. They could see several of the fish at the edge of the current. Some robins had come in for the winter and were calling. They could see their fire-red breasts shining in the sunlight. "I'll drive you to Moffitt early, Jack. If we leave here at 4 a.m., we should be there by 7:30."

"Honey, you'd have the trip back alone. It would be easier on you if I took the evening bus out of Calistoga."

"Jack, we'll have about fourteen more hours together. God knows when I'll see you again."

"If you want, dear."

Visiting with the children and the episodes with Anna in the bedroom made the time fly. Thursday morning at a quarter to eight, Anna and Jack arrived at Moffitt. When the marine guard stopped them, Jack announced his name. The marine consulted a roster and said, "Sir, you may proceed, but the car and lady are not permitted."

"I understand. Can she turn around this outpost?"

"Yes sir, if you exit the car."

"Yes, I'll do that." They kissed fervently. Then Jack grabbed his bag and said, "Hope to see you soon, my wonderful one."

"I miss you already," Anna said, tears sliding down her cheeks. As she pulled away, in her rear view mirror she saw Jack striding into the military complex. When the thoughts of Jack faded, Anna wondered about the coming resort season. She stopped in Santa Rosa at the wholesale grocery warehouse. She was greeted by Abe Rosenberg.

"Anna, good to see you."

"Good to see you, Abe. I think I'll pick up a few staples instead of going to the resort with an empty car."

"Good idea, Anna. In fact, if you want a word from an old man, you better think about stocking up right away on certain items that may become rationed."

"You really think so, Abe?"

"Yes. Things we don't grow here will become the hard-to-get items."

"Like what?"

"Coffee, sugar, spices. Tires and gas, which I don't handle. But I'll build some storage tanks right quick and stock pile some tires."

"Abe, thanks for the advice."

"Do you have the room to store a lot of coffee and sugar?"

"Yes."

"I'll send a truckload up in a couple of days. You can pay me later."

"Thank you, Abe."

As she drove up Mark West Road, she thought, "There's a lot of honey raised in the area." She would contract for a good supply since it kept so well and was used in so many recipes. By the time she arrived at the ranch, the girls had left for school.

George was raking up fallen leaves and twigs. "Good trip, Anna?"

"Yes, but I was sad to see him go. We'll miss him."

"A nice man, Anna."

"He really is, George."

"You've been lucky, Anna."

"I really have. I picked up some groceries at Abe's."

"I see you got a good load in the car. Looks like you could have used the truck."

"I could have. This was a spur-of-the-moment decision. Abe's sending a truckload of coffee and sugar. Will you make a safe place for it in the storage shed?"

"Yes, Anna."

"Start on it in the morning."

"I may need some sheet metal."

"Get it in town. Put it on the account." Anna carried some packages into the dining room.

Stella was sitting at the bar with a glass of wine in front of her. "Can I help, dear?"

"No, Stella. I'll have a couple of the men finish unloading it. What were you sitting there thinking?"

"Christmas is in a couple of days, Anna. What are we going to do?"

"We'll do just like always. Dinner for everyone and their families."

The holiday was nice, but not as cheerful as it had been. The war had created so many questions in everyone's mind. The day after Christmas, Ray told Anna he would be leaving to join the service. He felt it was his duty. "I understand, Ray. Your job is here when you come back. Or some job. I don't want to lose you or your family."

"Thank you, Anna."

The girls often asked Anna where Jack was and she would tear and say, "I wish I knew. Just say a prayer he's safe."

Alicia said, "Mom, he's a good pilot. He'll be safe."

"I hope so, dear."

By the time the resort season started, Anna knew old Abe had been right about the rationing. Several people who had been coming to the resort in their cars were now taking the bus up. They were staying longer, but business had dropped off that first summer, especially the Sunday dinners.

In late summer, Anna was approached by a former guest who had stayed, with his family, the three previous seasons. He arrived in uniform and was wearing an eagle on his shoulder. "Mr. Winslowe! I almost didn't recognize you."

"I shaved my mustache and beard, Anna. I am still Lyle to you."

"Yes, Lyle."

"How's Jack?"

"He's flying brass. I expect to see him in uniform, too."

"You're probably right, Anna."

"What brings you here, Lyle?"

"Anna, the army is looking for a place to train and quarter men for warfare in Germany. They would live in tents and practice maneuvers on the hillsides. They'd use the bar during some off duty time."

"Maybe I could get some of the single ladies up for a weekly dance."

"That's a good idea, Anna. The army would pay for the use of the grounds and if anything was damaged they would repair it."

"I'd want them to be very careful of the steelhead stream."

"I'll make arrangements to post no fishing signs and that it's a breeding area."

"That would be good, Lyle."

Six hundred men and their officers came to the resort in mid-October. Several of the officers were quartered in the hotel, eating meals and using the bar. When Jack, who was in uniform as a colonel, first heard of the soldiers being quartered there, he had some second thoughts. But Anna explained how she knew Lyle Winslowe, and Jack became more comfortable with it. The dances were well-received and several men were always assigned to guard duty to keep everyone in line. Some of the local girls developed friendships, and letter-writing started. Anna explained to the women that the soldiers were only around for four months and then there would be a new group. Still, passion sometimes reigned and a few pregnancies did result.

Jack was still flying the brass and had safely put a plane down with engine trouble in a harvested wheat field in the Midwest. He got to come home for a week's leave following that episode. Anna was so delighted she said, "I am ashamed, but I almost wish for another safe accident, my pilot man." They enjoyed their week.

Four months later when Jack called from God-knows-where, Anna said, "I have a gift for you, Jack."

"What is it honey?"

"You'll get it in about five more months."

"How come so far away?"

"Because that's when we'll have a child."

"Oh, Anna. Really?"

"Yes, dear. I am having an easy time."

"I can't wait to see you, darling."

"I love you, Jack. This makes us the perfect family."

"Yes, my dear." He asked about the soldiers and how things were going.

"It's been good, Jack. Lyle has really stayed on top of everything and we're making some money in the off-season."

"I hope to see you for a few days next month, Anna."

"I'm looking forward to it. I love you so very much."

"Me too, darling. I have to run."

"Yes, love. Goodbye for now."

"Goodbye, dear."

That summer the guests who brought children up for the summer season were thrilled to be around real soldiers. The men catered to the children as much as they could. Mrs. O'Malley had passed on that spring so Anna planned to have her child at the Calistoga Hospital. The war was taking a turn for the better according to the newscasters and the local paper. There were Italian prisoners of war working in some of the vineyards. They were brought in each day and returned to their prison at Vallejo each evening. The vineyard owner said that almost to a man they would try to return to America after the war ended.

Late one night, Jack arrived in a staff car with a driver. He said he had two days and asked Anna if she could lodge the driver. "We're fully occupied, Jack. Maybe George could find a spot in the tents with the other soldiers. The army has built complete lavatories for them."

"That would work."

Anna's pregnancy was quite evident now. Jack complemented her. "Honey, you're beautiful."

"Thank you, my love."

That night in bed he was very tender, and Anna said, "Darling, I think we can still do it, but carefully."

"I don't want to hurt you or the baby, Anna."

"You just lay back and let me do what I can." She engulfed him and they reached several orgasms before Anna tired.

"Honey, you are so wonderful," he said. They fell asleep with Jack wrapped around her back.

Anna woke and gently untwined from Jack. She showered, looked at her sleeping man, and went to the kitchen. Uncle Gus, Eva's brother, had come to America for his sister's funeral and had stayed on. He was now doing the cooking for the resort and doing a very good job.

"Morning, Uncle Gus. I am very hungry. How about a stack of your pancakes?"

"Yes, Anna. An egg on top?"

"Fine." Anna poured a glass of orange juice.

"Go sit down, Anna. I'll bring the pancakes to you."

"Thank you, Gus." Lyle was at a table drinking coffee.

"Can I join you?"

"Yes, Anna. I was going to look you up today. The army wants to close this operation down when this last group of men completes their training."

"Oh. Kind of sudden, isn't it?"

"War, Anna. Things can change pretty rapidly. That means about six weeks and we'll be out of here. I am sure I'll be reassigned to the Pacific theater. I was wondering about having my family stay on here for the duration of the war. I discussed it with the wife and she'd like to. She calls it her second home."

"I am sure we can work something out, Lyle. I'll hate to see you go."

"Me too."

Jack came to the dining room about noon and found Anna doing paper work. He went over and kissed her as she sat. "Hungry?"

"Yes."

"Food or me?"

"Both. I ate, but I'll need some more of you."

"You sure?"

"Yes, while I have you here for such a short time."

She got up, saying, "I'll have Uncle Gus cook you a steak. And some eggs too?"

"Yes, please."

"Coming up. Order something from Stella. I'll have a small glass of white."

When Anna returned, she could see Jack was sipping on a martini. "Early, isn't it?"

"My nerves are a little edgy. Just something to settle down." Anna sipped her wine. "Jack, Lyle told me the army men will be leaving soon."

"They always do."

"No, he said they're going to close this operation down."

"I'm surprised. The end of the war isn't really in sight yet."

"Lyle said it's kind of the army's way. They get something going good and someone has a different idea, or some congressman wants the men stationed in his state."

"There's some truth to that. That was quite a welcoming you gave me last night, pretty lady."

"Just call it my war effort, which I hope to continue tonight."

Gus put the food on the table and saluted Jack. "I should be doing the saluting, Gus. Thank you for this feast."

"Nothing too good for a soldier."

That night was a repeat of the night before. The next day Anna and the girls were kissing Jack goodbye.

Chapter 21

Nicholas

Anna and Judy were in the dining room, Judy drinking a glass of wine and Anna, Calso Water. They talked of the past season, and laughed about one of the soldiers who had taken one of Judy's horses, ridden down to the steelhead stream, removed his clothing, and gone swimming. He had tied the horse to a large Poison Oak bush, brushed against it, and ended up with Poison Oak all over. The sergeant wanted to know if he had had sex with the bush. Ending up in the Calistoga Hospital for ten days, when he was released Sheriff Roy served him with a fake summons to appear in court for horse stealing. Everyone had gone along with the gag. Despite the poor soldier's hearing stories that they still hung horse thieves or sentenced them to a minimum of twenty years at San Quentin, the judge sentenced him to six more months in the U.S. Army. Lyle told the soldier it was because he was such a good defense lawyer that he got off so easy. The poor guy was the absolute last to realize it had been a joke.

That night they had a big party at the resort. It had been fun and lightened up things for everyone. The visiting girls really enjoyed the joke.

Judy was dating one of the junior officers, a nice, quiet young man from Wyoming. An excellent rider, he and Judy would go off on rides that eventually led to overnight dates.

"You're serious about this guy, Judy?"

"It's starting to look that way, Anna, but I have some misgivings."

"What about, Judy?"

"Anna this is very hard for me, but I need advice before he proposes, which I think he's going to do. A couple of days ago he made a ring out of a vine we were playing around on a picnic. When I eventually took it off to go swimming, I caught him saving it in his shirt pocket."

"Clever man. What's the problem, Judy?"

"That day at John's monument when I said I thought Dad had killed John…"

"I remember and wondered for a long time about that statement."

"Anna, Anna. My father had started molesting me when I was quite young. In time I accepted it and eventually enjoyed it. I feel so ashamed."

"Judy, I am lost for words. What father would do that?"

"I've read about it, Anna, and it's more common than you would imagine. But I am still very ashamed, and it's the main reason I've tried not to be serious with any man."

"Since you say I am the only one you told, it's our secret, Judy."

"Should I tell Dale, Anna?"

"That's a heavy trip for a man to accept, Judy."

"I've slept with a few of the guests when I've had a few drinks, and a few of these soldiers."

"It's normal to want to be held and loved, Judy. If Dale knows you're not a virgin, I wouldn't tell him anything. Just be the loving person I know you are."

"I've seen Alfonso and Rosalie so happy together, even with their simple life. I'd like that, Anna, someone to share with. Dale and I love to ride and camp."

"Do you think he'd want to stay in California?"

"He says he loves it and the mild winters we have. He says he'd like to never shovel snow again or be so cold your teeth rattle."

"Then if he asks, Judy, accept him and try to forget what happened with your dad. You were young and couldn't do much about it. Don't feel guilty. Many things sexual are enjoyable. Only it's a lot better with someone you really love and you have some of the control."

"Do you really enjoy it, Anna?"

"Very much." Anna started to get up from the table to use the restroom and two steps away from the table her water broke.

"Oh Judy! It's time."

"I'll drive you to the hospital."

Stella was alongside Anna, helping her out to the car. "I'll tell Dr. Massie that you're on the way to the hospital."

"Good, Stella. I wish I knew where Jack was stationed. He's probably in the air somewhere."

"Anna, if he happens to call, I'll tell him what's happening."

"Yes, Stella."

Judy was driving carefully down the twisting road to town. "You better speed up a little, Judy, or I'll be having my baby here in the front seat."

"Just hold on, Anna."

Anna was rushed into the hospital in a wheelchair. A young intern told her, "Dr. Massie will be here in about twenty more minutes." They wheeled Anna into a room with a bed and put her into a hospital gown. The pains were now coming quite quickly. A minute after Dr. Massie arrived, he was welcoming Jack's and Anna's son into the world. He was a healthy boy with good lungs.

Five days later, Anna and the baby left the hospital. Jack had called and was expected to be home in two days for a three-day leave. When he arrived at the resort, it was close to 2 a.m. In the morning, Anna heard Rags barking and thought it must be a raccoon. Then she noticed car lights in the front yard and knew it was Jack.

She was just going to get up to feed Nicholas, a name they had picked out if she had a son. Anna went to the bureau, brushed her hair, and quickly put on a little make up. Jack was coming into the room as she turned.

"Darling, I got here as quick as I could. I wish I could have been here for you."

"I love you," Anna whispered.

She pointed to the crib.

"It's something new in your life, Jack."

She kissed him again. "He's due for his two o'clock feeding in a couple of minutes. He's quite regular, and a hungry little guy.

"He's healthy?"

"Yes, he's fine. The doctor's pleased, and I am really pleased."

"What do the girls think?"

"They fight over holding him."

"Good girls."

Nicholas woke with a cry. Anna picked him up and handed him to his dad. Jack had the biggest smile.

"Hi, little guy." Nicholas cried louder. "What did I do, Anna?"

"Nothing, dear. Bring him over here." As she sat on the side of the bed, she opened her nightshirt, exposing her full breasts.

"Wow," Jack exclaimed.

"Yes, they are loaded. I've never had so much milk before and it's good the way he eats." Jack watched, enthralled.

"This only takes a little while. He'll soon fall back to sleep."

A few minutes later, Anna was leading Jack to the dining room. "I'll get you something to eat."

"No, dear one. Maybe a glass of wine."

"Okay."

"Tell me everything," he said. She told of the trip to town with Judy, and Dr. Massie arriving at the last minute so that she thought the young intern was going to have to help her deliver.

"I am glad he made it. I know you had confidence in him."

"Yes, Jack. He has a good reputation with the women in town."

"It's so good to see you, dear lady. You make me so proud. You and the girls were enough, but he is ours. This is the fulfillment of our wonderful love. Thank God I came here for a vacation."

"I thank him too, Jack. I just want this war to get over and have you home."

"That's all I want too, Anna dear."

They went to bed and Anna said, "I want you, Jack, but I am still healing."

"I've heard this takes a while to get over, Anna. Just holding you will be enough."

They fell asleep in each other's arms. Jack did not even wake for the six o'clock feeding.

The girls were happy to hear Jack was home. They would see him after school since he would be home for three days. George came into the dining room, telling everyone that America had bombed Japan. All were astounded.

"How?" some asked. "No plane could fly that far."

George replied, "Carriers launched the planes."

Anna thought she should wake Jack. She went into the room and he was just swinging his legs out of bed. "Jack, they've bombed Japan."

"Where did you hear that?"

"George said he heard it on the radio. We turned the radio on in the dining room and they were still talking about it. Will the war be over?"

"I don't think they'll give in with one bombing. I'd better try and call the brass I fly."

"Will you have to leave?"

"I don't know, Anna."

That night Jack finally reached Admiral Ryan. "It's a morale-raiser, Jack. We're waiting to see the outcome. Jimmy Doolittle and his crew pulled it off. Lots of good fliers are lost, I fear. I'll call you as soon as I know if there is any change of plans for us."

"Thank you, Admiral."

Anna was glad to hear Jack would still be here. There were kisses from the girls and a grand dinner that night with the whole crew and the officers quartered at the resort. Anna also invited Judy and her crew.

After dinner, there was a lot of war talk, and drinks at Stella's bar. Anna left to nurse Nicholas when Michelle came and told her he was waking up and Alicia was changing his diaper. Anna said, "Thank you, dear." She then excused herself.

Jack said, "I'll go with you." She took his hand and led him to the room. Nicholas was crying.

"Here Nickie," she cooed, opening her blouse. Jack had a smile on his face.

The girls left the room, saying, "Good night, Mom."

Nickie fell asleep, and Anna put him back into the crib. "Do you want to go back to the others, Jack?"

"No darling. I just want to be with you." They undressed for bed and came together, their kisses very passionate. Kneeling between her thighs, Jack started to have an orgasm. "I'm sorry, honey."

"It's all right, my love. You know where I wish it was."

"It's your fault. You're just so beautiful." They soon fell asleep. Jack woke up for the two a.m. feeding. He held Anna on his lap as she nursed

Nickie. "Jack, I wish we had a picture of this for our old age."

"That would really be cute, darling."

When Admiral Ryan called two days later, he told Jack he could take an extra day and then meet him at Moffitt Field. That day Jack was shown around the army camp by Lyle. He said the staff and a couple of sergeants were going to have a poker game that night, and asked if he would like to join. Jack mentioned it to Anna and she thought it would be good for him.

He ended up coming to the bedroom just as Anna was finishing nursing Nickie.

"Sorry I missed the feeding. I stayed a little longer than I intended. It was good to relax with the men. It's always so straightlaced with the brass."

"I'm glad you're here, Jack. I need you."

"Is it okay?"

"It's got to be."

He was very gentle kissing her breasts. She wept a little. "Taste me, darling." He did. "Am I stealing Nicky's breakfast?"

"It's okay. I have so much this time, darling."

When he entered her, he could feel the difference, but she encouraged him.

"Easy, honey. Don't hurt yourself. I just crave it and you." Their passion lasted and lasted.

Jack had to wake Anna for the six a.m. feeding. She was a little sore going to the crib. "Honey, I was too hard on you."

"It's not your fault. You were doing what I wanted and needed."

A few minutes later, Jack left for Moffitt Field. She did not hear from him again for three and a half weeks. It was a quick phone call. He was all right. How were she and Nickie and the girls?

Everyone was fine.

It was raining, but he did not say where he was. They exchanged "I love yous."

CHAPTER 22

SPRING 1943

Anna had just finished with Nicholas' morning feeding, showered, and gone to the kitchen where Dianne, Colonel Lyle's wife, was preparing coffee. "Dianne, whatever are you doing up so early?"

"That time of the month and I needed a cup."

"Good for you. I think you're on your way to becoming part of the crew."

"Your girls have sure matured into pretty young teenagers. I know they're starting to ask about boys. God, mine will be there soon."

"Dianne, do you think this war is going to get over so we can have our men back?"

"Anna, I have a good feeling about our two guys. They seem to be on top of everything." Anna asked if she could fix Dianne something to eat. "No, I'll wait and eat with the girls."

"The season starts this weekend and the reservations are light. I guess with the gas rationing and the war, it's making life a little harder for everyone."

Gus came in. "Morning, ladies. Breakfast?"

Both replied they'd better go make sure their girls were starting to get up for school. Then Dianne said, "See you later."

"Okay, Dianne."

Anna went to the office for a moment to see if she had answered all her mail. She had. She was getting a little absentminded with all the things that had been coming her way. The girls were still sleeping. She could see a little of Don in each of them.

"Come on, girls. Rise and shine, as the army says."

"Oh, Mom," Alicia said.

"Come on, Michelle."

She woke rubbing her eyes.

"Brush the teeth, comb the hair, and dress warm. It's still a little cold."

"Yes, mother," they replied.

Anna went out to the front yard to check the pickup for gas, and air in the tires. Dianne was coming back with her daughters for breakfast.

"Anna, I'll take the girls to the highway for the school bus this morning."

"That will be great, Dianne. I feel like taking a little hike. I'll ask Barbara to watch Nicholas for a little while."

Later that morning, Anna hiked down to the stream. It was running quite full since the rain had been heavy that spring. She hiked down to John's monument and rested. For the first time in her life, she noticed she was a little out of shape. She mused, "I must get out more. I love this country so much."

As she leaned against the monument, she noticed a yearling spike coming to water. He stopped and gazed at her. "I won't hurt you, little guy."

He continued toward the stream, moving off at an angle farther downstream. She didn't move until he finished his drink. Then she moved up the hillside.

As the yearling watched her, she hiked up to the old Indian ruins, looked around, and noticed a rattler sunning on lava rock. She'd have to remind guests to be wary. Thank God no guest had been bitten. She arrived back at her office and felt a little weary, but refreshed. "I've got to do that a couple of times a week," she thought. The phone rang and it was a former client.

"How are you, Mrs. Lawrence? Is the family well? That's good. What can I do for you? You want reservations the first two weeks of July? You and the three children, and your husband will be up on weekends? You're coming on the bus and he'll come up weekends on the bus? Okay dear. We'll pick you up. Let me know what time your bus gets in. Yes dear, looking forward to seeing you."

By the end of the week several more phone reservations had been made. In the past the majority of reservations had been made by mail. Anna guessed it had become practical to do it by phone.

Randy, Gus, and George were now the male crew. An older woman was doing dishes and waitresses were still being supplied by the high school. Stella was still running the bar and doing a great job. Because George was really overworked, Anna had to call Jim Bond to see if he could find a helper for him. Jim said he had a good prospect and hard worker, who was black, fifty years old, and thus safe from going to war. Anna asked, "What was his crime, Jim?"

"Burglary without a weapon. That's why he got off with only seven years and is being paroled after five years. He's Christian and said he did it just to buy food for himself and his mother. She died while he was in prison. No family…just a couple of brothers down in Texas older than him."

"I wonder what the guests would think. I'll have to talk to Randy. He's from the south."

"Let me know, Anna?"

"Yes I will. Goodbye."

Anna wondered. She knew how scarce help was right now. And she respected Jim's opinion. All the men he had ever sent worked out pretty well except maybe that rogue, Lance. That night after dinner, she talked to Stella and George at the bar. George said, "Anna, I really need some help."

Stella interjected, "Yes, Anna. My man has been quite tired getting ready for the season. He has been doing a lot of work by himself."

"I'll talk to Randy to see if he could be comfortable working with him."

"Good idea, Anna."

"Thank you, George."

The next morning she drew Randy aside before he went to his various projects. "I worked with those boys down south a few times, Anna. I've gotten along. God made all of us."

"Thank you, Randy."

The next day Anna called Jim Bond. "Jim, I think things will work out fine. Bring James up at your earliest convenience." James turned out to fit in perfectly with the guests and crew. He came to love this place full of friendly people.

Chapter 23

Second Honeymoon

Jack had come home for the first time in eight months. He looked quite haggard and slept a lot the first five days except for some intense lovemaking. He had told Dianne he had run into Lyle in Australia. He looked well, lost some weight, and was growing a beard and mustache. "My god, I won't know him."

"We compared notes and had a few, warm, Australian beers. We were both counting our luck that we were safe. A lot of the wounded were in Australian hospitals. They were treated well by the nurses. The Aussies had had heavy casualties wherever they fought."

Dianne asked, "How much longer, Jack?"

"I'm afraid a couple of more years, and if we have to invade Japan, God forbid, maybe longer. They're good soldiers, but we might be able to keep their supply lines closed with some bases near Japan while we build an armada."

Anna asked, "Jack, do you really think so? These separations are terrible."

"Honey, we're lucky. I fly and get around some. It may be a couple of years before Dianne sees Lyle." Tears came to Dianne's eyes. "I'm sorry, Dianne. I hope I am wrong."

"I know, Jack. Just as long as he comes back to me and the girls."

"And that goes for you too, Jack."

"Yes, Anna. I sure want to."

Anna and Jack flew over to Reno for four days of a second honeymoon. Stella and George were caring for Michelle and Alicia, and Barbara was caring for Nicky. They caught several shows, played the slots, made love, and relaxed. Then they returned to the resort.

A couple of days later on a visit to the Fire Mountain cave, Anna asked Jack to tell her how things really were. He told her of the constant flying of the admiral to Washington and then back to CINPAC in Hawaii. Plans were continually being made and changed, and getting Joint Chiefs of Staff to agree on combined operations seemed to be the major problem.

"What do you do in your free time?"

"Sleep, play poker with other pilots like myself, have a few drinks, talk about the war, our wives and children, show the pictures we're all so proud of, and talk of what we're going to do after the war."

"Well, you know what you're going to do. Be here with me."

"Honey, you run this place so well…"

"Yes, but you could be a help."

"I want to help you all I can, but I was thinking of going back to Pan Am."

"I almost forgot. I thought you just might be tired of flying."

"Honey, this has been hard, but I still love to fly."

"More than being with me?"

"No. If I go back to Pan Am and finish out my twenty-five years, I'll have a nice pension. We'll still be young. We can travel the world on Pan Am quite reasonably, and when the war is over we can take our family on trips to Hawaii."

"That does sound sensible and wonderful."

"You should see the poor beaches in Hawaii right now. They're entangled with barbwire and covered with foxholes."

"Do they think the Japanese will invade?"

"At one time they probably could have. Now that we have them on the run as we recapture islands, it's less likely."

"I'm sorry I brought this up."

"It's okay. I think it probably does some good for us to talk about it. And you, my darling wife, have a right to know about her husband and his thoughts." She slid into his arms and they were once again in a familiar place.

When they returned to the resort, Stella told them Alicia had fallen during a basketball game and broken her arm. Dr. Massie was with her and Michelle at the Calistoga Hospital. Barbara and Randy had gone to the hospital also. "Okay, Stella. We are leaving now," Anna said, as she and Jack hopped into the truck and headed for town. They arrived at the hospital, where Randy and his children met them in the lobby.

"Anna, Jack, she is doing fine. She is quite a little trooper. Barbara and Michelle are with her and Dr. Massie. He said he will put a cast on it in a couple of hours."

"Okay, Randy. Thank you for filling in for me. You and Barbara can head back to the resort."

"Thanks, Randy," Jack echoed. They went into the receiving room and saw Alicia propped up in bed. Anna and Michelle moved to the bed and kissed her. "How are you, sweet?"

"I'm okay, Mom. It hurt at first and I cried a little."

"That's okay, honey, I know it hurts." She then kissed Michelle and Barbara. "Thanks, Barbara. I really appreciate your coming to Alicia's rescue."

"Anna, I'd do anything for you and the girls."

"Thanks again, Barbara. I told Randy that you and the kids should head back to the resort. Jack and I will stay until she is released."

Four hours later, they were all back at the resort and Anna was in the kitchen, making sandwiches for the four of them. "The doctor said the cast should come off in about eight weeks and the arm would be as good as new. I'll have to join the team again next year."

"I'm sure you will, Alicia. By then Michelle may be playing too."

"I don't know, Mom. I may go out for track."

"Whatever you want," Anna said as she placed a platter of sandwiches on the table. "Milk, girls?"

"Yes Mom," they echoed.

Jack interjected, "Anna, dear, if I open a bottle of wine, will you share it with me?"

"Yes, dear."

After they both tucked the girls in, Anna said, "Tomorrow you both can stay home and the four of us will drive into Santa Rosa for a movie and some light shopping. Then we'll go down to Penngrove to the Greenmill for dinner."

The girls exclaimed excitement at the news.

Following shopping and going to the Greenmill for a leisurely dinner, they came back home on the Mark West Road. There were quite a few deer out on the moonlit night and, as they neared their place, several times they caught glimpses of Fire Mountain reflecting its flames of orange and gold. After they put the girls to bed, Anna and Jack went to their room and got ready for bed. Anna went to the window to stare at Fire Mountain. Jack came to her and they stood face-to-face. Soon she was moaning, "Oh Jack, Jack," as she caressed his locks and they slipped to the floor.

Morning found them in bed with Anna caressing him. "You've had enough sleep, soldier." He smiled and rolled over to her.

Two days later Anna was driving Jack to the bus depot. The girls were in a play at school and she had to hurry back to see it. "I'll write or call whenever I can, Anna."

"Please do as I love to hear from you and just want this thing over with."

"Me too, darling."

She followed him onto the bus and sat on his lap until the bus was ready to leave. The old driver said, "Sorry, ma'am, I do have a schedule to keep."

"I understand, thank you." She watched and waved until the bus left the lot.

CHAPTER 24

SECOND THOUGHTS

As Anna was walking to the car on main street, Sheriff Roy pulled alongside her. "Hello, Anna."

"Good to see you, Roy. How's Owen?"

"We hear he's in a hospital in Australia. Shrapnel wounds in his foot and hand. He'll be okay although they say he may carry a couple of pieces in his foot."

"Sorry to hear that. But thank God he's alive."

"Yes, that's for sure."

"Roy, I've seen your car parked down by the end of the road leading to the sulfur baths a few times over the years. I kind of wondered what you were up to."

"Once in a while I still think about Indian John being killed there and how whoever shot him could not have seen him. I've even made a cutout of cardboard of John, a buck, and the shooter, and placed them where they had to be. Assuming there was a buck there, I find it hard to believe that John had not been seen. Who could have wanted that boy dead, Anna? No one that I knew of at the time. The one who did most of the hunting around here had been Frank. I know he had a scope on his rifle, but it couldn't have been him, I don't think. Why would he kill that boy? Did he hate Indians?"

"I don't think there is anyone around in the country that actually hates them anymore. I think that died out as they were mostly killed off or died from diseases."

"That's probably right, Anna. It had to be almost a perfect situation for John not to have been seen. The sun in the hunter's eyes, John rising up from a squatting position, and the deer in exactly the right spot. It still makes me wonder, Anna."

"It does, Roy?"

"What brought you to town, Anna? Kind of late in the year for guests."

"Yes, Roy. Jack was home on leave. I just put him on the bus. God only knows when I'll see him again."

"Coffee, Anna?"

"I'd like to, but maybe next time."

"Whatever, Anna. 'Til next time."

"Goodbye, Roy."

Anna had kept her promise to Judy to say nothing. The fact that Frank was now dead made her believe that there was no harm in not telling Roy. Moreover, he should eventually give up on the idea as time passed.

In mid-July, Dale and Judy were married at the resort with Alphonso giving the bride away. Anna had arranged a large wedding. Even guests staying at the ranch were invited. Dianne and her daughters, Anna and her daughters, and Stella had knocked themselves out arranging flowers and food. Anna and Stella had prepared one of the rooms as a bridal room. Dale and one of the other gunnery officers from Fort Ord had a 72-hour pass. At three o'clock Saturday afternoon, the wedding was held at the campfire site where amateur hour occurred each week. Father Charlie conducted the ceremony without his collar on.

"Non denominational," he said. They would have to have a civil ceremony later. Dale was in his dress uniform and Judy in a wedding dress closely matching her husband-to-be's uniform.

After the service, there was a sit-down dinner for all in the dining room and music by George, Randy, and James. The party lasted until three in the morning with the bride and groom exiting about midnight. Anna, Stella, and George were the last to leave the dining room, happy that everything had gone so well.

The next day, departing guests were saying how much they had enjoyed their stay and especially the wedding of Judy, since some of the guests had ridden with her over the years. When Anna said, "I don't know when, but there'll be more weddings here in the coming years," a couple responded, "Let us know when. We'll take time out of our schedules to make them." Anna laughed and wished them good trips home.

The rest of the summer went well. Judy made a few trips to Fort Ord on weekends and the girls filled in for Judy on the rides. They were becoming a real asset to Anna. If a waitress failed to show, they were thrilled to fill in. They were starting to learn to drive and would have their licenses soon. In September, Jack called and wanted Anna to meet him in Monterey in the middle of the week. She said she could leave Dianne to take care of things. Jack said he'd reserve a room at the Carmel Hotel. Anna should ask for his room in their name and he'd be in sometime Wednesday. He'd have three days leave.

Jack was late getting to the hotel and Anna spotted him as he approached the desk. She saw him from a table near the bar where she had been waiting for him. Quickly moving toward him, she called, "Jack, Jack." He turned and she was in his arms, kissing and hugging him. They made a spectacle of themselves, but it was wartime and these sights were common.

Anna opened her eyes and looked closely at Jack. He looked haggard. "Darling, are you okay?"

"Just a little worn, sweetheart."

"What do you want to do?"

"Rest, shower, eat."

"Darling, we better eat. The dining room closes in a few minutes."

As they approached a table, you could see the unhappy look on the waiter's face as he looked at his watch. They ordered butterflyed lamb chops, salad, and baked potatoes. Jack said, "That order will be quick. We must not keep the crew overtime. Wine, honey?"

"I was nursing a couple of Old Fashions before you arrived. I think I'll stay with the same, then I'll order a double Manhattan." Both kept saying how wonderful it was to be together.

When dinner finished, it was up to their room. A tired man came alive as Anna came to bed stark naked. Love and lust—where did they begin and end?

They slept late, bathed, and then Jack said, "Anna dear, I am going to order breakfast sent up with some champagne."

"Jack, whatever you want. I just want to spend every minute with you."

They showered and washed each other intimately. As Jack stepped out of the shower, he heard a knock on the door. He grabbed a towel, went to the door, opened it, and a busboy wheeled in breakfast. "Just a minute. Please excuse my dress." After wrapping the towel around himself sarong-like, he got his wallet, took out a few ones, and gave them to the man, just as Anna entered the room in the raw.

"Oops. I thought you were alone, darling."

The bus boy smiled and backed out looking at Anna.

"You bad girl. No pride."

"Oh, honey. It was for you."

"I know. I'm kidding. He'll have something to tell his fellow workers."

They ate, drank the champagne, cuddled, and slept again. Later that afternoon they walked the beach. The ocean was beautiful and they saw otters eating abalone. Then they returned to the hotel, changed, and went to the lounge for cocktails. After a few drinks, they went into the dining room for dinner. They ordered abalone steaks with wild rice, seafood salad, and white wine. After dinner, they danced to a trio's music with a few other couples. Then they nursed after-dinner drinks and retired early for some intense lovemaking.

The three days passed too quickly. After driving Jack back to Moffitt, Anna parked a half block away well off the driveway. "Jack, I just have to have you one more time."

"Lady, I like how you think. Even quick passion has a place at times."

As Anna pulled up to the guard's post, Jack said, "This is the second time I leave you here, my darling."

"I know the routine," Anna said as the guard started to give his spiel. Then she pulled around the post and stopped. Jack kissed her deeply, grabbed his bag, and said, "I love you, lady." Then a quick kiss and he was gone.

Anna drove straight back to Calistoga. As she drove into the resort, everything looked the same. She entered the dining room where Stella was talking to two couples at the bar. She waved and went to the office. Dianne was behind her desk, talking on the phone. Anna greeted her, "Hi. You're busy. I'll go look for the girls and talk to you later." Dianne returned to her phone conversation.

The girls were in their room doing homework when Anna came in. "How're my beautiful girls?"

"Hi, Mom," they echoed. "How is Jack?"

"He's doing great. It was so good to see him. I wish it was longer, but the darn war goes on."

"When is it going to be over?" Michelle asked.

"No one's sure, Michelle."

Chapter 25

Missing Pilot

Anna was looking at the glow of Fire Mountain from her balcony. It was cold, but she wanted a breath of fresh air. It had been a long day. She noticed a dark object falling and a second later an explosion on the side of the mountain. A large area was immediately covered with fire. She wondered whether it was a meteor. The rains had been heavy recently and she couldn't imagine a fire spreading.

She wondered what could have happened. The next morning Sheriff Roy was at the resort asking anyone he saw if they had seen or heard anything unusual the night before. No one had. When he visited Anna in her office, after hellos were exchanged, he said, "Anna, the army called and said they had a plane down in this area."

"Oh, my God, Roy. I saw an object falling and then an explosion of flame on the side of the mountain in the area we call Eva's Goat Canyon.

It's just to the left of Fire Mountain. I watched for a little. The flames were fierce for awhile and then died down. I must have watched it longer than I thought. My God, maybe that was a pilot parachuting out of the plane."

"Did you see a chute open, Anna?"

"I don't think so. It was close to the earth."

"Anna, I'll call the army. I am sure they'll get someone right up here." "Roy, I better go now. I know the area."

"I know you do, but you shouldn't go alone."

"I'll take a gun. I need to move quickly. Tell George what's going on and where I am going. He'll lead whoever comes to the area. I'll fire three shots every so often if I find anyone."

"I'll get an ambulance up here. George can guide the crew to the area."

Sheriff Roy called the army and the Calistoga Hospital and contacted George at his quarters. Anna was already moving at a dog trot. She had a 22, water, and a first aid kit. She crossed the stream at the ripples. The water was waist-high with winter run off and cold. She worked her way along the side of the stream up into Eva's Goat Canyon. It took her a good two hours to find the downed man who was being pawed by a mountain lion.

She could hear a low moan escaping from the man who was tangled in a half open chute. She fired two quick shots and the lion moved off into the nearby ferns. Then she went to the downed man. A big man, he was semiconscious and had been bleeding from the cuts on his face and hands.

"Soldier, I am going to help you. You're going to be okay." She didn't think he understood her because he was delirious. She cradled his head and gave him a little water. It ran out of his mouth. He was lying on a bed of lava exposed from run off.

"God, he must have hit this ground so hard," she said to herself. She noticed he became silent. "No, no. Don't go. No." She put her ear to his lips. There was the slightest hint of breathing. She took the rifle and fired three shots which echoed in the canyon. A 22 was not that loud. Maybe no one was on the way yet. She heard an almost inaudible moan.

"Come on, soldier. Hang in there." Anna tried to give him a little water and thought he retained a little of it this time. She held him and asked God to help him until someone arrived. She felt so inadequate.

Eventually she fired three more shots. This time there was an answering three shots. She waited and waited and then fired again. The shots which were returned were now very close. In a few minutes she heard Roy and George calling, "Anna, Anna."

"Over here," she yelled. Two minutes later they appeared with two other men carrying a stretcher. The medic looked at the soldier cradled in Anna's arms. "Ma'am, he's gone."

"No! Are you sure?"

"I am." She started to cry softly. Roy and George tried to console her. The medics put the man on the stretcher, tying him tightly for the trip back to the resort. George had his arm around Anna, talking to her softly. On the way back, Roy spelled the medics on the long carry.

At the resort the army had just arrived. They were insisting on being led to the area where the body had been found. They also wanted to know if the crash sight had been found. Sheriff Roy replied it hadn't. The only effort had been to find the pilot. Anna had told Roy the explosion had been to the left of where she had seen the object falling. George agreed to lead the army to where the pilot had been found, but wanted half an hour to catch his breath and get something to drink.

With Stella behind the bar, George ordered brandy and told her what had happened and what he had to do. "Honey, you take it easy. I am worried about you."

"I'll take it slow and easy. There is no rush now. The poor guy is dead. His poor family! And it wasn't even in combat."

Judy, Barbara, and Randy were also there. Anna told them of finding the soldier and the mountain lion pawing him. "Thank God he was delirious," she said as she finished her story.

Anna subsequently gave the same story to a couple of lieutenants. Several days later, the army was again questioning her. A month later, an older gentleman came into the resort asking for her by her married name. He was the father of the downed pilot. He asked to see where it had happened. Anna replied, "It's a good hike."

"I know. I look old, but I am fit. I'm a farmer from Washington. Apples and pears and some sheep. I work every day, Mrs. Collins."

"Call me Anna. Everyone does, and if we make this hike it will make it easier."

"I'm sorry. I am Mr. Walters. Please call me Allen."

"Yes, Allen. It's late. I'll put you up for the night. You'll eat with us and we'll leave in the morning."

"Whatever you say, Anna."

After breakfast the next morning, Anna and Allen met before leaving. Anna was carrying the 22.

"Why the gun, Anna?" She explained how she had found his son.

"My God. If that lion had dragged him off and eaten him. Anna, Anna, I owe you a debt of gratitude."

"Allen, I was glad I found him. I just wish there had been a happier ending."

When they reached the spot where Allen's son had been found, they could see a small white cross. "Someone from the army must have placed it," Anna said to Allen. He had tears easing down his cheeks.

Eventually they were back at the resort. Allen insisted on buying Anna and everyone at the bar a drink in memory of his son. He toasted, "To Jimmy, my son. He was a good boy." Several others had tears in their eyes. Mr. Walters stayed overnight and left the next day.

About a month later, Anna received a beautiful card from Mr. Walter's wife, thanking her for her efforts. For several years following, Anna would receive a case of premium Washington apples and a "Thank you" note.

CHAPTER 26

LONELY CHRISTMAS

When Jack called several days later, he mentioned that he heard a pilot had died in a crash near Fire Mountain. Admiral Ryan had told him. "I hadn't heard about it before. The admiral said he had seen the guy play baseball and thought he'd make it to the big leagues. He really felt it was a shame to lose the young man."

"Yes, Jack. I wrote you about it in my last letter. It evidently hasn't caught up to you yet."

"No, it hasn't, dear one."

"Jack, I found the pilot after a search in Eva's Goat Canyon. He was severely injured because his chute didn't open properly. The army inspectors thought he had been too low when he bailed out. They were up here often and asked lots of questions. George and Sheriff Roy helped the medics bring him out. The boy's father came here and I led him to the site of the accident. There had been a fire, but the area was quite wet from winter rains so the fire from the crash only burned about half an acre."

"Geez, Anna. What a sad experience!"

"Yes. I was depressed for several days. The poor boy died in my arms. I thought about how often you fly and I thank God you're safe."

"I'm careful, Anna. I fly, trying to keep all my options open. I'm friendly with the mechanics and I think they go overboard to keep the planes I fly well-serviced."

"I hope so, Jack."

"Honey, it's war and pilots go down for many reasons. I'm lucky having these easy runs with the admiral. He says he has to be at Moffitt Field for a week next month so I'm hoping to see you for a couple of days. He's pretty decent about letting me off when I'm near home."

"Jack, I hope so. I miss you so much. The children do too. Nicky is talking now."

"Kiss him and the girls for me. I've got to run, dear one."

"Oh, Jack."

"I'm sorry, Anna. I love you, my wonderful lady."

"I love you too."

When Anna saw Stella, she asked, "What are you doing here so early?"

"Inventory, Anna."

"I just got off the phone with Jack. I told him about the pilot who crashed. He had already heard about it from his admiral. I'm sad he can't be here."

"I know, honey. It's so good when your man is with you."

"Stella, please give me a glass of wine."

"Red or white, dear?"

"Whatever you have open."

Barbara suddenly came into the room with Nicky. "Mama, mama," he cried as he ran to Anna.

"Nicky, Nicky," she said soothingly as she picked him up and held him.

"You're holding me too tight, mama."

"I'm sorry, little guy."

"I'm getting big, mama."

"Yes. Yes, you are. Barbara, can I interest you in a glass of wine?"

"No thanks, Anna."

"Thanks for dressing him, Barbara."

"He came over, knocking on our door in his pj's, so I took him back to your place and dressed him. He wanted to see you and also said he wanted cereal."

"Well, I'll get some from the kitchen. Can I get you anything?"

"No, Anna. I have to get the children off to school."

"Okay, dear. Thanks again."

"Anytime, Anna."

Anna took Nicky to the kitchen where Gus was starting breakfast for the help. "Customer here for you, Gus."

"Morning, Anna. That's a big guy."

"He sure is."

"Just a bowl of cereal for him. I'll get it."

"No, I've got it, Anna." He poured shredded wheat into a bowl and added milk and a little honey.

"Thank you, Gus. What do you say, Nicky?"

"Thank you, uncle Gus."

"You're welcome, Nicky."

Anna sat down at a table with Nicky. Stella brought her unfinished glass to her. "Thank you, Stella."

"You're welcome." Dianne then came in with her girls and good mornings were exchanged.

"Anna, I think I have all the office work completed."

"Thanks, Dianne. Maybe I'll run into town. Could you keep an eye on Nicky for me?"

"I'd be delighted to, Anna."

Later Anna drove into Calistoga, dropped off mail at the post office, did some banking, and went to the local creamery for a cup of coffee.

Then she ran into Sheriff Roy and they talked. He told her his son was in the Pacific with the marines and he was quite worried about him. "He's a tall boy and makes a big target."

"Yes, Roy. But he's also a superior hunter and stalker. That should stand him well in those jungles."

"I hope so, Anna."

"I feel positive about this, Roy."

"How are things at the resort?"

"Good. It's the quiet time of the year. Not like spring and summer."

"The town's also quiet, Anna. I'll be glad when this war is over so we can get back to normal."

"I'll be glad when all our men are home, Roy."

"Me too, Anna. I'll leave you now."

"I'll walk with you, Roy."

Anna got into her pickup and drove over to Pacheteau's. She didn't know why. She had been living here all her life and had heard about the mud baths and massages, but had never tried them. Why not now? The owner was at the desk and recognized her from having been to the resort many times over the years.

"Anna! You finally come to my place. Hello. I'm Steve Margolis."

"Yes, Steve. I thought I'd try to use your facilities for the first time."

"You're most welcome, Anna. My wife runs the mud baths. She'll be glad to attend to you. Just go through these doors. Her name is Mary."

"Thank you, Steve."

Anna went through the doors and down a short hallway to an open room with nice couches and tropical plants. There was a desk with a bell on it and a sign saying, "Please Ring," which she did. Two minutes later a dark complexioned woman appeared.

"Mary?"

"Yes, Anna. I recognize you from Fire Mountain Resort. I've eaten at your place and attended several parties. I look forward to going to your place."

"You'll have to come up as my guest sometime."

"That would be nice, Anna, as I don't get away from here too often. You can shower through that door. Put a robe around yourself and I'll come for you shortly."

Anna showered and put on a robe, which was hanging from a rack and fit her loosely. Then she sat down and picked up a Life Magazine. She had read a few pages when Mary came for her and led her to a tiled room with two large tubs. Taking her robe, Mary asked her to get into a tub. Anna soon was covered with the warmest mud imaginable. It felt strange at first, but after Mary placed a pillow behind her head, she fell asleep for several minutes.

Mary woke her, saying, "I've been watching you so you didn't slip down too far. I think you've had enough. I'll help you out." Then Mary removed most of the mud which was on Anna. "Now you can shower over there and we'll get the rest of the mud off of you. Then, if you want, you can take a steam or a sulfur bath."

"I think I'd just like to go for a massage after the mud is off."

"Yes, I'll bring you a massage towel." Then she led Anna into a room with a massage table. "Lie down here. A masseur will be right here to attend to you."

Shortly a tall, Scandinavian man entered the room and introduced himself.

"Arne Bjorkman at your service, madam."

Anna was a little shy, even after all her nude swimming. Maybe it was being a mother. After the massage, she left the baths wishing Jack was waiting for her at home. Returning to the resort in the late afternoon, she walked into the dining room and over to Stella's bar.

"My God, Anna! You look pink." Anna laughed. "Stella, I had my first mud bath and massage. Please make me one of your good Manhattans."

"Yes, deary. Coming right up." Anna took a big sip. "Good. Good! Thank you."

"The mud baths are really relaxing. I took them a few times when I lived in St. Helena. I'll have to get George to go to town and we'll take one together."

"I really enjoyed it, Stella. It's kind of sexy."

"I think so too."

Dianne came in with Nicky. "Mama."

"Hi, my big guy." She scooped him up again, showering him with kisses.

"Thank you, Dianne. Was he a good boy?"

"Anna, he's a pleasure. He wants to help with whatever you're doing. My girls are crazy about him. They say, 'Mom, when Dad gets home, we want a little brother.'"

"That's cute, Dianne."

"Well, I'll go and help the girls with their homework."

"Thanks again, Dianne."

"You're welcome, Anna."

Alicia came into the room. "Hi Mom."

"Hello angel. How was your day?"

"Good. Mom, you look pink."

"I took my first mud bath and had a massage."

"Was the mud gooey?"

"It's different at first, but it was very nice. I'll start recommending it to our guests. Where is your sister?"

"She's at Judy's. They were going for a ride."

"It's so cold."

"She had on that flight jacket Jack gave you so she should be okay."

"You're right. That will keep her warm."

That night at dinner, Michelle said she and Judy had ridden over to the Petrified Forest on a trail Judy had developed. It was steep in spots and slippery on the wet ground, but it was fun.

"I really don't worry when you're with Judy," Anna said.

344

Christmas arrived. Gus and the girls made many cookies for guests. Jack had called and said he wouldn't be home. He thought he would be spending a warm Christmas. Anna took it to mean he would probably be in Hawaii. She told him, "I wish I was there with you, my handsome man."

"Me too," he replied. Because he had to hurry his call, he expressed his love and then there was a click.

Hans, George, and Randy had brought in a large Christmas tree from Shaw Flat. Everyone had helped to decorate it. Christmas day had been wonderful and Hans had given large bonuses from his share of the profits. He had little need of money now. He also had beautiful charms of gold made for the women and their daughters.

There were a lot of happy faces Christmas day. War or no war, Christmas was important. Gus had spent the previous night and most of Christmas day preparing a great feast.

At the day's end when Anna and Hans were the last people in the dining room, she said, "Dad, you are wonderful. It was so considerate what you did for everyone."

"Why not, Anna? Things are so good. I just wish your mother was still with us."

"Me too, Dad."

Anna fell asleep on her pillow wishing Jack was in her arms.

CHAPTER 27

JUDY

Late spring one evening when Anna had the children in bed and had finished some work in the office, coming into the dining room she was surprised to see Stella behind the bar and Judy drinking. As she approached, Stella said, "Anna we have some very bad news." Anna could see the telegram on the bar in front of Judy.

"My God, Judy."

"Yes, Anna, it's true. He's gone. I received this at noon. I was stunned for quite a while. Then I went riding to some of our favorite places. I was careless and didn't get back until dark. I just walked over to talk to you, but I saw Stella getting ready for the coming season. I really needed a drink."

"You poor girl. Dale was such a nice guy, Judy. I can understand your loss."

"Thank you, Anna, you've always been a good friend. You and Stella, the two of you have helped me in so many ways."

"Judy, we love you dearly. Let me fill your glass."

"Thank you, Stella. Here, take my money."

"No, Stella. I've got this. Stella, please give me a glass of white."

"Yes, Anna. I may as well join you girls."

"Do," Anna said.

The three of them talked to late in the night.

Several days later, Judy came into Anna's office. "Anna, I am sorry to bother you."

"Judy, you're never a bother. What can I do for you?"

"Anna, I got this letter from Dale's parents. They want me to come and see them as soon as possible."

"I wonder what the rush is?"

"I really don't know, and they live way back in a small town about one hundred fifty miles from St. Louis."

"Do you want to go, Judy?"

"I would think that Dale would have liked me to meet them, although he rarely mentioned them."

"Judy, you have to be the one to decide this."

"I know, Anna, and the season's coming right up. I wonder if your girls could handle the rides with Alfonso's help?"

"Judy, you say they ride so well and they know all the trails. I'll ask them and get back to you right away."

"Thank you."

"You're welcome."

"I'll see you later then."

"Okay, Judy."

The phone rang and Judy waved as she left. Two days later, she was back telling Anna she was going to visit Dale's parents. "I'll be gone about two weeks. I really appreciate the girls taking over for me."

"Judy, they're thrilled."

The girls did real well with the rides and the guests all seemed quite happy, but Alfonso had noticed the horses coming in a little more sweaty. He was sure the girls were sometimes indulging some guests in their desire to let the horses run.

When Judy returned several days earlier than expected, she got to her place and found Alfonso feeding the horses. "Senora, welcome home. It so good to see you." Rosita came out of the house with her little one also excited to see her. They had dinner together and Alfonso told her how well everything had gone. She thanked him and Rosita for their help.

"I am going over and thank the girls and see Anna." Goodbyes said, Judy left. When she arrived at the resort, she went to Stella's and ordered a drink. Eventually Anna came to the bar and went right over to kiss Judy. "Hi, my dear friend."

"Anna, it's so good to see you."

"How was the trip?"

"That's one of the reasons I came over to see you. I wanted to give this envelope to the girls and tell them to go ahead and finish out the weekend as I have a few things to take care of."

"Okay, I will. They will be thrilled with this money."

"It's not that much, Anna, but I think it's fair. Anna, my reception by Dale's parents was cold and they implied I had been a gold-digger. I was moved to tears and left their house. I stayed at a cheap hotel until I could make connections to come back home."

"You poor dear."

"I can't believe Dale came from such cruel people."

"Judy, it does take all kinds."

"They were so worried about my getting his death benefits, especially because we had only been married for seven months. Anna, I never even thought about life insurance. A letter from the war department was in my mail when I returned saying I was the beneficiary and would be receiving 10,000.00 in a few weeks."

"I know that doesn't make up for losing Dale, but it's yours, Judy."

"Anna I still have to think about it, but I wanted to ask you. What would you think about burying Dale's remains down by John's monument?"

"That would be nice. That's quite an idea. I am really surprised."

They talked until late in the evening. Stella finally said, "Goodnight, ladies," as she left. She knew Anna would close up.

Six weeks later there was a little ceremony at John's memorial site. Two good men would be remembered there.

CHAPTER 28

SECRET?

Anna's daughters were really becoming part of the crew, having helped with Judy's horses, filling in as waitresses, and leading an occasional hike. The summer was quite busy. Everywhere the war was going more and more in the Allies' favor. Spirits were looking up and a few of the women were starting to be a little more discreet, hoping husbands would be home soon.

Jack had not been home in several months. Anna was spending the late hours talking to Stella or telling her to retire for the evening because she would close for her. Stella protested, but she always looked forward to cuddling up to George, the gentlest man she had ever known. Judy often came over to the resort and the three women would talk about their lives. Anna consoled, "You have to go on, Judy. You are an attractive woman. There will be someone else for you."

"I was so happy with Dale. He was so easy going. I was just so comfortable with him."

Late one night as they were sitting alone, Sheriff Roy stopped by. He said he'd been in the area because he had had a complaint of some continued gunfire. "Probably just someone spotlighting a deer for a little stamp-free meat. Really a game warden problem."

Joining the women for several drinks, they talked about the war and he offered Judy his condolences for the loss of her husband. A few months ago, he had read of it in *The Calistogan*. Eventually goodnights were said and Roy offered to drive Judy home. The sheriff took to dropping in more often late in the evenings and, as time passed, Judy and he would leave earlier. One evening Anna asked Judy if Roy was becoming part of her life.

"I guess it's starting to show, Anna. We were trying to be careful. He is married and his reputation is important in this little town. He says he and his wife have slept in separate rooms the last ten years. She's into every woman's club in town and the entire Napa Valley. He admits his long hours and irregular sleeping habits had something to do with it. Since Owen went into the service, she's been extremely nervous. For her, the sun rises and sets on the boy. Three or four times a year has been the extent of their lovemaking and it's like she's not there. My own loneliness has led me into this situation. Anna, I think I am pregnant!"

"Judy, you'll have to know for sure."

"I'm going down to Vallejo next Tuesday. There's a young woman doctor starting a pediatrics practice that I read about in the Calistogan."

"Keep me informed and I'll help in any way I can."

"Thank you, Anna. I know I can always count on you."

"Does Roy know yet?"

"I want to be sure before I tell him, Anna. I wonder how he'll handle it?"

"He's really a good man, Judy. I think he'll stand by you."

"I sure hope so Anna, I'd like to have a baby. I'd have to give up riding for a while."

Anna laughed, "Judy, that's for sure."

"I guess I better give up drinking, too."

"I think so, Judy. Maybe an occasional glass of wine would be all right."

The season was winding down and it had been a good year. Jack had still not been home and his few phone calls had been short. Anna could understand with the war going so favorably and island after island being recaptured in the Pacific.

Judy came by one evening and told Anna she was definitely pregnant. The baby should be born in April—about the 15th. She should be able to handle the summer rides and Rosita would care for the baby. Roy had been surprised. He said he would marry her when the war was over. He had come to love her deeply and wanted to be with her for the rest of their lives. Owen would be home from the war, God willing, and Roy would divorce his wife then.

"Judy, I am happy for you."

"You know, Anna, I am only a little older than Owen."

"I never thought of that, Judy. You are so much more mature."

"Thank you, Anna. I have just fallen so hard for Roy that I have not done that much thinking."

"Yes, Judy. It can really consume your every thought. It did mine twice."

"Anna, your men were very special individuals. I mean Don was, and Jack is."

"You're right, Judy. I was lucky to meet each of them."

Two nights later Jack put in an unexpected appearance. Anna was overjoyed, but saddened when he said it was only for forty-eight hours. He told her they had landed at the Alameda Air Station. One of the crew who lived in Alameda had lent him his car so he was only two hours from having landed to seeing her. Everyone was happy to see Jack. Nicky had grown so much. Anna offered to fix something for Jack, but he only wanted some red wine. The girls and Nicky eventually went to bed and Stella and George said their goodnights too.

Anna took Jack's hand and said, "Come, my warrior. I am ready to be ravished."

"Yes, fair maiden, let us adjourn to the battlefield."

A couple of hours later, as they lay together, Jack said, "I knew something wonderful was missing in my life."

"Thank you, my darling. Don't expect to leave this battlefield. I will bring you breakfast in bed in the morning when I am through with you."

"What a wife I married!"

After breakfast, Jack had gone back to sleep, not rising until late afternoon. When the girls came home from school, there were kisses and hugs. Nicky asked several times, "You're my daddy?"

"Yes, Nicky. I am your daddy. I have been away at the big war most of the time since you were born and when it's over you'll see a lot more of me."

Gus cooked a large dinner and they all had a great evening. When Jack left the following day, Anna insisted on riding back to the base with him. She would catch a Greyhound back home. Their parting at the Alameda Depot was tearful for Anna because she had no idea when she would see her man again. It took her five hours to make it back to Calistoga. She called the resort and George came down to pick her up.

Chapter 29

John Roy

After a very wet winter, as Anna and the crew started to prepare for the early opening of the resort that spring, Judy gave birth to a little boy. Anna had driven Judy to the hospital in Vallejo. Judy's water broke as they put her into bed. Contractions started strongly. The doctor, Nancy Petersen, arrived and was attending Judy. Anna went to a phone and called Roy who had just gotten into his office.

"Roy, it's Anna. I just brought Judy to the hospital and the baby is due shortly."

"Thank you, Anna, I didn't know anyone else knew."

"Roy, everyone knew she was pregnant. They just didn't know the father."

"I know what close friends you two are. I should have realized she'd have to confide in someone."

"Roy, she told me of your plans and I respect what the two of you are doing."

"Anna, I'll get down there as soon as I can."

"Take your time, Roy. She'll need a little after the baby comes."

"Thank you, Anna. For everything."

The baby arrived five hours after Judy's arrival at the hospital. Everything had gone well and the baby boy was healthy. It was seven pounds, eight ounces and had lots of hair and great lungs.

Anna had stayed for the second feeding of the new baby and was just going to leave when Roy walked in with a luggage-sized bunch of roses. The nurse, who was just taking the baby from Judy and Anna, said, "This is the father? Would you like to hold him, officer?"

"Please, just a second." He went over to the bed, kissed Judy, and placed the flowers on her lap. "Hi, Anna," he said as he kissed her on the cheek. Then he turned and took the baby into his large hands, cradled him in his left arm, and walked back over to Judy.

"He's a handsome boy, Judy, I am proud to be his father." Judy smiled radiantly.

"Thank you, Roy. I really appreciate your coming and the flowers are beautiful."

Anna said goodbye to Judy and Roy and left the room. She decided to wait at the entrance of the hospital until Roy left twenty minutes later. Surprised to see Anna, Roy asked, "What are you still doing here?"

"I thought you might like a drink. I know that wasn't easy for you, even though I know you love her."

He smiled and shook his head.

"Anna, it *was* a little rough. I love the girl, but I am still married and it has to stay a secret for all of our sakes until I am divorced."

"I know, Roy. It's a secret I'll keep."

"Now, how about that drink?"

"Where shall we go? Vallejo Inn?"

"It's pretty public there, Anna. How about The Vine on Silverado Trail?"

"That's good, Roy. I'll follow you there."

Twenty minutes later they were parking alongside of The Vine, an old hunters' watering hole. Anna ordered a glass of cabernet, Roy bourbon and water. Anna lifted her glass, "Roy, here's to you and Judy and the baby. Happiness and a long life together."

"Thank you, Anna. Your happiness too."

"Do you and Judy have a name for the baby?"

"We were concerned about names and the birth certificate. We decided to use Judy's last name as mother and my first name and her last name for the father's name, then when we're married, we would have it corrected."

"That sounds like it should work."

A couple of drinks later, they left. Roy gently gave Anna a large hug and said, "Thank you for everything you've done to help. I really appreciate it. Please call on me for anything."

"You and Judy are two of my special friends, Roy."

Goodbyes given, they got into their cars and headed for Calistoga.

As he drove, Roy was thinking about everything going on in his life and wondering what his son Owen would think about the divorce and having a new brother. When he reached Calistoga, he stopped at the arterial sign just as someone ran it. He could see them looking back, but today no one was going to get a ticket, thanks to his new son.

Anna reached the resort and went into the dining room and over to the bar where Stella was pouring George a glass of wine.

"Hi, Stella, George. It's a boy."

"How did it go for her, Anna?"

"Fine, Stella. About five hours of labor and, thank God, a healthy son."

They toasted the baby and Judy and George asked if she had named the baby.

"It's up in the air, but I think she's favoring John."

"That's a good solid name," George proclaimed.

Anna excused herself and went to her office. Dianne was just leaving. Hellos exchanged, Dianne mentioned to Anna what she had done, answering letters for reservations and working up a new ad for the coming season. "Thank you, Dianne. Judy had a little boy. She's quite happy."

"I am glad for her, Anna. Did it go well?"

"Yes, it really did. I'll check my children and see you at dinner."

"See you then."

That night at the dinner table all the talk was about Judy's new baby. Anna's daughters wanted to go and see him. "They will be home in a couple of days. You can see him then."

"Yes mother," they echoed.

Four days later Anna brought Judy and John home. Judy said she had named her son, John Roy.

When they got to Judy's home, which had had an extra bedroom added to it two years ago, Alfonso and Rosita had spring flowers placed everywhere. They also had purchased mosquito netting to hang over Judy's bed and the baby's crib. Judy thanked them for their kindness and put the baby into the crib. He started to cry and Rosita picked him up and started a lullaby. He calmed right down and a few minutes later he was asleep.

"Judy, these two came from heaven. They're such a dear couple."

"They really are, Anna. And wonderful help."

"Well, Judy dear, I'll let you get settled and see you later."

"Anna, thank you for everything. You've been so good to me."

"What are friends for, Judy?"

As Anna drove back into the resort, she thought, "Another season coming up. I wonder where my flyer is right now. What's he doing?"

CHAPTER 30

BEARS IN THE NIGHT

The season was only a week old when victory in Europe was declared by the Allies. It led to celebrations all over the country. A few even got out of hand. The guests who were now coming to the resort early were older and more reserved, but Anna told Stella the drinks were on the house that night.

The children wanted to know if Jack would be right home. Anna explained the war in Europe was at an end, but the war with the Japanese was still raging in the Pacific. Even the men in Europe wouldn't be home right away as it took time to work out peace agreements. The girls understood Anna's explanation, but Nicky was still too young.

Everyone indulged that night and talked about the war in the Pacific, saying that it should be expedited by moving European bombers and men to the Pacific. As the season progressed and the news in the Pacific became more hopeful, guests were enjoying the summer in a more festive way. People were warmer and everyone seemed to be drinking more. Anna found herself taking more and more of the guests for hikes, even making more overnight trips to Mount St. Helena.

Dianne was running the office to Anna's complete satisfaction. Thus Anna was able to devote more time to her own children and occasionally drop over to see Judy and her new baby. Roy would sometimes drop in at the bar for a quick drink. Anna knew why his visits were so short. Once in a while she'd see him and Judy riding. Anna and Roy talked and kidded, but it was always short-lived.

On one of her hikes to the water cave, Anna found Max coming out of the cave. "Hello, Lipshun."

"Max, you old he bear, you're in late."

"I am not as fast as I used to be, Anna. Slowing down."

"You look good, Max. I'll tell Dad you're camped down here."

"I'd appreciate that, Anna. I didn't get my usual list off to him."

"What do you need, Max?"

"Coffee, dried fruit, wheat flower, brandy, two bottles, socks, and matches. That should do me."

"Max, Dad or I'll be back in two days with what you asked for."

"That will be good, Lipshun."

When Max was out of the hearing range of the guests, Anna explained who the old man was and what a legend he was in the mountains of the Sierras. That night the guests were explaining to family and friends their meeting with the old man.

Just as Anna was leaving the office before going to the bar for a nightcap, the phone rang. It was Jack.

"My darling man."

"Anna, I am glad it's you and you were still up. I love you and miss you so much."

"Me too, Jack."

"How are the children?"

"Thank God they're all healthy. Nicky had chicken pox, the girls, a couple of colds. But it's been a good spring and the season's off to a good start."

"Glad to hear that. I am three hours earlier than you."

"Wish I was there with you, darling man."

"Me too, Anna. That's good news in Europe. It should expedite things out this way."

"I sure hope so, Jack. We all miss you and want you with us."

"Anna, we're leaving within the hour. I just had to talk to you, pretty lady. It may be awhile before you hear from me again, but I think it's pretty safe."

"I hope so, Jack. I do worry about you. I know how qualified you are at what you do. Is it far away?"

"I can't say, sweet."

"Dreaming of when we can be together again."

"Yearning, no; craving you, lady."

"Jack, it's mutual. I think of all the places we've made love and I want us to be in those places again when you get home."

"Anna, that sounds great. It can't happen too soon, my passionate one. I've got to run, I love you, Anna."

"Jack, I love you. I need you. Good night, my darling."

"Good night, Anna."

Anna went to the bar. Stella was preparing to close as Anna saw the last guest leaving the dining room.

"I see a half-smile and a couple of tears, Anna."

"I just got off the phone with Jack. God, I miss him."

"I am sure you do, dear. Let's hope he's home soon."

"Evidently he's on another assignment, Stella. I think he was calling from Hawaii and he said he was moving on. Our conversation is so restricted for fear we'll be cut off."

"Damn wars."

"I agree. Stella, please pour me a glass of red."

"Yes, Anna. How's Judy's little John doing?"

"He's a cute baby. Has Roy's blue eyes."

"Let's hope he's as handsome as his dad."

Stella poured herself a glass of red and added to Anna's glass. They talked about the season, the guests, the girls in school, and their lives, in general.

Anna fell asleep in bed dreaming of Jack, wishing he was there. The next morning she parked at the trout farm entrance on the southern side of Mt. St. Helena with six guests for an overnight camping hike. The farm manager greeted them as they passed the porch where he was enjoying his morning pipe. He asked Anna to come to him for a minute. She told the guests to wait a minute and she'd see what Mr. Sands wanted.

"Wayne, you old fish breeder. What's wrong?"

"Anna, I don't mean to alarm you, but I can see you're taking an overnight hike and carrying your food bag. The bears have been troublesome the last two weeks. They raided my cabin for the first time in years while I was down in Calistoga shopping. I know where your camp is below the crest and slightly east. I am worried you'll leave the food and gear there, hike to the top, spend some time there and return to a ravaged camp site."

"Wayne, I've never had a problem in the past and I've always tied the food up in a tree."

"Anna, these bears are hungry. I think it's a sow and a couple of late yearlings. The young ones can climb if hungry enough. They can do it easy."

"Thanks Wayne. What do you suggest?"

"Leave your food and gear here. Me and the mule will bring it up to you early dusk."

"That would be nice of you, Wayne. Figure on eating with us. I've got plenty of food as I had two guests cancel out at the last minute."

"Sounds good, Anna. See you in a few hours."

Anna led the hikers on up the mountain. At the campsite, she had everybody help gather some wood for the campfire that night and explained Mr. Sands would bring the food and gear up later.

The guests rested at the campsite for a while. Then Anna led them to the top of the mountain. They loved the view which was crystal-clear. They could see to the Sierras and far down into the San Joaquin valley. Anna led them to the fire tower which was not occupied yet because it was still a little early for fire watching. The gate at the bottom of the stairs prevented their climb up the tower so she led them to a nearby artesian stream to quench their thirst and refill canteens. They looked at small trout in a pond fed by the stream and then she led them back to the campsite where she announced food time was getting close because Mr. Sands should be here in about half an hour.

Wayne and Kippy arrived right on time. "Everyone, this is my friend, Kippy. He saves me a lot of backpacking. I got him two years ago because my old back was getting tired."

"I'll take the backpack, Wayne; you folks grab the sleeping bags."

Anna removed a grill from over a pit and placed a small piece of candle on it. Then she lit the base and fed small twigs to it until she had a good fire going. Then she took out utensils and tin plates. She opened a couple of bottles of red wine and filled paper cups, passing them around. A little later as the fire died down and the pit was filled with hot coals, she returned the grill to its place and placed the nine steaks she had brought on it. She had also opened three cans of tomatoes and peaches, and had a dozen and a half rolls—what she called a cowboy dinner. Steaks ready, dinner was consumed by all along with some more red wine. A sing-along soon was in progress and a star-filled night was enjoyed. Just as the guests started to crawl into sleeping bags, a bear roar sent a chill through the spines of all.

Wayne looked at Anna and said, "I'll bring in some more wood."

"Stay close, Wayne. I should have had them gather more wood."

Wayne was gone quite awhile, but returned dragging in a big snag of branches.

"I'll make one more trip, Anna."

"Do you think you have to, Wayne?"

"It's a long night, Anna. I better."

"Wayne, you're still one hell of a man."

"Not quite, Anna. I'm going to ask you to stand the first watch."

"Sure, Wayne. Get some rest. I'm awake. Caring for these people, I didn't drink too much."

"Thanks, Anna, give me about two hours."

Anna went over and kissed Wayne on the cheek. "Thanks for the help and the protection. This could have gone badly."

"You're welcome, Anna. Anytime for you."

Everyone was fast asleep as Anna continued to feed the fire. She heard a couple of more roars and eventually she could see three forms moving in a circle in the moon light. She kept the fire going by burning the little food left in camp. Wayne woke after about four and a half hours. Anna was feeding the fire. He got up, went over to the edge of camp, relieved himself, and walked back to her.

"You should have woken me sooner, Anna."

"Wayne, we've had company for the last few hours. I've spotted them several times."

"You should have gotten me."

"I would have if they got any closer."

"Try and get a little rest. It'll be light in a couple of hours."

"Yeah, I am ready to fall asleep." She kissed him on the cheek again and crawled into the sleeping bag he had just left. Enjoying his male smell, she fell asleep.

When morning came, the guests were peering around, remembering the bear roar.

"They've gone off to sleep, too. You are safe," Wayne said.

One of the men said, "Thanks to your keeping that fire going all night."

"Anna kept it going most of the night while the bears were prowling around. You will see a lot of tracks when you check the ground around here."

Anna sat up, "Hi, everyone. Welcome to breakfast in Calistoga."

There were a couple of cheers and ten minutes later they left camp. Arriving at Wayne's cabin, everyone thanked him for his help, Anna especially. "I owe you, Wayne. Bring your lady friend up some night for dinner, drinks, and a sleep-over at my place."

"I just might do that, Anna."

Goodbyes given all around, twenty minutes later they were ordering breakfast at the Calistoga Creamery and talking about their adventure on the mountain.

Chapter 31

Peace

September 2, 1945. Victory over the Japanese! Admiral Ryan called down to the hanger for Captain Jack Collins. Jack had been talking to the head mechanic, Master Sergeant Art Fagundes.

"Thanks Art, I know she's in good shape when you tell me she's ready to fly."

"That she is, captain."

"Telephone for you, captain," a corporal called from the nearby office.

"Thank you, corporal."

Jack entered the nearby office and picked up the phone.

"It's over, son. You can go home soon."

"Thank God, admiral."

Anna filled his thoughts, and then the children. He hoped for an early release from the service.

Stella came into the resort's office. "Anna, Dianne, it's over. The war has ended. It just came over the radio." Anna and Dianne hugged each other. Then Stella joined in.

"Oh Stella, we will have our men home."

"I think you need them, you've both looked haggard from male loneliness." Grins came to Anna's and Dianne's faces.

"Stella, does it show that much?" Dianne asked.

"Yes. I'm glad Lance wasn't still here to weaken you girls any further."

"Stella, lets have a drink to their quick return."

"Sounds like a good idea, Anna. Dianne, no tears."

"Stella, they're tears of happiness."

They joined other guests coming to the bar in celebration of the good news. Smiles on their faces, they were coming in from the pool or their rooms. Anna was buying drinks for those who would imbibe.

Alicia came to Anna, "Now will daddy Jack be home?"

"Soon I hope! Where is Nicky?"

"They'll probably be here soon, Mom."

"Thank you."

No one left the dining area. The joy of the day led into an evening of gaiety.

Later that evening Anna and Dianne each heard from their husbands. Jack confirmed he was at Guam and Lyle told Dianne he was back in Australia.

That three weeks the resort did a thriving business with guests and local people coming in for evening drinks and dancing. The locals were really starting to use the resort as their meeting and entertainment spot. More and more people started to book for rooms on the weekend right into mid November. The local Lion's Club wanted to rent the facilities for a big New Year's Eve party. Anna said she would get back to them. She talked to Hans, Dianne, Stella, and George and told the Lions' directors to "give us a count and we'll give you a great party. Everyone must agree to stay the night and no one leaves the resort after 9 p.m." The exit would be blocked at that time for everyone's safety. There were a few grumbles, but most saw the good sense in Anna's demand.

Jack arrived home for a thirty-day leave the first of November. He was a little gray around the temples and his hair had receded a little, but to Anna he was still quite handsome. Jack had not called, wanting to surprise her, but she knew he was stateside again. He walked into the dining room just as she came out of the office.

She froze like a startled doe. Jack dropped his suitcase and rushed to her. Her tears were flowing and their lips and arms were entwined. Stella was in the middle of pouring a glass of wine and it ran over at the beautiful sight in front of her. Anna guided Jack to the end of the bar where Stella came around and gave him a big kiss.

"Good to have you home, captain."

"Stella, it's good to see you again."

"Champagne?"

"Yes, Stella," they both exclaimed.

As Jack took Anna back in his arms, she melted, clinging to his body.

Later the children were almost ecstatic to see Jack. They had a party that night. Nicky sat on his daddy's lap all through dinner. Anna could not get him to return to his own highchair. Jack said, "Leave him be, darling. I don't mind."

That night when they finally made it to bed, it was magnificent discovering each other again. They almost journeyed past exhaustion in their craving for each other, but sleep eventually came to them.

Noises of the day awoke them and they crawled next to each other. Anna asked, "Can we always be this close, Jack?"

"Anna, let's try to keep this as great as the last few hours. We feel deeply for each other and respect each other. If we keep these priorities, we can."

"I hope so my wonderful man. Are you hungry?"

"Starved."

They showered, held each other, and then headed for the dining room. Meeting Dianne in the dining room, good mornings were exchanged.

"I got the girls off to school with my kids. Nicky is with Barbara."

"Thank you, Dianne."

"You're welcome."

"Dianne, join us for breakfast."

"Anna, I've eaten. I have a few things to do in the office."

"Thank you, dear lady."

Anna got Jack coffee and asked what he wanted for breakfast.

"Honey, real eggs and some bacon and a loaf of toast."

"Really?"

"Maybe half a loaf of the toast." They ate a leisurely breakfast and talked about the last month of their lives.

Jack was surprised about the Lion's Club New Year's Eve Party. Anna said, "If you're discharged by then and if you feel like it, you could help bartend."

"Whatever I can do to help, Anna, I'll only be too glad to do."

Later they walked down to the stream. A doe was watering and moved slowly off as they got closer. Going to and returning from the stream, they necked like teenagers.

Lyle made it home to his family in late December. Dianne and her children were ecstatic. They decided that when he received his discharge, they would return to San Francisco.

One evening when Roy dropped in, he said his son was going to stay in the service. He was a sergeant now. "You'll probably see him when he's home on leave."

Anna replied, "That would be nice, Roy. How are Judy and the baby doing?"

"They are fine, Anna. I love them both. It's going to make it a little harder to leave the wife with Owen staying in the service, but maybe a few days after he leaves, I'll ask her for the divorce. I know it's not going to play too well in this small town, but I want to enjoy Judy and our son."

"It's a shame when anyone has to be hurt, Roy, but I think Judy and the baby need you the most."

"Thanks, Anna. What you say is right, and I'll do right by the wife."

"Tell Judy I said Hi."

"I will." He tipped his hat and left.

On December 31, 1945, forty Lions and their wives or friends sat down to a sumptuous dinner. The good Napa Valley wines were served and Randy and George and a couple of local musicians provided dance music, with Randy's golden voice making for a wonderful evening. A few minutes to midnight, Stella and Jack started to open bottles of champagne, letting corks fly to the ceiling. The party lasted till 3:30 A.M. and a great time was had by all.

Anna and Jack got to bed just as dawn was breaking. "Lady, I have not had you since last year."

"Sorry it's been so long, mister."